One Potato, Two Potato, Dead

One Potato, Two Potato, Dead

A Farm-to-Fork Mystery

Lynn Cahoon

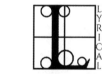

LYRICAL PRESS
Kensington Publishing Corp.
www.kensingtonbooks.com

LYRICAL PRESS BOOKS are published by

Kensington Publishing Corp.
119 West 40th Street
New York, NY 10018

All Kensington titles, imprints, and distributed lines are available at special quantity discounts for bulk purchases for sales promotion, premiums, fund-raising, educational, or institutional use.

Special book excerpts or customized printings can also be created to fit specific needs. For details, write or phone the office of the Kensington Sales Manager: Kensington Publishing Corp., 119 West 40th Street, New York, NY 10018. Attn. Sales Department. Phone: 1-800-221-2647.

Lyrical Press and Lyrical Press logo Reg. U.S. Pat. & TM Off.

First Electronic Edition: March 2019
ISBN-13: 978-1-5161-0385-0 (ebook)
ISBN-10: 1-5161-0385-8 (ebook)

First Print Edition: March 2019
ISBN-13: 978-1-5161-0386-7
ISBN-10: 1-5161-0386-6

Printed in the United States of America

To my restaurant partner in crime, Jessi, thanks for helping me keep track of my monkeys and ignoring the rest.

Acknowledgments

The Farm-to-Fork series allows me to visit home. Set in the rural landscape of Southwestern Idaho, the places where Angie and her crew live and work are all made a little softer by the paint strokes of time. You may or may not be able to visit the same park where Angie and Dom like to walk, but you'll get the feel of the warm summer days that made this area such a delight to remember.

I'm always grateful for the solid advice and support I get from Esi Sogah and the Kensington crew. And of course, I am grateful for Jill Marsal's advice and belief in this project.

Chapter 1

Angie Turner shivered as she all but ran to the barn to feed her only hen, Mabel, and the newest member of the Turner household, Precious, the goat she'd found earlier that year. Fall had come hard to the little farm town of River Vista, Idaho. She'd known when she moved north from San Francisco the moderate weather wouldn't hold long, but she wasn't quite ready for winter yet. She didn't know why, but she always worshipped days like this that started cool, then turned into a sunny afternoon. The chill made her appreciate the warmth that arrived later in the day.

The best thing about fall was the produce that came out of the farmers market. Her options had turned from the leafy greens of summer to the deep oranges of fall. And the potatoes she'd been cooking with lately were amazing.

Today she was planning on experimenting with a few different takes on the Canadian staple poutine. Hope Anderson had been talking about the dish since her classes started back up last month. Angie thought that maybe her dishwasher/chef-in-training was more interested in the Canadian visiting professor than the food he was teaching them to make. A bleating from the middle stall brought her out of her musing. Precious, the not-so-baby goat she'd adopted in early spring, was standing on two legs, looking at her over the top of the gate.

Angie hurried over and waved the goat down. The last thing she needed was Precious learning she could jump or climb the gate into the main barn area. She wasn't afraid the goat would take off; instead, she was more concerned that Precious would find the grain stored in the barn. Mabel, the lone black-and-white hen from Nona's last flock, wouldn't be pleased with sharing her corn.

Angie's boyfriend Ian had suggested they put up an electric wire to shock Precious when she got close, but that just seemed cruel, especially since the goat hadn't got out of her pen. Yet. However, it looked like Angie might be running out of options.

She rubbed behind the goat's ears. "Hey, girl, how was your night?"

Precious bleated out a few sounds, lifting her head to sniff Angie's hair. When Angie had first gotten the new addition, she'd set up a baby monitor in the barn so she could hear if anything went south. But now that Precious was older, she'd turned off the monitors and trusted the barn to keep her safe.

She fed the goat, cleaned out her stall and water trough, and then turned to where Mabel liked to roost. The hen eyed her warily as she spread out corn. Angie figured Mabel might warm up to her in a few years, but she wasn't holding her breath. The chicken had loved Angie's grandmother. And maybe that was enough.

Taking one last look to make sure she'd finished her chores, Angie headed back across the yard where Dom, her St. Bernard, sat waiting for her on the porch. Dom and Precious didn't quite get along. The goat liked the dog well enough, but Dom? He was scared of Precious. He'd been that way since the day Angie had brought the baby home from Moss Farms. Back then, she thought the goat was just a visitor. When she became one of the family, Dom hadn't voted for the change.

"Good morning, mister." Angie climbed the stairs to the porch and turned to study her neighbor's house. Mrs. Potter was visiting her son and daughter-in-law this month, so no one was in residence across the street. The house had a sad look to it. Dom glanced that way and sighed. "Don't worry. Mrs. Potter and Erica will be back soon."

As they walked in the house, Angie wondered if Mrs. Potter would even come back from California or if she'd stay down for the winter. And maybe longer. She was getting up in years and didn't have anyone here except her granddaughter, Erica, who was going to school at Boise State. Angie wanted her to be happy, but even now, she missed seeing her come over with her walker just to chat.

Angie tied on an apron and pushed the sad thoughts out of her head. It was time to cook. By noon, she had a pot of tomato basil bisque on the stove, chili-braised short ribs in the pressure cooker, and she'd tried two different versions of poutine using a variety of potato types.

A quick knock on the back door and then Ian stepped into the room. His dusky red hair and rock-star build only made his blue eyes sparkle that much more. Ian McNeal was the town do-gooder. He ran the farmers market, helped Mildred run Moss Farms, and taught Sunday school. Definitely not the type Angie usually went for. Todd, her last boyfriend, had been more of a bad boy type. She didn't think he'd ever stepped into a church, let alone taught Bible study. Thanks goodness she'd gotten that type out of her system.

"Are you about ready?" Ian paused after closing the door. Mostly he had to stop forward movement because Dom had come and sat on his foot, wanting attention. Next to Angie, Ian was the dog's favorite person. Angie suspected it was because Ian snuck bits of human food to him when she wasn't looking. "What is all this? We don't have to bring anything. You know we're cooking this afternoon, right?"

Angie stirred the soup, the smell of the sweet basil she'd harvested from her garden last summer filling the room. She then set the spoon down on a plate. "Cooking? The County Seat isn't open today."

"You forgot, didn't you?" Ian leaned down and gave Dom a quick hug, moving him off his foot. Then he stepped to the table and snatched a French fry from one of the poutine dishes. Dipping it into the brown gravy, he ate it before nodding his approval. "This is really good. Are you putting it on your menu?"

"Not sure yet. I've got two versions there." She handed him a plate. "Do you have time for lunch? I'd like your opinion."

"Sure. We had planned on picking up takeout on the way into Boise, but lunch here sounds better. Besides, you'll need to put all of this away before we go." He went to the sink and washed his hands. Standing next to her, he gave her a light kiss as he dried his hands. "You still don't remember, do you?"

"We're going somewhere in Boise to cook." Angie thought about where they were going to cook as she filled two bowls of soup and took the pot off the heat. There was no way this would be cool enough to package by the time they were done with lunch. Then the answer hit her. "Crap, today's the day we're volunteering at the mission."

"Give the girl a cigar." Ian took the bowls to the table and went to the fridge. "Want a soda or water?"

"Water, please." Angie got plates, silverware, and napkins out and put them on the table next to the bowls. "I even put it on my calendar, but I haven't looked at it since Saturday. How do you keep all this in your head?"

"I check my calendar each day. I don't have to keep it in my head." He sat and took a minute of silence before starting to eat.

Angie knew he was praying, but he didn't make a big deal of it. He'd invited her to attend his young adult Sunday school class several times, but with her having to work every Saturday night until late to close the County Seat, she'd begged off. Besides, she wasn't sure what she believed. Not like Ian. He knew who he was and what he believed. It was kind of overwhelming at times. She waited for him to pick up his spoon.

"So how long are we there today?" She took some of each poutine to try. One would have a beef spare rib topping that was still on the stove. The other had a chicken gravy and would have grilled chicken with a spicy sauce. Of course, she hadn't completely finished the creating of the topping, but she still had a week or so before they changed their menu at the restaurant.

"You're wanting to get back to work. I get it. But you have to admit that the people we'll be feeding will be appreciative of your talents, just like your customers are." He grinned as he picked up another fry. "Besides, we'll finally get to meet Felicia's boyfriend. She's been spending a lot of time with this Taylor guy."

"I'd like to say my intentions in signing up to cook were pure, but meeting Felicia's guy is the main reason I agreed to this." Felicia was her best friend and partner in the restaurant. If some guy was going to be taking up Felicia's time, Angie wanted to make sure that he wasn't a flake. "I'm not sure she has her eyes open on this relationship. I know feeding the homeless is a worthy occupation, but according to her, this guy has trust fund money. Why would he be running a homeless mission?"

"Because he wants to serve mankind?" Ian held up a fry with the beef gravy. "If you want a vote, I'd go traditional with this. The chicken gravy just seems a little flat compared to the richness of the other."

"Still, it seems suspicious." She let her worries about Felicia go for a minute and focused on the food. "I was afraid of that. I'm thinking instead of gravy, I might change it over to a barbecue sauce. But I don't want to overwhelm the potatoes."

"You're always looking for a new path. At least with food." Ian focused on his plate. "I have to say I'm enjoying my frozen dinners you supply me with much more than my usual ramen soup I had before we started dating."

"Don't tell me that you're dating me for the food!" Angie said with a laugh. She finished her soup and glanced at her watch. "I guess I better put this stuff away so we can get going. Remind me who else is going to be there?"

Ian listed off the staff from the County Seat who'd said yes. The only one who hadn't agreed was Nancy, and she was still working a second job. Angie hoped by next summer they'd be able to open the restaurant full-time and get Nancy down to one job. "And Hope called. Her class got canceled for this afternoon, so she's coming as well."

"So the full gang, almost." Angie ladled the soup into freezer containers. Mrs. Potter would be happy to have a pot of this going when she returned and the weather turned chilly. Maybe she'd make her a corn bread to go with the soup when she took it over. She looked up and saw Ian grinning at her.

"Earth to Angie? I asked you where you wanted the leftovers twice." He held the two plates of poutine.

"We'll have to compost those. I'd hoped we'd eat most of it, but it's so filling." She put the soup pot in the sink and turned off the water. "I'll do dishes when I get back."

"I'd help, but I have a meeting with the farmers market board this evening. It's our last meeting until next spring when we reopen." He scraped the scraps into her compost bag and rinsed the plates. "Maybe we could do a date night next Monday? I've got you penciled in on my schedule."

"I feel so honored." Angie took a rag to wash off the table and eyed Dom, who was watching the food move out from his reach. He whined and laid his head between his paws. "Sorry, dude. You have your own food."

Ian came up behind her. "You're always on the top of my list. We're both just so busy, and when I'm free, typically you're working."

"Well, at least we have the car ride to and from Boise to chat." She took off her Kiss the Cook apron and glanced at her capris and T-shirt. "Do I have time for a shower and change of clothes?"

"If it's quick." Ian walked over to Dom. "I'll take him out and do a lap around the barn with him so he gets some exercise today."

"Give me fifteen and I'll be ready." She grazed her lips over his. "You're the best, you know that?"

"I've been told that by many beautiful women. I'm just happy you think so." He grabbed Dom's leash off the key holder by the door. "Come on, big guy, let's go see what's going on outside."

As she got ready for their adventure, she glanced at Nona's picture on her dresser. "You would have loved Ian."

Traffic downtown was crazy busy, but they made it to the mission fifteen minutes before they were supposed to meet Taylor and the group. Sitting in the car, Angie eyed the building. It looked more like a warehouse than a shelter. "Are you sure we're at the right place?"

Ian laughed and turned off the engine. "I keep forgetting you just moved back into the area. They started here about five years ago. And besides, I know it's the right spot because I've come here with my class several times to help serve. But this is the first time I'll be helping in the kitchen."

"It's really not that much different. Except the kitchen staff works harder."

"Don't say that in front of Felicia. I think she could take you. She's been taking a martial arts class." He nodded to the woman who had just walked inside the mission. "There's Hope. Let's go in so they won't think we're making out in the car."

When they got into the building, they almost ran into Hope, who stood frozen at the edge of the room. Two men were yelling at each other in the middle, and as Hope turned to escape, her face lit up as she realized Angie was right behind her. Tension filled the large room.

"I'm so glad you're here. I'm not good with conflict." She moved between Ian and Angie. "Should we stop them? Or maybe we should just leave?"

Before Hope could spin around and escape, another man walked over to the uproar and put a hand on each man's shoulder.

"You know we don't solve our issues with loud voices or violence." The man's voice was calm and comforting.

"He stole my paper. I was looking at the jobs section and Harrold took it." The taller man poked a finger into Harrold's chest. "I told him to leave it alone."

"I was just looking at it. George was in the bathroom. He didn't need it in the bathroom." Harrold slapped the man's hand away from his chest. "And don't poke me."

"Don't touch my stuff and I won't poke you." George poked the guy again.

Angie stiffened. "This isn't going to end well."

The guy trying to stop the fight turned and smiled at her. An unspoken challenge danced in his eyes. He mouthed the words *watch this*.

He stepped between the two men. "What's our motto?"

"We are all friends and soldiers in the war against poverty," the two men chanted.

Angie watched as the man smiled and tapped both men on the shoulders. "And who do we fight?"

"We don't fight others, we fight discrimination, injustice, and hunger." This time their voices were stronger, like they really believed what they were saying.

"And what do we do when we've hurt someone else?"

Now George shuffled his feet. "We apologize. I'm sorry, Harrold, I shouldn't have yelled at you."

Harrold held out a hand, "I shouldn't have read your paper without permission. I'm sorry, friend."

As they shook, the other man smiled and nodded. "Great job. Now, both of you head out of here. We've got a dinner to get ready for."

As the men shuffled past Angie and the others, she could hear the mumbled threat from George. "Next time you take my stuff, Taylor's not going to be in earshot when I take you down."

"You're the one who should be glad he stopped me." Harrold glanced back at Taylor and waved. "I would have crushed you."

"Taylor..." Felicia popped out of the kitchen, her blond hair pulled back into a ponytail. "Oh, I didn't realize you guys were here already. I was going to ask Taylor to keep an eye out for you. I know first impressions of this place and the guys can be a little intimidating."

"Intimidating isn't the word. Scary as heck is more accurate." Hope almost ran toward Felicia. "If I wasn't getting extra credit for this, I'd be running home right now."

The man now known as Taylor smiled. "We all need a little help now and then. Let me introduce myself. I'm Taylor Simpson. You must be Felicia's friends."

Chapter 2

Ian held out his hand. "Ian McNeal. And this is Angie Turner, head chef and partner in the County Seat with Felicia. And that over there, quivering in fear, is Hope Anderson. She's usually stronger than she appears today."

"I think you're overestimating my character, Ian." But Hope smiled and waved.

"We're still missing a few, but we can get started and the rest will come in as they arrive. What's on the menu for tonight?" Angie walked toward Felicia and gave her a quick hug.

"We have tons of chicken and potatoes. What you do with that is up to you." Taylor joined the group heading into the kitchen. "We like our guests to have freedom to create. Besides, the guys are thankful for any meal they get. Sometimes, they don't eat for days. I can't even imagine that. And with all the food that goes to waste in America."

"You don't have to lecture me on food waste. I work with the River Vista Farmers Market, and I've seen a lot of perfectly good produce go to the compost heap because it's not sold or not perfect. Maybe we could work out a deal?" Ian studied Taylor with interest. "We're shutting down the market this Saturday for the season, but I'm meeting with the board tonight. Maybe I could come up with a proposal."

"You're always saving the world." Angie gave Ian a hug. "Let's just feed this group, and you and Taylor can talk after we get dinner set up. I wish Estebe was here, I'd like to run a few ideas off him as we look at your pantry."

As if she'd called him, her sous chef and the other cook, Matt, walked in the door. Matt waved at Angie. "Boss, you take us to the nicest places."

"Just be happy you have a job and a home. Some of these people would be thrilled to have your life. Although I'm not sure who would want to be you." Estebe turned from the shocked Matt, headed to the stoves, and nodded his approval. "This looks adequate. What are we making?"

Angie waved him over to the pantry. "I want to try something. But you make sure I'm not off my rocker."

Ian smiled as Angie and Estebe headed to the pantry. "You'll get more points for taste here than creativity."

"Oh, I don't know." Angie threw a look over her shoulder. "A little gourmet food never hurt anyone."

Hope glanced up at Ian as she went to put on an apron. "She's kidding, right? I don't think these guys want fancy stuff."

"Relax. When have you known Angie to make something that just looked good? She's all about the taste." Felicia pursed her lips as she started stacking plates from the dishwasher. "At least, I hope so."

By the time Angie and Estebe returned from the pantry, they had a plan. She called the group together and started breaking out the chores. "Hope, you and Ian are on potato peeling duty. Felicia, you can focus on dessert. Matt, you help Estebe with the protein. And I'll handle the gravy and the other toppings."

Ian walked over to the pantry. "I take it we're doing another take on the chicken poutine I vetoed at lunch?"

"It's a good dish. It just needs some tweaks." She turned toward Felicia. "Hey, could you ask Taylor how many he expects us to be feeding tonight? I'd hate to underprep."

"I already did. Two fifty was his rounded number. Sometimes a little less, sometimes a little more." Felicia still sat at the table, a pen and paper in hand. "What will work better, chocolate brownies or some sort of cake?"

"If you make brownies, they can add vanilla ice cream and melted chocolate over the top." Hope grinned. "Okay, so that's my favorite dessert ever. So sue me."

"That's enough of a sway vote for me." Felicia headed to the pantry. "When I've got the brownies in, I'll come help peel potatoes."

Matt plugged in a stereo Angie hadn't seen him bring in with him, and the too-quiet kitchen now almost sounded like their own kitchen at the County Seat. By five, their prep was done and they had an hour before dinner service. The group gathered around the table in the kitchen, and Estebe brought out a pot of soup with three loaves of round bread.

"I figured we wouldn't have time for a real meal before it was time to cook, so I brought lamb stew and fresh-baked bread for us to share." He tilted his head down toward the table, but not before Angie saw the tinge of pink on his cheeks.

Felicia came from the back of the kitchen with a plate filled with peanut butter cookies. "I thought we might need these to keep up our strength, but now that Estebe brought real food, I'm not sure anyone will want one."

"You're kidding, right? Peanut butter is my favorite. I love making peanut butter jam thumbprint cookies during the holidays." Matt reached over the table and grabbed two of the cookies.

Estebe cut the bread and Hope went to the fridge to grab butter. He filled a bowl with the steaming soup and then set a slice of bread over the top. Passing it down the table, everyone waited for Estebe to fill enough bowls before they started eating.

The table quieted down and Ian looked at the group. "If you don't mind, I'd like to say a blessing."

Matt set his already-filled spoon back down in the soup bowl. "Go ahead, man."

As Ian prayed, Angie thought about her own childhood where she was taught to show gratitude for the food on the table and the hands that prepared it. Maybe that tradition had been the seed that had grown into her love of cooking.

The chatter died down a little as they all started eating. When they introduced a new menu at the restaurant, all the servers and kitchen staff shared a meal together. They called it a family meal. This felt the same, except Angie really thought of these people as family. This wasn't the kitchen at the County Seat, but it was home for at least a time. She was amazed at how fast the bonds had been made between these strangers. But not really. Bonds made over food seemed to be stronger and longer lasting. Food was the great connector.

"So how do you like your classes this semester?" Angie turned to Hope, who had been texting someone. The girl flushed and put away her phone.

"Sorry, my friend Morgan was just checking to see if I was going to the soccer game tonight. Her boyfriend is playing in the intramural season this fall." Hope glanced at the clock. "I told her I'd meet her at the stadium at seven thirty. We should be done by then, right?"

"If we're not, you can still take off. It's a volunteer activity. You can leave at any time." Angie stirred her soup. The smell that wafted up from the bowl was heaven. "But you didn't answer my question. How are classes? You're still liking your program, right?"

"Definitely. I'm going to be finished next May, and I don't know what I'll do with myself." Hope dunked her bread into her soup. "I'll have tons of free time."

"No, you won't." Matt elbowed her. "When you graduate, you have to come play with us in the adult world. There are three things in the adult world. Work, sleep," his eyes met Angie's and he shrugged, then changed his word choice, "and more work. You'll get used to it."

"Whatever. Then why do I hear you talking about your trips out to the desert with your four-wheeler? You play more than anyone I know."

"Who said I was an adult anyway?" He grinned, then turned to Estebe. "This is great. Want to share your recipe?"

As the men talked about the soup, Hope turned to Angie. "One of the professors is so amazing. He's tall, and has dark hair but blue eyes. And when he looks at you, it makes a girl's head spin. Not to mention his voice."

"His voice?" Angie hoped she was keeping the grin she felt off her face. Their Hope had a crush on teacher.

"He's Canadian. Whatever he says sounds so romantic." Hope sighed, then took a sip of water. "Not like the dweeb boys around here. All they want to talk about is hunting, fishing, and what the Broncos did last weekend. And who plays on blue Astroturf?"

"Apparently your football team." A slightly accented voice added to the conversation, and Hope actually gasped and looked around for a place to hide. "Good evening, Hope. I decided to come by and help serve tonight."

"Professor Monet. I can't believe you're here." Hope's eyes glowed but her face was bright red. She looked like a possessed Halloween doll as she jumped up from her seat at the table. "I was just eating. I probably should be doing something. I'm sorry, I'll get busy right now."

"Hold on, Hope, I'm not here to grade you. Sit down, eat. We all have to eat, right?" He winked at Angie. "It's what keeps us in our line of work busy."

Hope sank back into her chair like a balloon with a slow leak. "Everyone, this is Professor Monet. He's visiting this semester from Canada. Professor, this is my work gang."

"Daniel, Daniel Monet." He grabbed an extra bowl from the sideboard and sat in an empty chair at the table. "Do you mind if I join you? I didn't get a chance to grab dinner before I came over to help. Office hours seem to always run over."

"No, please. Hand your bowl over and Estebe will hook you up. I'm Angie Turner, Hope's boss." She pointed to Estebe and, starting with him, introduced the people sitting at the table. When she got to Ian, he shook his head.

"Ian McNeal. Originally from South London. Have you ever been there, Arnie?"

Angie could feel the tension in Ian's body, and as she watched, the two men's gazes locked. A sly smile came over Daniel's too-perfect face.

"Can't say I've had the pleasure. No, Canada's been my home for most of my life." He took the full soup bowl from Felicia with a nod. "And it's Daniel, actually. Not Arnie."

Everyone at the table was quiet now. They had felt the strain between the two men as well. Angie put a hand on Ian's arm, and he broke contact and turned a reassuring smile on her.

"We better get this meal finished. Service starts in thirty minutes." He leaned toward her and whispered, "Let it go, I'll tell you in the car."

Angie nodded, then finished her meal, watching as the newcomer ate and made small talk with Felicia and Matt. He was tall and slender, his brown hair cut short and a pair of wire-frame glasses set just right on his face. He was dressed in a solid turtleneck, what looked like new jeans, and a business jacket, bringing the look right to the perfect professor. And from the look on Hope's face, the girl had it bad.

Angie had fallen for one of her professors. A young girl's crush on a man who probably hadn't even known her name. He had taught philosophy, and the ideas they'd discussed in class had her mind spinning. Once, she'd dropped off a paper and her fingers had touched his. She had studied her hand for days, trying to remember the touch. But then the semester had ended and she'd started taking culinary classes. The professor left Boise the next year for some larger college in Texas—or had it been Seattle? The details escaped her now. But she remembered the feelings, and seeing Hope going through the same thing made it all that more tender.

Taylor burst into the room. "There you all are. I've been stuck in my office on a budget meeting conference call. You'd think I was housing these guys at the Owyhee Plaza or something the way the board complains about every expenditure." He sniffed the air. "You made soup?"

"For our dinner. Would you like some?" Estebe stood and went to grab Taylor a bowl. "Sit down, we have a few minutes before we have to get cooking."

"It smells terrific in here." He pulled up a chair between Felicia and Daniel. "Maybe you should all come every night. Sometimes the cooking crew don't quite get the point of feeding others. Food isn't just a meal, it's a gift."

"I've been saying that for years." Ian took his empty bowl and reached for Angie's. "Thank you for allowing us to come tonight and share our talents with your guests."

Matt grabbed the empty bowls from his side of the table. "What he said. Ian's got the silver tongue. He can charm anyone. Right, boss?"

"Now, what is that supposed to mean?" Angie turned a playful snarl toward Matt.

He ducked farther back into the kitchen. "Doesn't mean nothing. I wouldn't be referring to you. Your disposition is quite pleasant."

"Unless you're stuck on a recipe that's not working." Ian kissed her on the top of her head. "We should get this process started. We'll be needing to set up the hot tray out front soon."

She nodded. "You and Felicia handle that. I did two types of gravy, one more traditional and one more of a barbecue sauce, so we'll need two trays for sauces." She listed off the way she wanted the serving line to go, drawing it out on a sheet of paper. "The only ones who will need to be back here are Matt and Estebe. They'll keep us in fresh, hot fries, but if someone starts to run out of something, make sure you call it out. I'll run pans to and from the kitchen."

"I could do that." Hope took her bowl to the dishwasher station. "You don't need to be our runner."

"I want you to be on the line." Angie thought this would be a good experience for Hope. Working as the dishwasher didn't give her a lot of customer front experience. This would give her a different viewpoint of the career she was working toward. Even though most line cooks didn't interact with the front, if she wanted her own restaurant someday, she'd have to deal with them sometime.

Daniel stood and followed her to the dishwashing station with his empty bowl. "I'll serve next to you so you can tell me all about your job with these folks. They seem very friendly."

She smiled up at him, and Angie blessed the guy for not making Hope feel uncomfortable in her feelings. She just hoped he wasn't too invested in the young woman. Hope might be totally legal in the dating world, but she was still a kid and didn't need to be dating someone at least fifteen years her senior. Angie glanced around the room. Her stomach had butterflies, just the same as those moments before she opened the doors at the County Seat. She'd always been nervous before openings. Which probably meant she cared.

"You all did a great job with prep. I know we're not usually on the front of the house, but I hope you enjoy your time volunteering here as well as just cooking for others. Sometimes a welcoming smile or a friendly hello is just as needed as a hot meal." Angie blinked away tears. "I'm so proud of all of you to take personal time out of your busy schedule to be here. It means a lot to me and Felicia, and of course to Taylor and the mission guys. Thank you all."

Cheers and whistles filled the small kitchen, and now Angie did wipe at her eyes. She hoped she wouldn't mess up her mascara. She didn't wear it often enough to know, but she'd sneak away to the bathroom before they got started and check out her eye makeup. She didn't want to look like a raccoon as she was serving.

Two hours later, with everyone fed and the kitchen cleaned, the group was getting ready to leave. The food had been a big hit with the guys, and Angie thought she could tweak the recipe just a bit more before she added it to the menu. They all grouped together on the sidewalk outside the mission.

Felicia stood with Taylor, his arm around her waist. "Thanks for doing this, guys."

"It was fun." Matt reached out to shake Taylor's hand. "And good to meet you finally. Felicia talks a lot about you."

"Does she? What exactly does she say about me?" Taylor chuckled.

"Matt, you need to shut up and leave." Felicia pointed a finger down the street. "Don't forget, I've got some dirt on you too."

"Point taken." He waved and started walking toward his car.

"Anyone going near Warm Springs? I walked here from the campus, but it's a little far to walk home." Daniel came out to the sidewalk and met the group. A black SUV pulled up to the light, then sped off, turning right on the red to the horns and annoyance of the other drivers coming through the intersection.

"Heading out to River Vista, sorry," Ian said. Angie didn't think his voice said sorry at all. She was about to say they could make a detour when Hope spoke.

"I'm meeting friends at the JV soccer game tonight. I can drop you off first, Professor Monet, if you don't mind being in my car. It's kind of old." Hope looked like she wished she'd never offered the ride.

"Student cars are supposed to be old and falling apart. That way you study hard to better your property." He smiled at her, and Angie saw the girl's shoulders relax. He turned toward the group. "It was very nice to meet Hope's work family. I'm sure our paths will cross again."

As they walked away, Ian muttered, "I hope not."

Chapter 3

Wednesday morning, Angie stood in the kitchen drinking her coffee and thinking about yesterday's adventure. Ian had been quiet all the way home, turning up the music when she tried to talk. She'd invited him in for dessert when they got to the farmhouse, but he'd begged off. He'd said he'd had a headache, but she thought the more likely cause was his discussion with the professor. Whatever it was, Ian had made it clear he didn't want to talk.

Felicia was better at reading people, which made her a perfect front of the house manager. She probably could have told Angie what was going on with Ian, but Angie was pretty sure she might still be with Taylor, and she didn't want to wake her this early.

This week was their first trial at being open on a Thursday, so she should just go into the restaurant and make sure everything was ready for tomorrow. Estebe had told her last night that he'd come in early and set up the prep. Since she knew he was trying to work as many hours as possible, she didn't want to take that work away just because she was anxious over what her boyfriend might be thinking.

Dom raised his head from his bed on the kitchen floor and watched her.

"I think you're right. We need to make some donuts." She patted him on the head and headed over to the cabinet to get things ready. She washed her hands, refilled her coffee cup, and tied her hair up with a clip. Then she got lost in her creating.

She pulled the last batch out of the oil when a knock came at her door. Holding the dripping basket over the oil, she eased the donuts out onto the paper towels where they could cool. Then she hurried to the door. Probably some salesman with a freezer in the back of his truck stocked with beef.

Like she'd trust buying her meat from a beat-up F-150. She swung the door open. "Yes?"

Sheriff Allen Brown stood on her porch. The man looked like a small-town sheriff. His shirt was just a little too tight and the buttons strained against the fabric. He tipped his hat, showing hair that was more gray than brown and thinning on the top. "Good morning, Angie. I was wondering if I could have a word with you?"

She hadn't always been on the better side of the River Vista sheriff, but since she was dating his nephew, the tension that seemed to erupt every time he stopped by to talk had eased a bit. "Of course, come in."

He slipped his hat off as he entered the house. Stopping just inside the door, he gaped at the pile of donuts covering the table. "How many did you make?"

"A few." Angie cleared a spot on the table. "Sit down and I'll get you a cup of coffee and a plate full. Maybe you'd like to take a few back to the station?"

"That would be nice. The guys would appreciate it." He set his hat on a small portion of table. Dom came and sniffed his hands, then apparently approving of the newcomer, sat down in front of the sheriff so that he could pet him. The sheriff took his cue and obliged. "Who's a good boy?"

"If you start petting him, he'll never let you stop," Angie warned as she placed the coffee in front of him. "Black, right?"

"Perfect. Thank you." He leaned forward when she set a plate in front of him. He took a bite, then sighed. "I never thought I'd say this, but yours are better than your grandmother's."

"That's high praise." She set her coffee and a smaller plate with her donuts on the table. Then she sat down. "What has you driving out all this way before nine in the morning? Don't tell me someone's dead."

When he didn't answer, she sat up straighter and set the donut she'd been about to scarf on the plate. "Oh my God. It's not Mrs. Potter or Erica, is it? They've been traveling, so I haven't bothered calling, but I should have called."

He reached out and laid his hand on her shoulder, easing her chatter. "It's not Mrs. Potter or Erica. According to Ian, you just met this guy last night."

Her mind raced. "It can't be Taylor. Felicia would be frantic and already have called me if something had happened to him. One of the guys at the mission? They were fighting when we came in, did it start up again? I knew Taylor's little peacekeeping mission wasn't effective with those guys. They just brushed him off."

"No, it wasn't one of the residents." He held up a hand when she started to list off more people. "Look, let me ask you some questions and you'll figure this out. Okay? I'm the investigator here, although you seem to be trying to take over my spot lately. Are you planning on running for sheriff if your restaurant fails?"

"What have you heard about the County Seat? Are people talking? Don't they like the food?" Now Angie's mind flew into a panic about the gossip about the restaurant.

"Hold on, I was joking with you. Maybe interviewing you in the morning isn't the best time. You seem to be jumping from bad to worse." He sipped his coffee and pulled out a notebook. "My turn to talk, right?"

Angie nodded and picked up her coffee. The cup felt warm in her hands and seemed to calm her frayed nerves. "Sorry. I'll be quiet."

"I'm not sure you can, but we'll try this, okay?" Sheriff Brown looked down at his notes, then back up at Angie. "Tell me about meeting Daniel Monet."

"Hope's professor? Is he dead?" She covered her mouth with her hand. "Oh, no, is Hope all right? Did they have an accident?"

"Hope is fine. They did not have an accident. But yes, Professor Monet is dead." He let the information settle before repeating his request. "So tell me about meeting Daniel Monet."

"We were sitting eating lamb stew at the mission between prep and service. Estebe had brought in food for us, which is so like him. I'd forgotten we were even scheduled to cook. Ian came and got me that morning and I was all into recipe creation. I've been working on a new menu for the upcoming month. I think it's good to change up things so people never know what to expect. Of course, you have to also keep the favorites on the menu. It's a thin line to keep everyone happy."

As she paused, the sheriff put up a hand to stop her chatter. "Look, I know this is sudden, but let's start from the first time you met Daniel."

"I'm nervous. I don't know why, but I feel like I've been through the wringer already." Angie took a deep breath. "Okay, like I said, we were eating. Then Daniel came in and introduced himself. Hope has it bad for the guy. She went all red and flustered. It was kind of cute. Anyway, he sat down, ate with us, and talked mostly to Felicia and Matt. Ian mixed him up with someone else he knew before he moved here. Then we served."

"And that was the last time you saw or talked to him?" Sheriff Brown was watching her, not writing, just watching.

"I saw him all during service, but we didn't have time to talk. Then he came out of the building as we were leaving. He needed a ride home, and

Hope said she'd take him. I think she was embarrassed at her little car, but it gets her where she needs to go." Angie broke off a piece of donut and ate it before continuing. "And then we left and Ian dropped me off here. I was home by seven thirty, quarter to eight. Dom and I watched a cooking show I'd recorded, then I went to bed."

"Ian dropped you off and left?" Now the sheriff was writing in his book.

Angie nodded. "I asked him in, but he said he was tired. I couldn't even tempt him with a slice of apple pie, and you know how he loves that."

"Okay then, that's all I need to ask. Thank you for your cooperation and the donuts. Do you want me to help you box up some for the station?" He started to stand, but this time Angie held him down with her hand on his arm.

"Wait, I need some answers too. Daniel Monet is dead. Hope is alive. How did he die? Have you talked to her? Is she okay?"

"I haven't talked to her. An investigator over at Boise City interviewed her this morning around eight after Daniel's body was found by his housekeeper." He didn't look at her as he put his notebook away. "I think she's still at the station. They may have more questions for her as the investigation continues."

She watched as he went to put his plate and cup into the sink. "They talked to her this morning? Why? She just dropped the guy off at his house. Why would they think a young college girl would have anything to do with his death?"

The sheriff turned and leaned against the counter. He looked older somehow. Like the interview had aged him in the last ten minutes. "Because your friend's fingerprints were found on a wineglass in his living room. Right next to the body."

A cold chill ran down Angie's back. "You can't think Hope had anything to do with this man's death. She's friendly and giving and—"

He held up a hand. "Facts are facts. Now we just need to deal with the reality of the situation and figure out why she was there so if she's innocent, we can rule her out. You know the drill."

Angie did know the drill. But it didn't make her feel any better about Hope having to go through this just because she'd offered to take her professor home. Angie boxed up donuts for him to take and walked him to the door. When his car pulled out of the driveway, she sat down with the remainders at the table. She dialed Ian first but got voice mail. She then tried Felicia. Same result. Where was everyone? Finally, she dialed Hope's number, not expecting to actually get her, but she could leave a message of support. The girl must be scared out of her mind.

"Hello?" Hope's voice rang in Angie's ear.

"Are you all right? Where are you? They let you keep your phone? Have you called a lawyer?" Angie didn't know how long she'd get to talk to Hope before they snatched her phone away. At least that's what they did in the police shows she watched.

A tiny laugh came over the phone. "Angie, I'm all right. Relax. I'm not at the station anymore. I called Estebe and he got his cousin who's a lawyer to make them release me. They didn't charge me or anything. Just kept asking me questions."

"Oh, good. I was so worried when I found out. Are you sure you're okay?" Angie heard the sniff before Hope answered.

"Professor Monet's dead. And they think I killed him."

"No, if they thought that, you'd still be at the jail." Angie hoped her statement was at least a little true. "Besides, all you did was give him a ride home, right? You had the soccer game to get to."

"Actually, there's a bit more to the story, but we just arrived at my apartment. Estebe drove me home. Do you mind if I call you later? I've got a class in thirty minutes and I need a shower."

"Sure. Just call me later." Angie heard the click in her ear.

She started to box up the rest of the donuts and clean the kitchen. Ten minutes later, her phone rang. She ran to answer it.

"Hello?"

"She's all right. Shaken but all right. I take it you'd already heard about the death?" Estebe's voice was tight, and from the background noise, she could tell he was in his vehicle.

"I got a visit from the sheriff this morning asking about meeting Daniel last night. Do you know what happened?" Angie sank back into her chair.

"No. She was frantic when she called me. I got my cousin out of bed and brought him down to get her out of there. They have no right terrorizing a child that way."

It wouldn't do any good explaining to Estebe that Hope wasn't considered a child even though she agreed with his statement. A young woman, yes, but in the eyes of the world and the law, she was an adult. "So she didn't tell you anything else?"

"It was painfully obvious last night that the girl worshipped this man. Maybe he went too far. That's not for me to say. All I know is Hope needs us right now." He cursed under his breath. "Driving on the freeway is getting more and more dangerous. People are idiots."

Angie didn't even want to bring up the fact that Idaho traffic was nothing compared to San Francisco traffic. During the five years she'd lived there she hadn't even owned a car, using Todd's when they were living together and then Felicia's for the few times she had to get somewhere that wasn't within walking distance of her apartment or the restaurant.

"Where are you going?" She didn't think he'd give her any more information about Hope. The good news was she was back on her normal schedule and could move on with her life.

"I'm heading out to Javier's farm. He wants to talk marketing with me." Estebe cursed again. "I will talk to you tomorrow. Are you coming in for prep?"

"I'll be there." She glanced at the box of donuts. Maybe she could take them in to Felicia and Ian. Anything was better than sitting here and thinking about eating all of them.

"See you then." The line went dead. Estebe Blackstone wasn't much for long goodbyes. The guy was direct and to the point. And that was one of his good points. But he adored Hope like she was his little sister. Even though Angie had been a little put out that Hope hadn't called her, she was glad that Hope had felt comfortable calling Estebe. Daniel had called the kitchen crew a work family, and he'd gotten that right. The group had been together less than a year, and still, they were bonded.

Angie stood and finished cleaning the kitchen. She grabbed a quick shower, then loaded the donuts and Dom into her SUV. In separate sections, of course. She'd installed a wire barrier between the back seat and the cargo section of the vehicle, just so Dom couldn't help himself to groceries or, in this case, donuts while she was driving. Dom sat in the back seat; the food, in the cargo area. Everyone was happy.

When she reached Ian's office, she parked in the front and stared in the window. The office looked deserted. Of course, there were only four rooms: Ian's office in the front, a small meeting room in the back, a bathroom, and a storage room. Angie could see Ian's desk and it was empty. Of course, he could be working in the meeting room. She turned toward Dom. "You stay here for a second while I check and see if he's working."

Dom whined but sat, leaning his head on top of the passenger side seat watching out the front window. Six months old and the guy almost took up the entire back seat of her vehicle. She might have to consider buying a larger model just so her dog would fit once he reached full size. The trouble with owning a St. Bernard, she mused. But she wouldn't give up the pile of lovable fur for anything. Dom was family now.

She went to the door with River Vista Farmers Market painted in black letters on the glass and pushed. It was locked. No sign. No handwritten note that Ian was so fond of. Just locked. She knocked. No answer.

"Hey, Angie." A woman called to her from the sidewalk. "Looking for Ian?"

She turned to see Beth Lee standing to her left, a bag of laundry in her hands. Beth ran River Vista Laundromat and Cleaning Services. Her business was between Ian's office and the Red Eye Saloon. "Hey, Beth. Have you seen him?"

"He went out this morning. Dropped off his laundry, which he usually does on Friday, and said to let anyone who was looking for him know he'd be gone for a few days." She glanced over to the bank. "I was just picking up the dry cleaning from the bank and on my way back to the laundromat. Did you need help?"

"Actually, no, I was just looking for Ian." She glanced at the locked door again. It was strange that he'd just taken off like that. He hadn't said a thing last night. "I guess I forgot he was going out of town."

Beth hiked the bag up onto her hip. "According to him, it was last minute. Maybe he forgot to mention it. You know how men are. My late husband would forget what day of the week it was if I didn't mention it. Then he'd be all bent out of shape because I'd said something. I can't count the times he'd say 'I know,' when really, he'd totally forgotten. God rest his soul."

"Well, I'm keeping you from your work." She thought about the three boxes of donuts in the vehicle. "Hey, do you like donuts?"

After she'd dropped off a box of donuts with Beth, she got back into her car and drove less than a block to the County Seat, where she parked in the back. Felicia's car wasn't in its normal spot. She looked at Dom. "I know, you want out."

She let Dom out, and he did his business on his favorite tree that grew between the sidewalk and the street. Either that tree was going to thrive with Dom's attention or it would be dead in a year. She got out one of the boxes of donuts since she was pretty sure her partner wasn't in either the restaurant or her apartment upstairs. She opened the back door, juggling the keys, the leash, and the box, and managed to turn off the alarm before it went off.

The inside was cool and she led Dom to her office, where he plopped down on his bed. Since her office was separate from the kitchen and dining room, the health inspector had reluctantly agreed that Dom could visit, if he stayed put. She flipped through the mail Felicia had stacked on her desk and checked her answering machine. No red light, no messages. She'd brought the machine from Nona's when she'd installed the landline at the restaurant. When recording a new message for the restaurant, she found she could also leave a second or third version. As she had at the start of each week since she opened the County Seat, she sat down at her desk and pushed the option for listening. Her Nona's voice filled the office and Angie felt the tears behind her eyes. Dom came and put his head on her lap. A tradition now. The dog could feel and identify her emotions probably better than she could. She stroked his soft ears as she listened.

When it was done, she shook her head. "Well, this isn't getting us anywhere." She ran upstairs to knock on Felicia's door, but no one answered. She took the piece of paper she'd grabbed from her desk and taped it to the door. Donuts on the expediting station. Then she went back downstairs and got Dom.

Two stops, two strikeouts. She'd been hoping to get rid of all the donuts. As she walked out to the car, she saw Barb Travis, owner and bartender at the Red Eye, standing outside the back door to the bar smoking. Maybe the woman had a sweet tooth. Angie already knew she had a strong coffee addiction.

She grabbed the last box and, with Dom still on his leash, walked over to greet Barb. She held out the box. "Do you like donuts?"

"Why?" The woman didn't even reach out for the offering.

Angie pushed the box closer. "Because I made too many this morning and I don't want to eat all of them."

"I saw you at your man's office. Where'd he take off to so fast this morning? I watched him shove a duffel bag into that truck of his and peel out of here like the devil was chasing him." She took the box and perched it on the iron railing that went around the top of her steps. "I suppose these were supposed to go to him?"

"I didn't have anyone in mind when I made them." She glanced over to the parking space where Ian's truck was gone. The little wagon he used for business sat alone in one of the two spaces. "What time did you see him?"

"It was early. I don't sleep much, so I head down here to have my coffee and read the paper. Sometimes I get lucky and see some action, even that early." She smiled, but Angie didn't feel like the emotion behind it was positive or friendly. "You two have a fight?"

"No. And don't be spreading that around. I hate the way gossip travels in this town." Angie tried to think of why Ian would take off, but the only thing she could think of was his meeting Daniel last night. He'd been weird since that guy had walked into the kitchen.

And now Daniel was dead. The two things couldn't be related. Could they?

Chapter 4

She left messages on both Ian's and Felicia's voice mail, then started the car. But instead of turning toward home, she decided to take a detour. When she arrived at the parking lot, she saw Dom's wiggle and smile in the rearview mirror.

Getting out at the base of the hiking trails that lined Snake River Canyon, she glanced up as a hawk cried as he flew over her car. She and Dom were the only visitors to the park based on the empty parking lot. She grabbed her backpack that had bottled water, a bowl for Dom, and a few protein bars. She tucked her cell phone into the front pocket and put the leash on Dom. Sometimes she let him off, letting him explore the area, but today she wanted him close.

Probably because she felt uneasy about not being able to find either her boyfriend or her best friend. She shook the negative thoughts away. They would call. Just because something happened to someone she barely knew didn't mean her friends were in trouble. Except maybe Hope. She hoped Estebe's cousin was a good lawyer. She didn't want to think the worst, but it never hurt to make sure you were protected.

Again, nothing she could worry about now. Right now she was going to walk up the trail and focus on getting some of this extra energy burned off. And if she saw some amazing scenery, all the better.

She locked the car and then tucked her keys into her backpack, making sure she zipped up the pocket. Being out here alone wasn't a problem. Losing her keys on her walk and not having anyone close by to rescue her, that might be more of an issue.

Dom and Angie wandered up the trail that did switchbacks to keep you climbing. By the time she got to the top of the canyon, both she and Dom were panting. She sat on a bench that provided an outstanding viewpoint for the entire canyon and river. If you could get here. Opening her backpack, she poured half a bottle of water into Dom's bowl and drank the other half. She absently picked up her phone and noticed she'd missed a text.

Clicking on it, she read Ian's message aloud to Dom. "I've got to go home for a few days. I'll call you when I'm back in the States."

Ian had grown up in England, where his mother had moved them when he was a baby. He had dual citizenship, but he didn't talk about England as home. Had something happened to his mother? He didn't talk about her or his childhood. She decided she'd call Sheriff Brown as soon as she got home and see if Ian had mentioned this trip when they'd talked that morning.

Wait. If he had, why hadn't the sheriff mentioned Ian's leaving when he came for donuts and information? Sometimes the guys kept things from her that didn't need to be a secret. It was like they had this family code that didn't include her. Well, that was going to be a conversation she had with Ian as soon as he got back. She needed to know these things.

Angie steamed all the way down the trail. But when she called the station, Sheriff Brown was out in the field. The only satisfaction she got was leaving a terse voice mail. She drove home and took care of her chores. Precious ignored the food and cried until Angie stopped working and paid attention to the goat. The animal seemed to know her moods. Angie sat on the stool and stroked her neck, telling her about all the weirdness that had happened that day. When she closed up the barn after feeding Mabel, she felt better. Dom sat on the step to the house watching her.

"You still don't like having Precious as one of us, do you?" She sat next to him and scratched behind his ear.

The only answer she got was a baleful look toward the barn. She guessed that was all he needed to say.

"Let's go inside and make dinner. Then we'll put on a movie and eat popcorn."

Dom stood and waited at the door. Apparently, he thought that was the perfect ending to this day. Angie glanced around the darkening farm and threw out good wishes to her loved ones.

She'd finished the dinner dishes and was about to put the popcorn in the microwave when her phone rang.

"Hey, just got your message. Thanks for the donuts. I spent the day with Taylor at the donation center going through stuff. You wouldn't believe what people think is worth donating. I swear we threw away more than we kept." Felicia sounded happy but tired. "What's going on with you?"

Angie wondered where to start. "I guess you haven't heard. Daniel Monet is dead. And Ian's taken off across the pond."

"Wait, what? Who? What's going on with Ian? Do I need to come over?"

"You don't have to come over, but I'd love to chat for a few minutes if you have time." Angie curled up into the recliner in her living room. Then she proceeded to tell Felicia everything she knew. "And Ian's taken off for England for some reason. You don't think it has something to do with Daniel's death, do you?"

"Of course it has to do with Daniel's death. You said Ian thought he knew the guy. Maybe he's going home to look at his high school yearbook or something." Felicia was quiet for a second. "He said he'd be back in a couple of days. Just talk to him then."

"Reasonable." Angie yawned and realized they'd been talking for over an hour. "Look, I'm coming in tomorrow. I'll stay out of the kitchen so I don't shorten Estebe's or Matt's hours by doing prep, but I want to be in the office working. I think it will help take my mind off this whole crazy mess."

"Sounds good. Do you think I should hire a temporary dishwasher?"

Angie considered the question. "I don't think so. According to Estebe, his cousin is dealing with the legal issues."

They said their good nights, but Angie didn't go up to bed. Instead she made that popcorn she'd promised Dom and put on a movie she'd watched too many times. But she knew how it ended, and she needed something proving that the world rewarded good and punished evil, even if it was only in the movies and novels she loved to immerse herself in.

* * * *

Thursday morning was bright and cool. Mornings like this always made her think of the song about Thanksgiving with the frost on the pumpkin, but she had no idea what fodder being in the shock meant. She could call Ian, but he was being a world traveler and not available for such inane questions.

Angie fed Precious and Mabel, then went inside to feed Dom and make her own breakfast before she headed into town. She tried to fuel up on workdays because she knew she'd be on her feet for hours once service started and, besides the tastings, she wouldn't eat much until after the restaurant closed. She insisted on a family meal between the prep and the service. It kept her kitchen staff from fainting during service and she got a feel for how her team was feeling.

She cut the last loaf of homemade bread into thick slices and made her French toast. She'd emptied a jar of strawberry preserves into a saucepan and let it warm while she made the toast. She fried bacon in another pan. Dom was lying in his bed watching her. She thought she saw him lick his lips.

"No bacon for you, big guy. You're going to be home alone way too long for me to chance it." She'd set up a dog door to the backyard and reinforced the fence, but she still worried about him being by himself so many hours. It couldn't be helped. Long hours were part of being the chef/owner of a restaurant, especially during the first few years when establishing the business.

She sat at the table, reading on her tablet to find any more information on the murder. The local paper had a small article buried on the third page of the local section. The piece hadn't mentioned Hope, just that all avenues of investigation were being explored. Angie wondered how Sheriff Brown had gotten involved in the investigation. Or maybe he hadn't been on official business when he came out to interview her.

She was going to make sure she popped into the police station today and had a chat with him. One, she was kind of worried about Ian, and maybe Sheriff Brown knew more about Ian's little disappearing act. But two, she wanted to know what his stake in this investigation was and why he'd come out to the farm.

Angie cleaned up the kitchen, checked on Dom's food and water, and gave him a chewy bone. She left the radio on so he'd have some company and leaned down to kiss him on the top of his wide brow. "You be good, boy. Maybe we can squeeze in a hike Saturday morning before I go into work."

Dom huffed and laid his head on the chewy. He wasn't happy, she could see that.

She locked the door and headed out to her car. Maybe Dom needed a friend, but she couldn't imagine having a second dog in the house. Unless it was small. And then she'd worry about Dom sitting on the puppy and smothering it while she was gone. No, for right now, she'd just have to deal with the guilt.

The drive into River Vista was relatively quiet. No dawdling farmers driving tractors in her way. No wandering farm animals to slow down the commute. Just the music on the stereo and the sun shining through the side window. If she didn't have so many worries on her mind, she would have enjoyed the pretty day.

She parked behind the County Seat and looked over at the building that held Ian's office and apartment. The windows were dark. Stupid, she thought, as her heart sank. She wasn't going to moon over a guy who didn't even see the need to tell her he was leaving. Yes, Ian was going to have a lot to account for when he returned.

Angie unlocked the kitchen door and was surprised to see Estebe already in the kitchen working. "Hey, I didn't see your car. How long have you been here?"

"I parked out front since I stopped by Pamplona Farms this morning and picked up the delivery. I'll move it now if that's a problem."

"No problem. Just move it before service. I'd rather have those slots available for our customers." Angie felt stupid correcting him. He'd probably planned to move it anyway, but she felt surly and the words were out of her mouth before she could soften them.

"Yes, ma'am." He watched her walk into the kitchen. "Hope is coming in after class. She's holding up well, considering everything."

How had he pinpointed one of her worries so fast? It felt like the guy could read her mind. Angie grabbed a cup of coffee and sat at the table. "I can't believe she's having to go through all this. All she did was give the guy a ride home and they're dragging her into a police station for questioning? Hope?"

Estebe set down the knife he'd been using to chop vegetables. He refilled his own coffee cup and then sat down at the table with her. He studied her face, not speaking.

"What? Do I have my makeup on wrong? Why are you staring at me?" Fear bubbled up in her stomach. "No, it's about Hope. You know something you're not telling me. What? There's no way she killed that guy. Not Hope."

"I do not believe she killed her professor. However, she didn't just give him a ride home." He sipped his coffee, now avoiding looking at her. "She told me she went into his house when they got there. He offered her a glass of wine and she went inside."

"She was going to a soccer game. She didn't have time for socializing."

Estebe shook his head. "You saw how nervous she got around Daniel. I believe she thought they might have a real relationship, so when he invited her inside…."

Angie finished the idea for him. "She thought it was so he could ask her out on a date." She shook her head. "What was she thinking? He's old enough to be her father."

"Some women like older men. They make them feel safe and they are more established in their careers." Estebe chuckled as Angie stared at him. "What? It's not uncommon for younger women to seek that stability. I've even been approached by girls much younger than Hope wanting to marry."

"But you turned them all away." Angie smiled and sipped her coffee. Estebe didn't talk about his personal life very much. She enjoyed seeing this side of him. And he was good at calming her down.

"I am not looking for a child to raise. I am looking for a partner for my life." Estebe shrugged, and she saw the pink tint his cheeks. "Anyway, Hope went inside, had a glass of wine, and the guy made a pass at her."

"What happened next?"

The door to the kitchen opened and Matt bounded inside. "Hey, good people I work with and like. Happy Thursday." He kept talking as he tucked his coat into the closet along with a backpack. "Angie, you don't know how much my budget appreciates these extra hours. I'll almost be at full time this month."

"I think you should talk to Hope," Estebe said in a low tone. He stood and took his cup. "Glad you could make it. I thought I was going to be chopping all these onions myself."

"You didn't look like you were doing much chopping," Matt teased as he grabbed a cup of coffee. Then he froze as he took in the scene. "Crap, I interrupted something, didn't I? Should I go into the dining room and let you guys talk?"

"No, we were done." Estebe looked at Angie, who nodded. "Besides, we don't have time to be sitting around talking. We have people to feed tonight."

As Angie left the kitchen, she heard Matt turn on the radio. The world was going back to normal. Hopefully this investigation would just blow over and not settle near her family. She decided to run over to the police station and see if she could talk to Sheriff Brown about Ian and what he knew about Hope and this guy. Maybe the case had moved on from the tiny blonde and she didn't have anything to worry about.

And maybe a dancing pig would be parading down Main Street when she walked outside.

The officer at the front desk looked up as she walked in and groaned. For some reason, this guy, Phillip, thought she was the bane of his boss's existence. Probably because Sheriff Brown never wanted to talk to her. He'd even told her that he thought she was bad luck for the town. No murders for over twenty years, and in the less than a year she'd lived there, three people had lost their lives to unnatural causes. Like that was her fault. She pasted on a smile and marched up to the desk. "Good morning. I hope you enjoyed the donuts I sent over yesterday."

The guy's eyes flashed but he nodded. "They were adequate."

Okay then, see if I send over any more. She smiled. "Always a pleasure to hear someone rave about my food. Anyway, is the sheriff in? I'd like ten minutes of his time."

"He's in Boise. He got called in as a special investigator for a murder case." He puffed up in what Angie thought was pride in his boss. "I'm not to bother him unless the town starts burning down or aliens appear."

"That's pretty specific." She shook her head when he just stared at her. "Look, tell him I need to talk to him."

"I'll put a note on his desk." Phillip almost smirked. "Thank you for coming in."

Angie turned and left the office. The jerk might not have the best customer service skills, but she knew he'd mention her visit and relay her message. He was a by-the-book type who wouldn't even consider not giving the sheriff a message. Even from her.

Dissatisfied with the way her day was going, Angie headed back across the street to the restaurant. She went straight into her office, turned on her computer, and opened up the accounting program. Nothing took her mind off her troubles like looking at the projections and monthly budgets she'd developed with their accountant. She'd found this little trick when she was in California. If—no, when—she had a fight with Todd, she'd lock herself in her office and work on the books. Normally, she hated the task. But she had to admit there was something calming about putting the numbers in all the right boxes and the whole thing balancing out.

Today she needed that level of distraction. With Hope in trouble and Ian AWOL, she could work herself up into a frenzy if she didn't distract herself. And she didn't want to go help out with prep, which would have been her first choice, because the team needed the work to make hours.

Running a business was harder than it looked. Especially when you had employees you cared about that you had to take care of...and keep out of jail. She shook off the thought and started working with the receipts.

An hour later, Felicia burst into her office. "Oh, good, you're here. I need you in the kitchen."

"Why? What happened?" Angie jumped out of her chair and followed Felicia.

Her friend shot her a backward glance over her shoulder. "It's Hope."

Chapter 5

Following Felicia into the kitchen, she glanced around. Matt and Estebe were standing at the table. As she got closer, she could see Hope sitting on a chair, bent over holding her head between her hands. Angie pushed Matt aside and knelt next to the sobbing young woman. "Hope, what's wrong? Have you cut yourself? Did anyone call 911?"

Estebe touched Angie's shoulder. "She's not hurt. At least not physically."

Relief flooded through Angie and she took a long breath. "Hope, tell me what's wrong."

"I'm responsible for Professor Monet's death." She hitched in a few breaths and started sobbing again.

"Wait, what are you saying? Did something happen? Did he hurt you?" There was no way Angie was going to let Hope take the blame for reacting if she had been attacked. "When you were in his house, did he hurt you?"

Hope looked up at her, confusion showing in her eyes. "Did who hurt me?"

"Daniel. Did he hurt you or force himself on you in any way?" Maybe this wasn't the time to be talking about a sensitive subject like this, but she needed to know so Hope wouldn't say something incriminating to the police the next time they interviewed her. Unless she already had. But if that was the case, she wouldn't be here, she'd be locked up in jail. "Honey, it's all right. Tell me what happened."

"No. Professor Monet didn't hurt me. He asked me inside for a glass of wine. He wanted to talk about my senior project and what I was thinking about doing for it." Hope wiped her sleeve across her cheeks, damp from tears. "He was going to be my advisor if he stayed another semester."

"So you went into his house."

"We had a glass of wine, then Morgan called and reamed me for keeping her waiting. I told the professor I'd talk to him tomorrow and left." She took a deep breath. "If I had stayed, maybe he wouldn't have been attacked. I could have saved him."

"You probably would have been dead too if you had been there when the killers came to the door." Matt handed her a paper towel.

"I didn't mean I could have fought them off, but maybe if I had been there, they would have gone to another house. I don't know. I just know I left, and now he's dead." Hope wiped her eyes with the paper towels. "Am I being oversensitive about this? I mean, he was only my professor and I hadn't even known him that long."

"It's hard to wrap your head around any death, no matter how long you've known the person." Estebe held out his hands, and when she took them, he pulled her to her feet. "Now, go wash your face, and when you come back, I will teach you how to make my green tomato steak sauce. We're trying it out tonight with the rib eye."

She nodded, then threw herself into Estebe's arms and gave him a hug. "Thank you for everything you've done. I really appreciate the lawyer and the ride and the advice."

"And now you'll appreciate the tutoring too." He patted her on the head and then turned her toward the restrooms. "Go on now, get cleaned up. We can't have you crying tears into the food. You'll make our customers sad."

No one said anything until Hope had left the room. Felicia sighed. "That girl has such a big heart, it's no wonder she's so upset. She wouldn't hurt a fly. The police have to know that, right?"

"From what my cousin told me, Hope has a solid alibi, as she was with Morgan and a couple of hundred others watching the game when Daniel was killed. They only called her in due to her prints on the wineglass." Estebe walked back and washed his hands in the sink. "The girl has nothing to worry about."

"Except she was in the dude's house." Matt followed Estebe to the sink. "She's probably toast. Maybe we should start looking for a new dishwasher."

"Matt!" Angie couldn't believe what she was hearing.

He turned and grinned at her. "Just kidding, boss. You know Hope's like my little sister. She's annoyingly good. All the time. To see her in a little bit of trouble? Well, it does my heart good."

"You better not let her hear you say that." Estebe picked up his chef knife and went back to work on the vegetables. "I think she can take you."

Felicia took Angie's arm as they walked back to the office. "Do we have insurance that could cover an employee's legal fees?"

"I don't think so." Angie rubbed the bridge of her nose. "You think it's going to be okay, right?"

"I hope so."

Angie tried to go back to working on the numbers, but now everything was running together. She turned off the computer. Too soon for family dinner, but she didn't want to go into the kitchen. Not yet. She grabbed a bottle of water from the mini-fridge and headed over to where Felicia was working on setting up the dining room.

"I'm going for a walk down Indian Creek." She glanced at her watch. "I should be back in twenty minutes if anyone comes looking for me."

"Like Ian?" Felicia knew her moods.

"No, like the kitchen crew. I told you that Ian's out of the country for who knows how long." Angie knew she sounded snippy, but she didn't want to talk about Ian, not now. "Look, I just want to clear my head for a while. I'll be back."

Felicia pushed a cylinder container into her hands. "Take this. It's pepper spray. Just in case."

"I'm just going for a walk." Angie tried to hand it back, but Felicia folded her arms. Angie sighed and tucked it into her pants pocket. "Fine, but I feel stupid."

"Better feeling stupid and being safe."

Nona had said something like that once when Angie had called home from California. Everyone in her life must think she was a flaming idiot. She ran into one of the servers who was coming in the door as she was going out.

"Sorry." The perky young woman smiled as she recognized Angie. "You heading out already?"

Emotion threatened to overwhelm her, so she just shook her head and kept walking. She'd be better with a walk. Calm down, cool down, and get her mind straight. What had Ian been thinking, taking off like that? Now she had two people to worry about, him and Hope. She kept seeing the fear on the girl's face. She knew Hope couldn't have killed anyone, but knowing that and proving it were two different things.

She needed to come up with a plan to get the attention off her dishwasher, sooner rather than later. She'd heard that you always need to look at the victim and that would lead you to the killer. Or at least that was the way it worked in her favorite mystery books. When she got home tonight, she'd look up Daniel Monet on the internet. That should give her an idea what the guy was like. Or had been like, she corrected herself. Then first thing Friday morning, she'd head over to the school. It was long past time for her to make an appearance, especially since one of her staff was working on her degree there.

And that should give Angie the access she needed to find out what Daniel Monet was doing in Boise. It seemed strange that someone would come here for a visiting professor position, but maybe he liked the Idaho climate and closeness to outdoor sports like skiing and hiking. The guy had looked like he kept in shape. But again, why leave Canada for a place that kind of mirrored where he came from?

She wasn't answering any questions, but at least her breathing had returned to normal and she didn't feel like punching something. She'd try to catch Sheriff Brown just before service started Friday night, and if she missed him, she knew where he'd be Sunday morning.

The Browns attended River Vista Methodist, just like Ian did. She could get there early and hang out in the parking lot until he and his wife arrived. Then he'd have to tell her what was going on with Ian.

By the end of the weekend, she should have both of these matters wrapped up into neat little boxes and tied with a bow. Feeling more settled and a lot more positive, she turned around on the greenbelt and headed back to toward town. A man in a black coat and ball cap was on the path behind her. When he saw her turn around, he turned and almost dove off the sidewalk and into the bushes.

Thinking something must have happened, Angie ran to the spot where she'd seen the man, but all she saw was him running up the road that went out of town. He turned back, and when their eyes met, he pushed forward faster.

"Were you watching me?" Angie fingered the pepper spray in her pocket. She'd never catch up with the guy and besides, why run toward trouble. Maybe she had just startled him. Maybe he was out for a jog and thought the path was empty. Or maybe her first instinct was the correct one. But if the man had been watching her, why? An alarm went off on her watch. It was time for family meal. The team would be worried if she didn't show up. Besides, what was she supposed to do with a stalker who took off running as soon as he was noticed? She'd tell the sheriff, but that guy was doing a great job of ignoring her for the last few days. She kept walking toward the County Seat.

When she got inside the restaurant, she saw worry in Felicia's face that quickly disappeared once Angie walked inside. She nodded to the kitchen. "They're in there, waiting for you. I'll be there in a few minutes. Can I bring my early shift in to eat too?"

"Of course." Angie paused at the kitchen door, her hand flat on the wood. She needed to be 100 percent here tonight. Otherwise, she had no business being in the kitchen. It wasn't the safest of work environments and she didn't want to get herself or worse, someone else, hurt by being in her head. She took a deep breath and settled her mind. She could worry about the rest tomorrow—or, more likely, when she wasn't sleeping tonight. Right now, all that mattered was the food, her team, and the customers. Pasting on a smile she didn't feel, she pushed open the door.

The team was already at the table. Nancy had joined them sometime during the day, and she and Matt chatted. Hope sat pushing her food around her plate, and Estebe had just brought over a dish of pasta with spareribs. The smell of the tomato sauce made Angie's mouth water. No matter how upset she might get, food always had the healing power.

"Come sit down. Tell us about the food we'll be cooking tonight. Is there anything special from your grandmother?" Estebe smiled and patted the chair between him and Hope. "Come and eat. You need the sustenance before we go into battle."

Hope looked at him, confused. "You see cooking as a battle?"

"And you don't?" He dished up some of the pasta, then held out his hand for Hope's plate. "Cooking is the ultimate battle. We have to gather the ingredients, sometimes from hostile areas. Then we have to master the art of the flame to cook the item. Then we have to hope our customers are as wooed by the taste of the food as the presentation our lovely chef sends out to the dining room."

Felicia and her servers had come in during this talk. She sat next to Estebe, probably because the other two were too frightened of the guy. "I can see that kind of logic. Especially from a man. But as a pastry chef, baking is like a chemistry experiment. Sometimes it works, sometimes you fail."

Angie loved listening to chefs talk. They all had such different perspectives on the craft. Some saw it as a job, some as a calling. The people who lived to cook, those were the ones she loved being around. And apparently, the ones she hired. She noticed Hope's eyes light up as the discussion continued. The girl loved cooking. She'd be fine, once this was behind her.

As they finished up dinner, Angie walked out of the kitchen and went to the reservations stand with Felicia. "So we're good for tonight?"

"We filled up as soon as we opened the slots and updated our hours on the website. I don't think we're going to have to worry about filling the restaurant, no matter how many nights we open for."

Angie shrugged. "I don't know. We're not into winter yet. I'd hate to slack off and think we're fine and have a snowstorm keep us closed until the spring thaw."

"We've been talking about opening a Saturday chef class. Can I schedule one for early November, maybe on locally sourced ideas for Thanksgiving, and a Christmas treat one for December?" Felicia paused and watched her.

"Maybe two in December? One for sweet and one for savory?" Angie took out her phone and made some notes. "Let's sit down on Monday and plan this out. We might even turn the sweets into a mommy and me class. I wonder if that will affect our insurance."

The doors opened and their first customers arrived. Angie stuck her phone back into her pocket and skirted out of the foyer. She'd let Felicia play hostess. That wasn't really her scene, although she was sure Felicia would pull her out of the kitchen sometime tonight to meet one of the patrons. She was excited about the cooking classes. She could bring in one or more of the kitchen staff and build up hours that way.

She stopped by her office and noticed the flashing light on her message machine. She took a minute to sit and let the message play.

"Hey, Angie. Sorry I'm not there. I know you probably have all kinds of questions. I might even have some answers when I come back." The message machine picked up Ian's laugh, but it didn't sound like he was truly having fun. "I just wanted to say I miss you and I'm sorry I didn't stop by before I left."

A train whistle blew in the background.

Ian came back on the line. "I've got to go. See you in three days' or a week's time, tops. I love you."

And then the message ended. Angie played it again. He had been waiting for a train. But a train to where? Where was he? Her heart ached a little as she stood from her desk and slipped on her chef coat. She didn't have time to wonder, except one last question hit her as she was turning off the lights and locking the office door. Why hadn't he called her cell?

Pushing thoughts of Ian out of her head, she went into her kitchen and got lost in the service.

At home she lay in bed trying to sleep. Dom was already snoring in his puppy bed that she needed to replace again since he barely fit inside. She picked up her phone and dialed Ian's number. It went straight to voice mail. She hung up without leaving a message.

Then she dialed again. This time after his cheery message inviting her to leave her name, number, and the reason for her call, she spoke quickly.

"Thanks for the message this afternoon. I miss you, lots. Be safe and come home soon."

She hung up the phone and set it on the bedside table. Then she turned off the light and cuddled into bed. Sleep didn't find her for hours.

* * * *

Friday morning, she dragged herself out of bed and, with a cup of coffee in hand, went out to feed the zoo. She didn't stop and talk to Precious and she almost threw Mabel's corn into her water dish. She had to get some sleep tonight, no matter what. If she didn't, on Saturday she might as well just call in sick since she wouldn't be any help in the kitchen at all.

Back in the house, she poured a bowl of cereal and opened her laptop. She probably should have done this last night while she wasn't sleeping, but she'd suffered through. She'd read somewhere that working on the computer at night tricked your body into thinking it wasn't time for bed. She didn't want to add to her insomnia.

She took out a notebook, turned it to a blank page, and started writing down everything she found on the handsome professor. He'd made a big splash at the college when he'd arrived a couple of months ago. He'd refused to give interviews, but that hadn't stopped the local journalists who liked a challenge. *Reclusive chef turned professor, he eats what he teaches* was one headline. Angie thought the author could have been a little more creative.

She found his official bio on the school website and wrote down the places where he'd taught before, where he'd gone to school, and where he'd been employed as a chef. The lineup was impressive, which led Angie to the same question she'd had yesterday. Why did someone with this type of background come and teach in Idaho? Not that Boise State wasn't a good school, but she knew the college wasn't paying him half of what he could have made in a larger town or staying where he was.

She went to the website for the last college listed on his résumé. He wasn't listed as attached to the school. Which wasn't unusual. He was gone on sabbatical or whatever they called it. But then she found no mention of the guy in any of the other places where he'd lived or worked, or even where he'd gone to school.

Daniel Monet was a ghost before he'd arrived in Boise. And maybe that's what had gotten him killed.

Chapter 6

She called the police station, and after a little bit of back and forth, she was sent to the sheriff's voicemail. Was it this case or Ian he didn't want to talk about? But she didn't have much time for wondering. Today she was going into Boise to check out the school. She might not find out anything, but at least she would have tried. And then she could put this worry away. There was nothing more she could do to help Hope. Besides, according to Estebe, Hope had an airtight alibi for the time Daniel was killed.

This visit was just for Angie's peace of mind. From what she had found or, actually, hadn't found on Daniel Monet last night, she was concerned.

She made sure everyone was fed and watered, as she wouldn't be home until late. On work nights, she refed everyone just before she left. Hoping that they wouldn't just eat everything all at once was a long shot, but at least she'd tried. She gave Dom a hug, grabbed her tote bag with her notebook and tablet, and headed off to school.

The campus sat just south of downtown Boise, on the opposite bank of one of the major parks for the area, Julia Davis Park. There was a footbridge that joined the campus to the greenbelt that ran twenty-nine miles east and west along the river. Angie had habitually run that path when she had attended classes. It was a great way to clear her mind. She pulled into visitor parking, put coins into the meter, and headed into the Administration Building to find out where the culinary school was housed.

The campus was so much bigger than it had been six years ago when she'd left for California. And from what she'd seen driving in, it was still growing. She got the alum magazine and sometimes paged through it before recycling. It wasn't that she didn't care, she just had other things on her mind, like growing a new restaurant and the business of that. Now she wished she'd paid more attention. She knew the school had been set to move to a different location, but she had no clue.

The rush of students in and around the quad made her homesick for her days as a carefree coed. She'd loved her time at the school. Learning new things, reading new authors, expanding her mind. But when she'd found her path through the world of cooking, she'd been laser focused on getting her degree and setting up her own restaurant, especially after she'd met Todd and Felicia. She'd thought the trio would be friends forever. Then she and Todd became a couple. Felicia had stayed a steadfast friend, even if she didn't like the relationship. And now, looking back, Felicia had been right.

Angie smiled at the thought. Her friend Felicia was right, if not always, then at least 99 percent of the time. She had a knack for reading people, which was why Angie counted on her to do most of the hiring. She climbed the steps to the building and glanced around at the signs. Finally, she picked new registrations. At least they might be able to give her a map, as they probably dealt with visiting prospective students and their parents all the time.

A young girl with black-rimmed glasses stood at the counter. She looked up from a copy of what Angie realized was a Hemingway novel. Angie pegged her for a work-study student and aimed toward her. Maybe she could give her some gossip that the more seasoned employees would know not to share.

"Can I help you?" The girl slipped a bookmark to save her place and moved the book to the side.

"Yes, I'm lost. I'm looking for the culinary school." She shrugged helplessly. "When I called, Professor Monet gave me directions, but I didn't actually write them down."

"Professor Monet?" The girl glanced around, but the rest of the desks were empty. Apparently, everyone was on break, which also worked in Angie's favor. She could see she wanted to talk but didn't want to look bad in the eyes of her coworkers. She leaned closer and lowered her voice. "I'm sorry to tell you this, but he's dead."

When Angie put on a look of shock she didn't feel, the girl nodded in sympathy. "I know, right? He was such a cutie too. He used to come in here all the time because he'd forget where his meetings were being held. He was as bad as some of the freshmen. Of course, he was Canadian, so maybe they do things differently at their colleges, but he never seemed to have a clue on what he needed to do."

"Oh, my. He's dead? What happened? Was it an accident?"

"No. He was murdered. Can you believe it? Right here in little Boise. I mean, I've never met someone who had been murdered. Or at least I don't know about it. Of course, I wouldn't meet them after they were murdered, well, you know what I mean."

Angie thought about what she wanted to know from the gossip train that surrounded the college. "Who killed him? Do they have the suspect in custody?"

"I guess they did, but they had to let her go." The girl glanced around again before she spoke. "They are saying it's a student and they were having an affair."

Angie thought the girl look more scandalized about the affair than Daniel's murder. "Really?"

"I know, right?" The girl twisted her hair. "I mean, I thought he was cute, but he had to be in his forties or something. Way too old for someone in college. Anyway, if your meeting was with Professor Monet, I guess it got canceled."

"I still need to go over and check in. Can you show me what building their offices are in?" Angie waited as the girl pulled out a paper map and with a purple pen, drew a walking path to the culinary school. "So the professor didn't have one of these maps?"

The girl looked up, confused. "What? Of course he did. I gave it to him the first time he came in looking for the library. Why?"

"You said he didn't know where he was going." Angie folded the map and put it in her pocket.

"For meetings. The departments are all required to come to meetings with their dean once a month. He was always forgetting about them. I guess they didn't have all-campus meetings where he came from. We always have one for the professors every quarter and the first week of every session. The president likes to put a face to all the policies." She straightened as an older woman with her gray hair pulled back in a bun came into the office from a side door. "Is there anything else I can help you with?"

Time to get back to business, Angie thought. "No. You've been most helpful. You have a knack for working with people. I hope you have a lovely day."

The girl beamed at her as the old lady shook her head. Angie's opinion had been noted and dismissed just as fast. Leaving the Administration Building, she pulled out her map. The culinary school was on the other side of the campus by the stadium. Instead of taking the straighter shot from where she was through the mass of student bodies, Angie instead turned to the greenbelt. Inside the campus, there was a path that mirrored the park greenbelt on the other side. It didn't go as far, but it would get her to the other side of the campus.

The trees had been busy dropping their leaves all over the blacktopped path. Angie's movement was accented by the crunch of leaves under her feet, and with every leaf she stepped on, a smell filled the area, reminding her of football games and bonfires that she'd attended during her college years. Thank God Hope and her friend had chosen Tuesday night to watch the soccer game. Otherwise, she wouldn't have an alibi at all. Angie heard someone coming up behind her at a fast pace. Now she wanted Felicia's pepper spray, but she'd given it back. She spun around to look the oncoming person full in the face. Her shoulders dropped almost immediately when she saw campus security coming toward her on a Segway.

Something must have shown on her face as the guy paused near her. "You okay, miss?"

Angie put a hand on her heart. "You gave me a start. I didn't think anyone else was out here."

"Typically they're not, but we do our rounds anyway. Especially on beautiful fall days like today. You be careful now. Maybe you shouldn't be taking deserted walking paths. You never know what might be lurking." He tipped his hat, then took off on his Segway again.

Angie stepped up her pace and checked her watch. It was almost noon. She'd see what she could find out at the college, then grab lunch at one of the drive-ins on the way home. She needed to be at the County Seat no later than two. She could hear Ian telling her to slow down. She always tried to fill her day too much for his taste. "Pot, meet kettle," she whispered as she marched the last few feet to where the path turned into the other half of the campus.

Was she missing him already? They'd only been dating a few months, but she thought she felt a hole in her heart because he wasn't here to talk to or hold on to. Man, she had it bad. She pushed thoughts of Ian away and made her way to the culinary building. Opening the door, she stepped inside into a heavenly smell. Someone was baking cakes.

She checked the directory and, again, pretended she was looking for a professor. Which she was, but she knew where Daniel was, just not where his office was. She headed up the three flights to his office. As long as the girl from the office hadn't called over, letting them know she was on her way, she could play dumb about Daniel's demise. She'd have to take the risk.

When she reached the third floor, she found herself in a narrow hallway with doors on either side. According to the building directory, Professor Monet's office was 309. The numbers were painted on the frosted glass window of the doors. Most of the offices she passed had open doors but were empty. As she passed by office after office, she noticed rows of book-lined bookshelves and desks stacked with paper.

Office 309 was no different. She glanced back down the hallway, but no one was watching her. In fact, the faculty seemed to be all in class. Or in a meeting. She eased into his office and shut the door behind her. She slipped on the garden gloves that she'd taken from the barn that morning. Going behind his desk, she flipped through the papers, all recipes and reports. Then she tried the desk drawers. Locked. Sitting in his chair, she glanced around the room. Cookbooks and travel journals lined the office.

She took out her phone and documented everything she saw. Then, tucking it back inside her tote with her gloves, she walked toward the door and froze. A body was outlined in the frosted glass. But instead of knocking or coming inside, it bent down and an envelope slid under the door. Angie watched as the shadow disappeared, then she picked up the envelope. She turned it over, but nothing was written on the outside. She opened the door and looked out into the hallway. No one was around. Whoever had dropped off the note had gotten out of there fast.

Glancing one more time around the office, she saw a second envelope that must have slid under the desk. She knelt and grabbed it. She considered opening them, but then she heard voices coming from the elevator. Quickly she tucked both envelopes into her tote and stepped out of the office. She made it to the stairs before anyone saw her.

Leaning against the wall, she listened to the conversations coming from the faculty offices.

"He was such a strange man. No wonder he's dead," a male voice said.

"Tom, you're just jealous because all the sophomores loved his classes more than yours," a different male voice teased.

"I believe professors should hold a certain level of decorum. He wanted to be everyone's friend. And if you ask me, a little more than friends with some of the younger, prettier students."

"That's just a rumor. The girls took his classes because he was drop-dead gorgeous. I remember having a crush on one of my professors. Okay, maybe more than one," a female voice added. "I guess I should drop the dead part."

"Who wants to grab a drink after classes end today? I'm feeling a little human after that over-the-top eulogy the dean just gave our departed friend. I'm pretty sure the Daniel I knew wasn't a saint." The second male voice chimed into the conversation.

"Sure. Grab me after class. I'd rather not walk by that empty office again. It creeps me out."

The hallway got quiet and Angie started down the stairs. When she reached the bottom floor she went outside and sat on the stone bench in front of the building. Daniel hadn't been well liked by his peers, that was certain. Angie wondered if any of them had done a Google search on the new guy.

"More questions than answers," she mumbled, then smiled at a young woman who was just coming out of the building. "Practicing a speech."

"Oh, well, good luck." The girl scurried down the stairs and headed toward another building.

Angie glanced at her watch. Even if she power walked back to the car and skipped the drive-in stop, she was going to be late. And she wasn't giving up food. She dialed Felicia's number and let her friend know her new ETA. Then she hurried to the car. She'd grab lunch and eat on the way.

And think about what she'd learned about Daniel today.

When she got to the restaurant, Felicia cornered her before she could even make it to her office. "Now, don't be mad."

Angie unlocked the office and put her tote under her chair. She had been going to sit for a few minutes and read the notes, but that could wait. They were more than likely condolence letters from his students, especially the ones who had, as the woman said, a crush on the guy. Probably sad, poetic goodbyes that no one but a young, heartbroken woman could pen. She remembered writing a few of them in the darkness of her dorm room during her college years.

"Why would I be mad?" She flipped on the computer so she could check her schedule. "How many covers are we doing tonight?"

"We're fully booked with two anniversaries, so I did a special dessert for both couples, but it's not that." Felicia slumped into the visitor's chair. "You know I have my yoga class on Fridays, right?"

"Please tell me you didn't sign me up. I'll pay for the class if you have, but there is no way I'm going to do that again." Angie rolled her shoulders back. "I just don't bend that way."

"No." Felicia's lips curved into a smile. "But now that you mention it, you should come to class. At least once a week. It would be good for your flexibility."

"No. And if that's it, I need to go help with prep." She scanned the list of reservations. "No special requests, except the anniversaries?"

"No special requests." Felicia waved her down when she started to stand. "But that's not what I need to tell you."

Angie leaned back in her chair and watched her friend. What was going on in Felicia's mind? Taylor? Was she quitting so she could volunteer full-time with her new boyfriend? Save the world together? Or had she signed the team up to do another day of cooking for the shelter? She decided to wait it out and let Felicia tell her what she was going to be mad about. "Okay, I'm listening."

"I can hear your mind working from over here in my chair. It's really not that big a deal, and we've already talked about doing this, but the date has been moved up for the first outing."

Angie felt the confused frown take over her face. "A date for what?"

Felicia took a deep breath to steady herself. "Like I said, I was at yoga, and those women have been asking for a cooking class for months. So when I mentioned we were starting the program, they talked me into one next Tuesday."

Angie flipped her gaze to the calendar on her computer. "Tuesday? We can't even get marketing out there to fill the class by then. I've done some preliminary numbers, and we need at least twenty students to make the cost worthwhile. And I haven't even talked to Estebe about working that day."

"I know there are a lot of details to get finalized before Tuesday, and I'll help with anything, including being your slave during the class if you need me." Felicia sighed. "I'm not sure how it happened. I was talking about the November class and someone mentioned needing new ideas for fall menu planning. And someone else chimed in about wouldn't it be nice to have a class for just this group once a month, and then they set a date."

"And it became Tuesday." Angie shook her head. Felicia was always getting pulled into other people's plans. "So not only do we have a new class this Tuesday, we'll be doing this group monthly? How many people are we talking about?"

"Twenty—twenty-five max. I told them they had to call me tomorrow with a final number. They've set up a little committee to handle the invite list." Felicia shrugged, her face a little red. "They have committees for everything. I'm on the Christmas party planning committee. We may be hosting that here in December."

"It's just a yoga class. Who does Christmas parties for a yoga class?"

"Oh, Angie, it's so much more than just yoga. I've had to turn down several invites for dinner parties, weekend outings to different local sites, and in January the whole group is going to Sun Valley for a week." Felicia glanced at the clock. "But I'm keeping you from the kitchen, and my servers should be showing up any time to set up for tonight. I'm sorry to drop this on you."

"No problem. Your sorority is welcome. I'll talk to Estebe and make sure he or one of the other chefs can work that day. At least it will increase hours around here." She tapped her fingers on the desk. "And we haven't talked about holiday parties. Maybe we should put it out there that we're open to private parties during the week for November and December. It's kind of late in the game, but we might get some parties."

"I'll talk to Tori. She's an event planner part-time. She could probably get us some bookings." Felicia started to stand. "You're not mad?"

"I'm excited to try something new. The fact you have a pre-made group to pay for the experiment is kind of a bonus." Angie's mind was already going to what she'd menu plan for the class. "Maybe we'll do a class on soups."

"You're the best. Every time life throws you a curveball, you figure out a way to knock it out of the park." Felicia walked toward the office door.

"Since when did you start with the sports analogies?" Angie turned off her computer and followed her out of the office.

Felicia laughed. "I guess I'm picking it up from Taylor. The guy loves his sports. Which is one reason I'm glad I work on weekends. Otherwise, I'd be in some sports bar watching some game I had no interest in just to spend time with the guy."

And the fact Felicia would actually consider doing that told Angie that this relationship was serious. She hoped for her friend's sake that Saint Taylor was all he was cracked up to be.

Chapter 7

As soon as she walked into the kitchen, Angie could smell the tomato basil bisque they'd added to their menu in August but would soon be replaced with a soup made of more fall veggies. They'd already added butternut squash soup. And on Fridays, they had a loaded baked potato soup. There were three that she could do with this cooking class easily. She went over and washed her hands, buttoning her chef coat as she took in the preparations. Her team was on top of things. Honestly, Angie could take a day or so off, and the world wouldn't collapse. Maybe if and when Ian returned, she'd suggest a weekend trip somewhere.

Pushing thoughts of Ian aside, she stood next to Estebe, watching him finish cutting the rib eye steaks they'd be serving that night. He set the knife down and put the last steak on the tray. As he wiped his hands on a towel, he looked at her. "Go ahead and ask."

Surprised, Angie looked up at his face. "Ask what?"

"You always have that look on your face when you think you're asking a favor. Do you need to leave us tonight? Or maybe tomorrow?" He grabbed the tray and headed to the walk-in. "I'm sure we can muddle through without you."

"I'm not leaving you tonight or tomorrow." But, Angie thought, this was a good sign for her possibly taking a weekend off soon. "Besides, you'll miss me too much."

"That is not possible. Now, Hope, if she asked for time off, her we would miss. She's a hard worker." Estebe gave Hope a smile as he passed by her workstation where she was chopping vegetables. "You are good at the boss stuff. But I can do the boss stuff fine by myself."

Matt chuckled. "Don't leave us, Angie. Estebe's mean when you're not in the kitchen."

Estebe gave him a flat stare. "I haven't been mean yet, but I can change that."

"Okay, guys, stop the bantering. I'm not leaving right now. But it's nice to know I can." She patted Matt on the shoulder. "And I'm sure you'll survive."

He grinned back at her. "Just seeing if you're listening."

As they walked back to the table in the middle, Estebe handed her a bottle of water and pointed to a chair. "Tell me what you need."

Angie sat and drank down half the bottle before she spoke. She needed to stay hydrated for service, a habit she harped on for all her chefs. And apparently, one that Estebe believed in too. "I need you to work Tuesday."

He raised his eyebrows, pulled out his phone, and after a few keystrokes glanced back at her. "What time do I need to be here?"

"Just like that? You can work?" Angie had expected a maybe or a full-out denial. Estebe volunteered with his Basque community kitchen on days he wasn't here at the County Seat. "I would have thought you'd have plans."

"I do, but I can change them. What's going on? And when do you need me?"

Amazed at the dedication, she told him about Felicia's yoga group class. "I thought we'd do a series of soups for them. Maybe some quick breads to go with the soups? We'd have to have batches made up in advance, but what we cooked in the class we could package and send home with the group."

Estebe nodded. "Good plan. I can be here first thing in the morning. Maybe we need one more chef? I'd ask Hope, but she's in class on Tuesday."

"Yeah." Angie turned and looked at Matt, who was watching them. "Hey, Matt, can you work on Tuesday too?"

"Of course. I live for your commands." He grinned, but when Angie didn't say anything, he nodded. "Seriously. I don't have anything going on Tuesday. I can come in. Besides, I'd love the hours. I'm looking at upgrading my apartment to a real house, but I have to convince the bankers I'm a good credit risk."

"Where are you looking to buy?" Estebe turned toward Matt. "I've got a few properties I would be willing to carry paper on."

Matt's eyes widened. "That would be awesome. I'd like to be closer to River Vista. Right now, my apartment is a few blocks from the shelter, and well, it's not in the best neighborhood."

"We'll meet up tomorrow morning before work and I'll show you what I have." Estebe turned back to Angie. "Is that all? I need to get the sauces completed."

"You own property?" Angie stared at him.

"Just a few. I've been putting money away since my first job, and a few of my investments have been fruitful." He shrugged, uncomfortable about talking about money. "We should do a family bread recipe. The sheepherders used to make it when they were out with the flock."

"Sounds good. Let's meet tomorrow for a few minutes and get a menu planned for this. I'll have Felicia make us recipe handouts for them to take home." Angie put her hand on Estebe's as he tried to stand. "Thank you for always being here for me."

"You are easy to please, Angie Turner." He gazed into her eyes. "It is my pleasure to work for you and call you my friend."

He stood and went back to the line. Angie had to sit for a minute, blinking away the tears that formed behind her eyes. With all that had been going on lately, she needed that touch of comfort. Estebe was a rock in her kitchen. One that made her steady in her business and her life.

She wiped her eyes and then went to find where she could help her team. Her team. She smiled as she thought of her group. Then she dove into her first love: cooking.

Friday night service went smoothly, and before she knew it, she was home with Dom cuddled on the couch. She'd run out to the barn, given Precious a bit of food, and checked on their water. Mabel had opened one eye when Angie came into the barn and then closed it again, returning to sleep on her roost. Everything was good in her zoo's world, so after giving the goat a few minutes of attention, including rubbing behind her ears and listening to the goat bleat out all the things that had happened that day, Angie returned to the house. She'd brought dinner home with her, so she unpacked the chicken and potato hash and put it in the microwave to heat up.

Dom glanced at his food dish, which still held over a cup of his food and then sniffed the air, capturing the smells of the warming food.

"Don't even think about it. This is my dinner." As she moved around the kitchen, she heard the ding of her phone announcing an incoming text.

She picked up her phone and read the message from Ian aloud. "Thinking about you. I'll be home soon, I promise. Tell Dom to watch over you while I'm gone."

Dom wagged his tail on the floor when he heard the name.

"Sorry, buddy, your friend isn't coming over tonight." She reread the text and then sent one of her own. She read it before she hit Send, hoping it didn't sound too needy. "Miss you."

She waited for the delivered message, then set the phone down on the table. Time for dinner while she watched one of her murder mystery shows she had on the DVR, and then upstairs to bed. Tomorrow would be busy, with a full dining room as soon as the County Seat opened as well as planning for the class on Tuesday.

Thinking about the class, she smiled. Felicia had gotten in too deep with this group. She always had groups of people she gravitated to that occupied her time away from the restaurant. Of course, that was before she had a boyfriend. Taylor seemed the type to keep Felicia busy all on his own. Life was changing for both of them. She just hoped that as much as their lives changed, they would always have time for their friendship.

As she finished dinner, she texted Felicia a short note seeing if they could get together for Sunday brunch. With Ian out of town, it was the perfect time for a girls' day. Maybe they'd even do some shopping or a spa day. Whatever they planned, Angie knew the two would have fun.

She didn't have long to wait for an answer. *Can't do brunch. Meeting Taylor at noon. What about dinner and a movie? There has to be a rom com playing somewhere, right?*

A smile creeped onto Angie's face as she texted back her answer. They'd finalize the plans tomorrow at work. At least Felicia was still there for her.

She cleaned up the kitchen, loaded her dishes into the dishwasher, and headed upstairs. Tomorrow was going to be a long day. She would need a girls' night after finishing this week's work schedule.

* * * *

Saturday morning the house was freezing cold when she got out of bed. The temperature outside had dropped and either she'd forgotten to set the furnace or, worse, the thing had decided to give out. Hurrying downstairs, she peered at the thermostat, which read a frigid fifty-eight degrees. "What the heck?"

She looked at the other switches and remembered she'd turned off the heat a week ago when they'd been having seventy-degree weather. Flicking the switch, her breath caught as she waited for the old heater to kick on. When it did and heat started flowing through the vents, she relaxed. She did not need the expense of replacing her furnace system right now.

Going into the kitchen, she started a pot of coffee and glanced out toward the barn. Mabel was already out in the yard, looking for her morning snacks. Angie scanned the pasture and found the black goat jumping to her own tune in the low grass. She'd bought the goat a few bales of alfalfa to get her through the next month or so, but she'd probably have to have more delivered as the pasture went dormant for winter.

She slipped on her farm boots and a coat over her pajamas and headed out to feed the troops while her coffee brewed. Then when she got back, she'd work on Nona's cookbook for a few hours until she got hungry. Then it was breakfast and another round of checking on the animals before she left for the restaurant. If Erica was home, she'd ask her to come over and feed, but since they were still out on holiday, Angie was on her own.

Chores finished, she glanced over to her neighbor's house that sat dark in the morning light. It felt like even the house missed its occupants. She'd give Mrs. Potter a call on Sunday to see how her vacation was going.

Two hours later, she looked up from her laptop and realized if she didn't get in the shower, she was going to be late for her planning meeting with Felicia. As usual, when she started working with Nona's recipes, she'd gotten lost in the past. Food did that. Brought back memories of the first spring peas that Nona would pair with tiny red potatoes from the garden. Or the strawberry rhubarb pie she always made in early June. No wonder Angie had gone into cooking as a career. She'd been raised with food both from her parents, and after they were gone, from her Nona. Food that came from the ground or the barn instead of from a box.

She thought about that as she got ready for her day and more as she was driving into town. Part of the cookbook was little essays about each of the recipes. Memories and stories that Nona told while she was cooking. Memories of Angie's mom as she cooked dinner while Angie did her homework at the kitchen table.

Kitchens had always been a big part of her life. And she was blessed that she could continue the tradition if not with a family of her own, then with her work family. She pulled into the parking lot and saw Barb from the Red Eye smoking a cigarette at the edge of the building, waiting for her.

"Hi, Barb, how are you?" She moved toward the woman, trying to stay upwind from the cigarette smoke.

"If I was any better I'd be shitting gold bricks," Barb croaked, then laughed at her own joke.

"That's," Angie paused, thinking of an appropriate response, "nice. How's business been?"

"People are still getting drunk and spending their money at my place, so I guess I can't complain." She put out a cigarette and immediately lit a new one. "Look, I heard about your girl and that professor dude. I hope she's going to be all right. I mean, what was he thinking, trying to get in her pants and all."

"I'm not sure." Angie stopped, realizing that Barb might have more information than she did. The bar got all kinds of people in there, and Barb heard a lot of stories way before anyone else. "What have you heard?"

A sly look came over Barb's face. "Maybe nothing, maybe something. What's it worth to you?"

She was trying to bribe her? Angie couldn't believe it. How badly did she want to help Hope? That one question answered everything else for her. "What do you want?"

"Some more of those donuts." Barb cackled. "You should see your face. You wouldn't have been surprised if I'd asked for money or your firstborn. But donuts? You never thought it would be that."

Angie laughed, the fear easing out of her body. "You're right. I'm sorry, I've been a little tense lately, what with this thing with Hope."

"Having your English boy toy out of town probably doesn't help much either." Barb shrugged. "I've been keeping an eye out for you, but so far, no movement up at that apartment of his."

Angie's gaze flicked up to Ian's window that overlooked her parking lot. Then she hated herself for giving in to the urge. "He texted me last night. I'm sure he'll be home soon."

Barb took a long drag off her cigarette, then put it out and lit up another one. Angie thought the woman must be single-handedly keeping the tobacco industry in business. "Look, I don't think he's messing around on you. But you don't want to talk about Ian. I need to get back to work anyway."

"What did you hear about Hope?" Angie quickly asked before the woman left.

Barb paused mid-step. "Oh, yeah, I forgot. That's why I came over to talk to you. See, there was this group of kids from the college over last night at the bar. They'd been drinking before they got there, but they weren't causing problems, so I let them stay."

Angie leaned against the wall of the building. Barb's stories were never short.

"Anyway, one of the girls is crying. I go clean off a table and I hear her say how she might as well have killed him. She told her friend she was so jealous and she'd seen him with other students."

Angie took a breath. "She was talking about Daniel Monet."

Barb nodded. "She said his name a few times. And then I heard her mention your dishwasher, Hope. I know that kid is a good girl. She's brought me home-baked treats most Saturdays she works. She's worried I'm too skinny."

A smile curved Angie's lips. That was so like Hope.

"Anyway, the girl said she saw them together Tuesday night and she went crazy." Barb shrugged. "Then a fight broke out over by the bar and I had to go kick some cowboy out of there. When I looked back, the group was gone."

"Do you know who was talking about Daniel and Hope? Did you get her name?"

Barb shook her head. "Her friend kept calling her Meg, but that's all I got. Dark curly hair, probably five five, skinny, and she carried a Vera Bradley purse or a really good knockoff. An expensive purse. I know, I've been trying to convince myself I deserve one."

Angie watched as the woman made her way back to her back door and slowly climbed the stairs. The years hadn't been kind to Barb, but she had a good heart. Angie figured donut making was first on her agenda Monday morning.

Right now, she had to get inside and write down what Barb had told her in her investigating notebook. She'd have a lot to dump on Sheriff Brown if he ever returned her calls. Angie wondered if ambushing him on the way into church was really the right thing to do. But then she thought about that guard dog officer he had in front of his office and decided she'd rather deal with the church ladies than that guy again.

She found Felicia already in her office, a notebook open and two cups of coffee on the desk. "Good morning. How did you know I'd be here before the coffee got cold?"

"I saw you drive in." She smiled. "What did our favorite local bartender want to talk about?"

Angie tucked her tote bag under her desk and sipping her coffee, told her what Barb had said. "This story matches what I overheard the teachers talking about at the college. Daniel was swimming in the college dating pool."

"That's just gross." Felicia flipped her hair back. "I told you about that professor who told me I could get an A in his class if I would stop by his office later."

"I don't think so. I bet that went over well." Angie knew she didn't put up with crap from anyone.

Felicia shrugged. "I told him that my father was a Boise cop and did I want him to come along to find out how exactly I was going to earn that A?"

"Your father is a pharmacist in Washington."

A smile came over her face. "Yeah, but the creeper didn't know that. And I got my A based on my work in class, not in his office."

"Professors like that should be banned from teaching." Angie set her cup down and booted up her computer.

"What are you doing? I thought we were going to plan the cooking class. We really need a better name than that. More punchy."

"I'm checking to see if there's a list of people who lost their teaching license in Canada. Maybe that's why Daniel came to Idaho as a visiting professor. He lost his teaching spot at the last college." Angie did a generic search, but all she came up with was newspaper articles about professors being charged. "There are over a hundred entries. Some of these are duplicates, but wow, that's a lot."

"And that's just the ones that made the news." Felicia shook her head. "Look, I know you're worried about Hope, but right now, she's okay and her lawyer thinks they'll leave her alone. We really need to work on this menu plan."

Angie turned off the computer. "You're right. I'm sorry. I just keep thinking that there's more to the story than just a jealous student."

"There probably is, but it's not your job to find out who killed Daniel. Besides, the last time you went snooping, it didn't turn out so well," Felicia reminded her.

Angie grinned. "I'm alive. Nona always said the angels take care of the brave and the stupid. Not sure which category I fall into, but I think I'm covered."

Chapter 8

Two hours later, they had a menu completed for the first County Seat Academy class— Soups to *Fall* in Love With. Angie was keeping all the menus in a separate file so they could repeat the class next year. "You know, we could put this out as a cookbook after a year. Make sure you get evaluations from the attendees so we can snip some quotes for marketing and the book."

"You're always thinking ahead." Felicia wrote something in her notebook. "If this goes as well as I'm thinking it might, we should think about hiring someone to do the administration part of the classes."

"I have a better idea." Angie tapped her pen on the desk. "What if we bring Nancy on full-time as soon as she can swing it? We'll be paying her a lot for admin work, but she'll be a great resource and we can give her some of these marketing assignments that neither one of us has time for."

Felicia brightened. "That is an awesome idea. I wasn't sure where I was going to find the time to be the headmaster for the academy and run front of the house."

"I'll pull her aside and talk to her when she gets here. If she's not interested, we can give the extra hours we've been giving to Matt to her and put him in charge of the school. Estebe's already at full-time, at least the weeks we have classes." Angie glanced at the computer. "We might be pushing our budget, but we should have a full-time kitchen staff, not including Hope, by the end of the month."

"Which is six months sooner than we planned." Felicia grinned. "Go ahead and staff. We'll wait a month and then I'll see what I can do with the servers. I'd like to up their hours too, but that means being open more days."

"I think we'll add a day in the spring. But if we do private parties, that should help with extra money for the holidays for your crew." Angie was getting excited. "I'll have Nancy look into that when she comes on too."

By the time the kitchen team came in to prep for dinner service, Angie was vacillating between glee and fear. She pulled Estebe aside first and let him know the plan.

"This is good. Nancy is competent in those types of skills. You have made good choices with hiring and staffing." Estebe sat in her visitor chair where Felicia had been just a few minutes ago. "The County Seat is lucky to have such a great management team."

Angie sat on the corner of her desk, drinking a bottle of water. "Okay, what do you want?"

A look of confusion passed over Estebe's face. Then he chuckled. "I could never hide anything from you. How do you read me so well?"

"You are never that polite or encouraging." Angie held up her hand. "I like your directness. It keeps me on my toes. And I know you'll tell me if something isn't working. So why are you blowing snow up my skirt now?"

"Excuse me?"

Angie shook her head. "Sorry, just something my Nona used to say. What do you want, Estebe?"

"We have a tradition on Christmas Eve. Everyone comes to the community center after mass and we have a Santa for the kids and a late meal. Typically, I and my family cook this meal." Estebe paused, watching her reactions.

"You want the night off?" She glanced at a calendar. Christmas Eve was on a Sunday, and the County Seat wasn't open. "Felicia and I need to make a plan for holiday nights. Are we open or not? I think we'll honor the holidays and close for most of them. But it's not something we've talked about. Anyway, we're closed this Christmas Eve and Christmas Day."

"Actually, I want you and the staff to come and cook with me. You all are part of my family now, and I want to share this tradition with you."

Tears built up behind her eyes. She'd spent Christmas with Nona or, if she couldn't come home, with Todd and Felicia. In either case, it had been a time of cooking and eating and laughter. Now Estebe wanted her and the team to be part of his tradition. She'd made the right decision coming home, and this offer made her understand that.

"I can't say yes for everyone, but I'll join you. Let's talk to the group today and they can see if the event can fit into their plans." She rubbed her face to make sure she wasn't crying. "Thank you for the offer. It means a lot to me."

"I'm the one who is honored that you accepted my invitation. Of course, Ian is welcome as well. We can put him to work peeling potatoes."

Angie laughed. "I'm sure he'll love it."

* * * *

The mood in the kitchen for service was lighter, happier. Angie didn't know if the news of more hours was the cause, but she figured it didn't hurt. She'd been a struggling chef once. Of course, she'd always been an owner of the restaurant. So for her, failure affected not only her paycheck but that of her entire team. She, Felicia, and Todd had pulled together all the capital they'd had to open el pescado. Most of that capital had been sweat equity into making the space they'd rented even passable for the health departments. She'd helped build that community into a thriving neighborhood. Then the landlord had taken notice and raised their rent after their first lease contract was expiring. But if el pescado hadn't closed, she wouldn't have moved to River Vista and opened the County Seat, and Todd would still be skimming off his part of the businesses profits after doing none of the work.

Life changed. Sometimes for the better. She pulled Hope aside after they shut down the kitchen. "You okay? You're quiet."

"Just busy. I've got midterms coming up, and the professor who took over for Professor Monet is a real hard case. I've had to resend three of my papers because he said he couldn't get into the class files so it must not have been turned in." Hope rolled her eyes. "Some people."

"Well, if you need off a shift, just let Felicia know. We can bring in a temp if we have to." Angie studied the girl's face. There was something more bothering her. "How are you with this whole thing around Daniel's death and being questioned by the police? Are you having nightmares?"

"No. Why would I? I dropped the guy off, drank a glass of wine, and left. That was it." She narrowed her eyes. "You aren't investigating this like you did the other murders, are you? Is that why you wanted to talk to me?"

"No. I wanted to talk to you to see if you were okay. That had to be hard." Angie figured Hope didn't need to know that yes, Angie was poking her nose in where it didn't belong, again. She didn't need the lecture from someone ten plus years younger than she was.

The wariness didn't leave Hope's eyes. "Well, I'm fine. Like I said, busy with school and work. And I've got to go home and get some sleep. I've got a study group early tomorrow morning."

Angie watched her hurry to grab her tote and head to the back door. When she reached it, Estebe stopped her and handed her a bottle of water. They exchanged words, and even from a distance, Angie could see Hope's shoulders drop. Whatever Estebe had said had calmed her, whereas Angie's conversation had just wound her up.

She waited for everyone to leave before she talked to Estebe. "What did you say to Hope?"

A slightly confused look settled on his strong features. "What do you mean?"

"When she left and you gave her the water. What did you tell her to calm her down?" Angie truly wanted to know. Her approach had been meant to comfort Hope, to let her know she had people who cared for her, but what she heard was someone spying on her.

"I just told her that my cousin wanted to see her tomorrow and that I would drive her to his office."

"On a Sunday?"

Estebe nodded. "He was a bit agitated too. He hasn't been able to reach her on her cell. I guess she's been in class a lot."

"Well, I hope everything's okay." For some reason, Angie had a bad feeling about this impromptu meeting.

"Now I have you worried. I will call you as soon as it's over if there is any news to report. Good or bad." He glanced over to the dishwashing station where Hope had worked that night. "We can't lose our up and coming star now, can we?"

When Angie got home, she was dead tired, but she still went to the barn to check on Precious and Mabel. This time both of them were asleep, and she only took a few minutes to check food and water. She'd spend some quality time with the goat the next morning before she went into town to talk to Sheriff Brown. The only thing Mabel wanted from her was food, water, and a place to roost. She heated up the short ribs and mac and cheese Estebe had packed for her. Dom cuddled up to her legs and laid his huge head in her lap, looking up at her with those soulful eyes.

"Hey, buddy. I've got a few errands to run in the morning. You want to go with me?" She'd stop by the store on her way home and grab a few items so she could try the sheepherders bread they'd put on Tuesday's menu. She didn't want the first time she made it to be at the class, even though she'd probably have Estebe make the bread. The women would love him. It didn't hurt the potential popularity of the classes to have a handsome chef in the kitchen.

Sex. The appearance or possibility of it was coming up a lot the last few days. She grabbed her tote she'd dropped on the table when she came in and dug inside until she found the two notes. She should give these to Sheriff Brown. And she would. Tomorrow morning. She opened them and laid them on the table, careful to hold them by the edges.

The notes were handwritten and most likely in the same hand. She wasn't a handwriting expert, but they looked the same to her. And they both started *Dearest Daniel.*

The first was an angry tome about how he'd been ignoring her and that she'd be at his door at seven p.m. on Tuesday wearing nothing but her red coat and black boots. Had this girl been waiting for Daniel when Hope dropped him off? And had she seen Hope go inside? Angie glanced at the signature. *Your one true love.*

This was probably the girl who Barb saw at the Red Eye the other night. Angie turned her attention to the second note.

We were destined to be together, but you had to stray. Now you've paid for your betrayal. I won't mourn you. Not now, not ever. Man, this girl had a bad case of the melodramatics. Would that have been enough of a reason to kill someone? Angie got a plastic bag and put both of the notes and envelopes into it and sealed it. She'd drop it off tomorrow and stay out of this whole mess. Daniel Monet had been a creep, and it was probably better for the entire lot of coeds from the campus that the fox had been removed from the henhouse. She ate her dinner, then headed upstairs to bed.

She was done playing Nancy Drew. At least for this victim.

* * * *

The next day, Angie stood outside the church doorway, her blue bomber jacket wrapped around her protecting her from the chill that had stayed around even after the sun rose that morning. She smiled and nodded as people greeted her going inside. A few tried to hold the door open.

"Whoever you're waiting for will find you inside just as quickly, and you won't be frozen." A tall older man nodded to the door he held open. "It's okay, we don't bite."

"Thanks, but I'd rather wait here." She put on as big a smile as she could manage. Her face seemed to be frozen as well.

"Okay then, but I don't want to hear from Ian how you caught cold from standing out here." The man nodded. "Remember, we have hot coffee inside."

That had almost tempted her, but she saw the sheriff pull into the parking lot just then. Hoping she wouldn't be struck dead by telling a lie in the church parking lot, she said, "Thanks, I'll come in soon if they don't arrive."

He nodded. "Okay then. I'm going inside. I'm not as weatherproof as you seem to be, Miss Turner."

She had a half second to wonder who the man was and why he knew both her and her relationship to Ian. Then Sheriff Brown stepped on the path to the church. He had his arm around a petite blond woman whose red lipstick was so harsh on her face, it made Angie blink.

"Sheriff Brown, may I have a word with you?" She stepped into his path, blocking his exit.

"Miss Turner, it is one of my rare days off and we are on our way to service. If you want to reach me, please call the station tomorrow morning." He tried to step around her, but as he moved, so did Angie.

"I tried calling the station. Several times. Don't tell me your guard dog didn't give you the message."

The woman squeezed Sheriff Brown's arm. "Is this the woman who's dating Ian?"

"Maggie, meet Angie Turner. Yes, she and Ian are dating." He turned toward Angie. "What do you want?"

She had thought about how to juggle the multitude of things she wanted to know, but she decided to get the evidence she'd collected on the murder out of her hands first. "I found these notes at Daniel Monet's office. I thought you should have them."

"What in the..." He paused and looked at his wife. With surprising tenderness in his voice, he said, "Maggie, go inside and get some coffee. You're going to freeze out here. I'll be right in after Miss Turner and I talk."

The woman moved up the stairs, then turned back. "You have Ian bring you by for Sunday dinner when he's back in town. I'd like to get to know you better. Ian's very special to me and my husband."

Angie watched her open the heavy wooden door and slip inside. "She seems nice."

"She's a peach." His face was hard, but his tone held a little softness for his wife. "You really need to stay out of police investigations. Can I ask why you were in the victim's office?"

"I wanted to make sure Hope was safe. But I realize that was stupid. She's already been released and is probably off the suspect list."

Angie saw the flicker in his face before he shut it down.

"Wait. She is off the suspect list, right?" She put a hand on his arm to keep him in front of her.

"I am not at liberty to say. Look, I know you believe that Hope couldn't have done this. Hel... Heck, I think the same thing." He pulled her out of the path of the stream of people entering the church. "If she didn't kill him, you don't have anything to worry about. So stop digging into this case."

She studied him and decided to switch tactics. "Where's Ian?"

"He's out of town, like my wife said. He'll be back soon." He pulled the collar of his coat up farther on his neck. "Are you coming in and worshiping with us or not?"

"You're sure he's okay?"

Relief flooded Sheriff Brown's face. "Yes, Angie. He's fine. I talked to him last night."

She hoped the pain she felt by the news hadn't shown in her face. Tears threatened to fall now. She had known Ian had been in contact with his uncle, but to hear it as a fact made her question their relationship.

"He'll be home soon. Come inside with us. Maggie would love to get to know you better." He put an arm around her and tried to lead her to the door.

She shrugged it off. "Please tell your nephew that he and I are going to have a long talk as soon as he gets back in town."

She left him and headed to the parking lot. Dom was in the car and she didn't want to leave him too long. Besides, he wouldn't take off to England and not call. She might have to buy him a box of dog biscuits when she stopped at the grocery store just to reward him for his loyalty.

A loyalty she didn't feel from the guy who was supposed to be her boyfriend.

Chapter 9

She'd just finished her quick shopping trip and was on the way home when she got the call from Estebe.

"Where are you?"

Angie felt her fingers tighten on the steering wheel. She'd known something was wrong when she'd talked to Sheriff Brown. Now Estebe's tone was verifying her hunch. "On my way home with groceries and Dom. I can't meet you anywhere until I get him back home and the ice cream put away."

She heard the chuckle. "You bought ice cream? I would have thought you'd have your own machine in that gadget-heavy kitchen of yours."

"I do own a machine, but this way I can sit on the couch and drown my sorrows in a quart without having to do any work. What's going on?" She might as well know the bad news sooner rather than later.

"I will be at your house in twenty minutes. That way you don't have to leave your couch or your ice cream." The phone went dead.

"Maybe I won't be on my couch with ice cream in twenty minutes," Angie said to the dead line. Dom whined from the back seat. Angie didn't know if he needed to go out or was just reacting to her bad mood. She softened her voice as she spoke and caught his gaze in the rearview mirror. "Hold on, guy, we're almost home."

After she got home and had the groceries unloaded, she still had ten minutes before Estebe was due to show up. Sunday was chores day, a habit Ian didn't approve of. He was always trying to get her to do something fun and relaxing instead, but he wasn't here to take her to dinner or occupy her time, now, was he? She put another load of clothes into the washer and had just finished cleaning the downstairs bathroom when she heard Estebe's SUV pull into the driveway.

The weather outside was beautiful, almost seventy degrees according to her temperature gauge on the porch. She met him at the door with a plate full of cookies she'd made earlier in the week. "I thought we'd chat outside. You want water, soda, or iced tea?"

"Whatever you're having." He took the cookie tray from her.

She quickly filled two glasses of iced tea and then held the door open for Dom. He went out, greeted Estebe, sniffed his shoes, then lay quietly on the other side of the porch. But Angie noticed his eyes were still open even though his head was on the ground between his paws.

"He's withholding judgment on me." Estebe took the tea and set it next to the tray of cookies he'd set on a table between the two chairs. "Trust but verify. I like your dog."

"He's good with people, but yeah, the first few times he meets someone, he's more reserved." Or at least he was now. A few months ago, as a puppy, Dom hadn't met anyone he didn't like. Including a killer or two. She was glad he was being choosier with his friendships with humans. "I forgot that you haven't been here before. I really should host a barbecue for the staff before the weather turns."

"That would be fun. The place is easy to find. My GPS didn't have a problem." He glanced around at the dormant garden and large barn. Mabel scratched at the dirt by the edge, looking for worms. "It's peaceful. I can see why you like living out here in the boondocks."

She laughed. "It's not so bad. Town's less than thirty minutes away. Although I'm not sure what will happen if we get ice storms this winter. I might be stuck out here for months."

"Then I will as your second-in-command come and rescue you and your animals. I'm sure we can rig something up in the parking lot for the hen and goat." He sipped his tea. "But no use worrying about tomorrow's concerns when today has its own."

"My Nona used to say something close to that." She picked up a cookie and broke it in half. She threw half to Dom and ate the other. When she finished, she brushed the crumbs off her hands and without looking at him, asked, "Why are you here, Estebe?"

"Small talk time is over, then? Good. I was never good at this part of conversations." He set his tea down on the table and leaned forward, resting his forearms on his thighs and crossing his fingers together, apart, together again. Angie could tell he was stalling. "I told you that my cousin asked to see Hope this morning. Apparently, the cops have a witness that puts her car at the professor's house an hour after she told the police she'd left."

"That's impossible, she was at the game with her friend." Angie searched for the girl's name, "Morgan, that was it. She was with Morgan."

"Well, she was, then she left the game to talk to the guy again. But according to Hope, there was a car in front and she could see figures in the window. So she felt foolish and went back to the game. Her friend had thought she'd run into someone she knew and had been talking for the twenty minutes she was gone."

"So that's a good thing, right? She can tell them about the other car and the other person." Angie's hands were freezing, so she set the iced tea down on the table.

"She lied to the police. Now she's changing her story because they caught her on camera leaving the parking lot, but she doesn't come back to the game according to the camera." Estebe rolled his shoulders. "She says she parked at Morgan's dorm, then walked the greenbelt over to the stadium. They're looking at the security tapes now, but this would have been easier had she told the truth the first time."

"Poor Hope. First she puts herself out there for a guy who's not worth the trouble, then she finds herself at the scene of the crime." Angie sank back into her chair. "Your cousin's going to be able to get her out of this, right? We both know she didn't kill anyone."

"I guess the police are looking at another student. One he did have an affair with." Estebe's face went hard. "If I'd known what kind of man he was that day we met, I never would have allowed Hope to drive him home."

Angie smiled at the protective streak he had for the girl. "You're not her father. And I should remind you that she's an adult."

"She's a child. You and I both know that. Our Hope is very naïve and innocent. And this man put her in a position that she never should have been in." He stood and paced the small porch. "Anyway, I told you I would update you, and I have. I am going to go work out at my gym. I feel the need to punch something."

Angie knew that if Daniel hadn't already been dead, Estebe would have been visiting the guy's house rather than the gym. "Thanks for coming over. I appreciate you taking care of Hope. She needs all of us on her side."

When he left, Angie went back to her laundry. As she waited for the last load to dry, she opened her laptop and started searching through the websites that she'd bookmarked for Daniel Monet. Again, nothing. She went to her email program to send Sheriff Brown a quick note about how weird it was that this guy had no internet presence. Instead she saw an incoming email from Ian's Farmers Market account.

"That's strange." She double-checked the from: address a couple of times. Yep, it was his address. Typically Ian emailed her from his Gmail account. Maybe he didn't have access where he was. She opened the email. There was nothing in the subject line. And the only thing in the body of the email was a link.

"What am I, stupid?" She closed up the email and her finger hovered over the Delete key. Instead, she went back into the email and forwarded it to Sheriff Brown.

She typed out her concerns about it not being from Ian and asked if he thought she should open it. Then she told him about not being able to track Daniel Monet through his last few jobs and educational background. Finally she finished with a plea for the sheriff to keep in mind that Hope was an impressionable young woman who had a good heart.

When she thought her plea had been crafted well enough, she hit Send. Then she went to her closest and got out her old laptop. She'd been reluctant to just give it away, but she'd already taken all the recipes and pictures off the drive. Now, it was more of a dust collector than anything else. She glanced at her email on her tablet, but she hadn't received anything back from the sheriff.

She closed out her tablet, then opened the link on her old laptop. It took her to a newspaper article from a London paper. A picture of Daniel Monet that must have been a booking photo looked out of the screen at her. The man wasn't smiling, not like the one who'd served the homeless that night with them. But it was Daniel, younger and thinner, she could see that. She scanned the article, which seemed to be a piece on what happened to children as they aged out of the foster care system. Arnold, no last name given, was an example of the failure of the system. He'd been in and out of jail since he was sixteen, according to the reporter.

So he had been a troublemaker. That wasn't unusual for a chef. Cooking seemed to draw in the ones who weren't able to handle their anger any other way. Maybe Daniel had turned his life around after this article and had chosen to teach others as his way of giving back.

Or maybe once a bad seed, always one? She sent an email to Ian using both accounts and then closed down the laptop. She'd spent enough time trying to figure out the guy and who had killed him, and as long as Hope wasn't on that short list anymore, she was done with the wild goose chase.

Dreams kept her tossing and turning through the night, and when she woke Monday morning, the alarm hadn't gone off and the bedroom was still dark. Checking her phone for the time, she noticed a text from Ian. No greeting, no formalities. It simply said *Running into a brick wall here. Coming home.*

She frowned at the small leap in her chest. The guy had taken off without a goodbye and now she was excited to see him? She was pathetic. She threw the bedcovers off and headed to the shower. Coming home didn't mean he'd be here today, but she wanted to talk to him. She'd missed his calm demeanor.

After chores were done, she sat at the table, drinking coffee and thinking about her day. What needed to get done? Tomorrow was their first class, but Felicia was handling the details for that. She'd buy the supplies and then tomorrow morning, before the class, Angie and Estebe would cook the soups and the breads. Then they'd demo the recipes as the attendees ate. So she didn't have anything that needed to be done for the restaurant. If Ian had been here, they might have been able to take off for a short trip, if he didn't have some sort of board meeting.

She glanced at her planner. She'd checked off all the house cleaning tasks yesterday. And there wasn't anything she could remember she needed to do, but still, something nagged at her. Maybe she should make some treats for the class.

"Treats." She slapped her forehead with the palm of her hand. "I told Barb I'd make her more donuts."

She got everything out and started the dough. As she worked, she turned the kitchen television on and watched the local programing. A screaming blonde was being forced into a police car. Angie turned up the sound.

"Breaking news: There has been movement in the ongoing investigation of the murder of local professor Daniel Monet. Police sources aren't talking, but News Center Seven was apprised of this upcoming arrest by an undisclosed source." The female anchor held the camera's gaze. "This is the second coed who has been brought in for questioning. Which leads us to ask, what exactly is going on over at the college? University officials failed to respond to our requests for an interview."

Angie turned the volume back down. She wondered if the girl who had been taken in for questioning was Meg, who Barb had overheard talking about Daniel needing to pay. Donuts were the currency to getting Barb to talk. She guessed she better get the batch going so she could make her way into River Vista on her only day off this week.

Dom sat on his bed and watched her. Somehow, the dog knew when she was upset. And unlike people, the dog always knew how to listen. "This whole thing might be over. If Meg's the killer, the case will be closed and our Hope will stop being the easy suspect."

Dom looked at her, his face showing his lack of conviction in her words. He lay down in his bed and let a sigh run through his entire body.

It was midafternoon before she reached town. She had three boxes in her car. One for Barb, one for Sheriff Brown if he was in the office, and one for Beth Lee. The woman saw everything. Maybe she'd seen this girl around town with Daniel. It was a long shot but worth a try.

Dom had stayed home. Angie had tried to get him to go on a car ride, but he'd just opened one eye, looked at her, then gone back to bed. Maybe he was in a growth spurt and needed to conserve his energy? She hoped he wasn't getting sick.

Anyway, she was alone on her trip, which was probably for the better. She could take time and talk to people without worrying about her dog getting too hot or too cold. Dom liked riding, but she didn't like leaving him in the car. And some people didn't love having a St. Bernard puppy in their place of business. She turned up the music and was just getting into a song when her phone rang.

"Miss Turner?" Sheriff Brown's voice was a sharp contrast to the happy song she'd just been singing.

"Oh, hey. You must have gotten my email." She rolled up the window so she could hear him better on the car's Bluetooth.

"I did. I'm not sure what you want me to do with this information. You know Daniel's the victim, not the suspect, correct?"

"Yeah, but…" She stopped herself. She'd just been going to say on the television shows they said know your victim. She needed a different approach for a real police officer. She knew from Ian's chatter that Sheriff Brown hated television police shows saying they always got it wrong. "Anyway, I was thinking that knowing Daniel might give you some clues in figuring out who killed him. I don't think he was the angel everyone thought he was."

"Looking into someone's juvenile record doesn't always give you a clear picture of who they are now." He paused, and Angie thought she might have lost him. Then he continued. "And it could accidentally hurt people who were around the guy during his problem teens."

"I don't think I said anything about looking up his entire life history, but don't you think it's weird that there is no internet fingerprint for the guy until he showed up here to start the semester?" Angie heard the hesitation in his voice before he even spoke.

"Just stay out of this. I understand your concern about your employee, but if Hope didn't do anything wrong, she'll be fine. No matter what you've read, innocent people don't get charged or convicted of crimes. The legal system does work."

Angie could have listed off several people who she knew for a fact had been charged and some convicted when they hadn't done the crime. Sometimes the technicalities of the law boxed them in. But it wasn't time for a discussion on the effectiveness of the current legal process. "I'm only trying to help."

"Run your business. Make cookies. Feed the homeless. Those are all ways you can help. Just stay out of this investigation."

He hung up before she could mention she had a box of donuts for him and his crew. She should find someone on the street to give them to rather than the grumpy sheriff. Instead, she parked in front of the Red Eye. She went to the laundromat first and found a sunny Beth folding towels.

"Well, good morning to you. What's got you out and about on a Monday? We typically don't see you in town until Wednesday." Beth set the towel in the basket and ran her hand over the top, a gesture Angie had seen her Nona do many times as she finished up folding a load. Appreciating the softness, she'd told her once.

"I have a delivery for you. I told Barb I'd bring in some for her and thought you might like some donuts as well." Angie sat the box on the table next to the folded laundry.

"Well, aren't you the sweetest thing." Beth opened the box and sniffed the air. "Sugar and spice and everything nice."

"Enjoy." Angie wasn't good at just throwing out questions, so she leaned against the table. "Anything new going on?"

"Well, let's see. Ian is still out of town, but you already knew that. Your restaurant is getting really good reviews by the country club set. They come in all the time with their laundry. You would think, with such big houses, they'd have their own laundry room, but those women are all so busy running around to different things, I guess they don't have time." Beth set the basket on the floor and lifted an empty one. "I shouldn't talk about them. I mean, I like the work. It just seems weird, you know."

"Yeah, I get it. I like spending time at the house doing my chores. It makes me remember my grandmother." Angie wondered how the class would be tomorrow with all these women.

"Anyway, at least I get all the good gossip. Like one of the group was apparently having an affair with that professor that was killed. I'd say her husband probably did the deed, but he's just a mild-mannered thing. He drops off their clothes on his way into work every Monday, even though that wife of his doesn't work or have kids to wrangle." She snapped a towel and then folded it. "Must be rough living the life of the rich and shameless."

Chapter 10

Angie managed to get the couple's name out of Beth before she left the laundromat. The woman had all the dirty laundry, so to speak, on the town's residents. Angie wasn't sure how she'd react to some of the women at class tomorrow with the secrets Beth had told her about the group, but the big one about the affair she wrote on a slip of paper, then tucked it inside the box of donuts she'd drop off at the station. Let Sheriff Brown worry about whether or not the rumor was true. She was out of it. She told herself that all the way to the Red Eye with the second box of donuts.

Barb sat at the bar in her usual spot. A cup of cold coffee sat on the bar to the side of an open newspaper. Angie started when the woman waved her over without even looking her way.

"Come in and sit down. I could smell those donuts as soon as you walked in the door." Now Barb did turn and look at her over the top of her reading glasses. "I appreciate you holding up your part of the bargain, even though you probably didn't get anywhere with the information I gave you."

Angie crossed the room, amazed her shoes didn't stick on the ancient wood floor. Who knew how many beers and cocktails had been spilled on this floor over the years. She sat the box on the bar next to Barb and slipped onto the barstool. "I always hold up my end of bargains, no matter what the outcome. Honestly, since I don't have a way to check up on people, that information went to Sheriff Brown. But I did have a follow-up question for you. Do you know Tanya Livingston?"

"She's one of the new group that moved into the old livestock processing plant that they turned into that overpriced subdivision a few years ago. She's come into the bar every once in a while, looking for a handout for one of her charity events. The woman is really into literacy and supporting the high school tennis team." Barb opened the box and took out a donut. "Tell you the truth, I didn't even know the school had a tennis team. Where are these kids going to play tennis? The barnyard?"

"Does she have kids?" Beth had said the couple didn't have children. In fact, Beth had told her specifically that they didn't have kids, which was why, in Beth's mind, the woman had started cheating in the first place. Angie didn't think it made much of a difference.

"No, she used to be a big tennis player when she was a kid. Her husband took her away from all that with promises of big towns and big money, but I guess he got stuck at Boise State." Barb held up her coffee cup. "You want some? I just made a fresh pot."

"I drank way too much at home this morning. I won't be able to sleep a wink if I drink any more." Especially of that black brew that she saw in the coffeemaker. "So she doesn't work?"

"Her highness work? Are you kidding?" Barb snorted a laugh. "She devotes all her time to charity, when she's not off sniffing around other men. I've heard the other wives talking over a few drinks about how much they wanted to kill her. I'm surprised she's never shown up dead. She's not very popular."

Angie pressed her lips together, trying not to smile. Barb had this woman dead to rights. "Did you ever see her with that professor who was killed? Daniel Monet?"

"That guy certainly got around." Barb took another donut out of the box. "I hear your dishwasher was sweet on the guy too. Men who know they're cute are hard to keep control of, just ask anyone."

Angie really didn't want to talk about Hope, so she tried to swing the conversation back to Tanya. "So you didn't see them together?"

"Now, I never said that." Barb got up, refilled her coffee cup, and put the box of donuts under the bar. "I'll eat all of these if I don't close up the box and put it out of my reach. You're an amazing cook."

"Thanks." Angie rephrased the question. "So you did see them together?"

Barb nodded. "Every Wednesday. They liked to come in midafternoon and drink until five, five thirty. I never knew if it was her or him that had to get back to something or someone."

"They came in here?"

"Yep. They were all secretive and such. Only holding hands when they thought I wasn't watching. But when you've run a bar as long as I have, you can tell who's just friends and who has a little something something on the side, you know?" Barb climbed back onto her chair. "I didn't realize it was him until I saw his picture in the paper. That's when I realized he was with Tanya as well as that girl who was way too young for him. I guess the guy had a liking for dangerous women."

"Yeah, I think he did." Angie got up from the stool. "Thanks for the chat. Enjoy your donuts."

"When that man of yours comes back, you two are going to have to come down after you get done with that restaurant some night. We have a really good house band right now. In fact, they're so good, I'm expecting them to leave for bigger pastures soon." Barb glanced over at the stand where the band set up on weekends. "It's getting harder and harder to keep this place going. Sometimes I wonder why I bother."

Angie didn't know how to respond to that, so she reached out for Barb's arm. "It's a great place. People need somewhere to go blow off steam after a long week."

"You're right, but it doesn't have to be me cleaning up after them." Barb waved her away. "Get out of here. I'm sure that dog of yours is probably waiting in the car for you."

"Dom's home but yeah, I've got to get going. One more stop, then I'm heading home and taking him for a walk out at Celebration Park. He loves chasing the rabbits." Angie pushed the door open and blinked in the bright light. She didn't know how Barb even attempted to read in the dim light, but as she glanced back, she saw she had gone back to studying her newspaper.

She took the last box of donuts out of her vehicle, then crossed the street, aiming for the small police station that shared a parking lot with the one and only drive-in in town. Traffic was nonexistent, and she hurried across the road more out of habit than necessity. When she opened the door, Sheriff Brown was manning the reception desk.

"You send your guard dog on break?" She set the box on the desk.

"Phillip is going to be sad he missed you. He enjoys your little chats. All he wants to talk about is you and your need to be involved." He lifted the top of the box and picked out the note, along with a donut. "You don't have to bring these every time you have a question."

"Actually, I owed Barb some." She nodded at the note. "Gossip around town says that Tanya and the deceased were having an affair. I figured you might want to know that."

He wadded up the piece of paper and threw it into the trash can in the corner. "Two points. And I'd already heard the gossip. She's coming in to make a statement tomorrow. Apparently she has a class at your restaurant at one, so she'll be here during my lunch hour."

"Sorry." Angie didn't know what she was apologizing for, but it felt like she'd stepped on the guy's toes.

"For thinking I'm an idiot and not doing my job or that her interview messes up my lunch?" He sipped his coffee as he waited for an answer.

Angie shrugged. "Maybe both. I don't mean to insinuate that you aren't doing your job. It's just people keep telling me things I think you should know."

"Maybe they keep telling you things because you're bribing them with these outstanding donuts?" He finished off the one he'd been eating and pulled a second out of the box. "I'll have to leave these here on Phillip's desk or I'll eat all of them by myself."

Angie felt her cheeks start to heat. She had kind of been looking for information when she'd come into town. So she was curious, what was the harm in that? "Well, I better be going."

"I'm picking Ian up at the airport tomorrow afternoon. I'd invite you to come along, but you have that cooking class thing."

Angie knew her cheeks were bright red now because they felt like they were going to flame up at any minute. "Well, I guess I'll see him when he gets back."

"Apparently, you are expected over at the house for dinner on Sunday. Maggie and Ian set it up last night on the phone. My wife is very interested in getting to know you better. She says anyone who can get me in a foul mood as quickly as you can deserves some support." He took out a third donut before he closed the box. "And since she seems to be taking your side in all of this, I'm taking another donut. Just don't mention these, okay? She might stop baking to try to keep me on my diet."

Sunday dinner? With Sheriff Brown and the wife? What was Ian thinking? She stepped back toward the door. "I'm not sure if I'm available Sunday. I might be..." She needed to think up a plausible excuse and quick. She grabbed at the first thing that came to mind. "Cleaning the kitchen at the restaurant."

His gray eyes twinkled. "She's not going to give up. You might as well get it over with."

Knowing she was defeated, she paused by the door. "When you talk to Ian, tell him we're going to talk about this."

The sheriff paused, raising the donut for a bite. "I'm thinking you all are going to have a lot to talk about when he gets home. It's about time he told you the rest of the story."

As she walked out to her car, Angie pondered what Sheriff Brown had said. The rest of the story? She would have never thought that Ian held any secrets from her or anyone. The guy was open and honest. But as she drove home, she realized there were a lot of times Ian had skirted the issue of who he'd been as a kid. What he'd liked in high school. Who he hung around with. Angie realized not everyone's high school memories were upbeat and positive, but she couldn't remember one story Ian had told her about that time of his life. It was like he'd been a child, then moved to the States full grown at twenty-five.

Yes, they were going to have a lot to talk about when he got back. She used her Bluetooth and called Ian to leave a message. "Hey, your uncle told me you're coming home tomorrow. Come by the farmhouse about six and I'll feed you. I hear you have some news for me."

She left it at that. Let Ian decide if the news was about the upcoming dinner with Ian's stand-in parents or something else she couldn't even guess at. Instead of worrying about tomorrow, she grabbed Dom's leash as soon as she got home. It was time for a nice walk to clear her mind and thoughts.

Halfway up Red Hawk Trail, she realized the walk was doing neither. Instead, she was ruminating on Ian and his secrets. Which led her to Daniel and his untimely death. Which led her to Hope and worrying that the girl's future was going to get cut short over driving a guy home and accepting a glass of wine. There had to be another answer. And she was going to keep stopping by the police station with more and more bits of information until they arrested Daniel's killer and Hope was in the clear.

She'd told Estebe that she'd make the potato soup for tomorrow's class. When she got done with her walk, she'd go home and cook. That would keep her mind off all of this. "Control the things you can and let the others go" had always been Nona's mantra. The problem was Angie didn't think she could control anything right at this moment.

But she *could* make soup.

When she got back to the trailhead, a man was standing outside what looked like a rental sedan. He was looking at a map and looked up with such obvious relief when they came down the path, Angie almost laughed.

"Can I help you?" She paused at her car, motioning Dom to sit. The dog was curious about the newcomer and wagged his massive tail on the ground, kicking up a mini dust cloud.

The man stepped toward her. "Thanks. I'm looking for the Indian petroglyphs that they recently discovered out here. Ancient Native American artifacts is my specialty. I'm a professor at University of Utah."

"I didn't think they were allowing people into the cave yet." Angie glanced upward, wondering who she could tell this guy to call.

"I got permission from the state historical commission." He stepped closer, holding out his hand. "I'm Evan Morris."

"You teach at U of U?" She kept her hand on Dom. The guy didn't look like a teacher. She would have thought he'd be more likely to be in construction or some kind of physical work.

"Mostly research. They make me teach a summer class every year, just to keep me considered facility rather than just research." He dropped his offered hand. "Sorry, I guess you don't know me from Adam."

"Not trying to be rude, but my dog isn't the friendliest. I think you should go down to the park office. They should be able to approve you for entrance and have someone show you the way. It's kind of hard to find." She knew where the cave was because she'd been the one to find it last summer. But he didn't need to know that. She pointed toward the road. "Turn left at the bottom of the hill, and the parking lot for the office is right there."

"Thanks." He turned, then turned back. "I didn't catch your name."

"Angie." She rubbed Dom's head. "This is one of our favorite hiking spots. Soon the weather is going to make it hard for us to get out here."

"You always bring your dog?"

Something in the way he asked made Angie question his attention, which Dom picked up and let out a low growl. She took her keys out of her pocket and unlocked the SUV. Then she patted her pocket. "Yep. My dog and my handy pepper spray. A girl can't be too careful."

A smile crept over his lips. "Point taken. Thank you for your assistance, Angie. I hope we run into each other again."

She stood where she was, and only when he pulled the car out onto the road did she load Dom up in the back seat. She didn't know why, but the guy felt creepy. Not a typical response she got from a university professor. And how did he know about the petroglyphs? The last she'd heard from Boise State was they were keeping the site under wraps until the paintings could be authenticated. But of course, they didn't run everything by her. In fact, they didn't ask her opinion at all. She locked the doors, then pulled the car out of the parking lot.

Glancing in the rearview, she saw Dom watching the road where the stranger's car had disappeared. Apparently, he had felt something too. Or he was just feeling her unease. Either way, she decided that she really was going to get some pepper spray for them to take on their walks. The canyon was deserted and remote. If someone decided to be up to no good, well, there wouldn't be anyone to stop them.

Who'd have thought that moving out of the city would be the final straw on her carrying protection? She made her way home, and once she had fed Precious and Mabel, she turned on all the lights on the bottom floor, locked the doors, and settled in to make soup. She hoped the chill she'd felt from the chance meeting would ease sooner rather than later.

Her phone rang at nine. She'd already packaged up the soup and played with a few other notes for the class tomorrow. Now she was ready to call it a night and find a place to curl up with a book. She didn't recognize the number as she picked up her cell. "Hello?"

"Angie?"

The noise from the bar made it hard for her to hear Barb, but Angie knew immediately who was calling. "Hi, Barb, what's up?"

"You need to come down here." The words were almost a whisper.

"Did something happen to Felicia?" Dread hit her like a ton of bricks. Maybe her unease today had been a premonition of tonight. "Is she all right?"

"Honey, Felicia's not here. You just need to come down."

Relief made her sink into a chair, the adrenaline rush she'd felt leaving her body weak and drained. "I'll come in soon. Ian will be home tomorrow and we'll make plans to come see your new band."

"You think I'm calling you because I want you to hear the band?" Barb laughed, or coughed, into the phone. Angie couldn't exactly tell which.

"Why are you calling, then?"

The bar noises faded and Angie realized Barb had probably walked outside. She could still hear the voices and the laughter, but they sounded far away. "The reason I called is to tell you to get down here. That girl I was telling you about is here with her group. They're singing karaoke tonight."

"I'll be right there."

Chapter 11

Angie threw on a coat and her tennis shoes and grabbed her tote and keys. Dom looked at her from his bed in the kitchen. "Sorry, buddy, you need to stay home. I'll be right back."

It took her twenty minutes to get into town. She parked in the County Seat back parking. Felicia's car was gone, which meant she was probably with Taylor. Again. Angie power walked to the bar through the alley. She swung the back door open. Instead of the dark and empty place she'd been in that afternoon, the neon signs lit up the large open room. People crammed around tables; a few were on the stage singing a really bad version of an Underwood song she really liked.

Angie wove her way through the crowd.

"Hey, beautiful. Want to dance?" A cowboy stepped in front of her and took her hand.

She shook him off. "Sorry, I'm on a mission."

"Everyone has time for a dance," he grumbled as she hurried past him right to Barb who was pouring drinks at the bar.

"That was fast," Barb said, as she loaded the three beers and two mixed drinks onto a tray. The waitress gave her the cash and she rang it up into the register before turning back to Angie. "Sorry, you want a beer?"

"No, I can't stay. I've got work in the morning." Angie glanced around at the people. "Where is she?"

"The girl I called you about?"

Angie nodded. Sometimes talking to Barb was a little frustrating. "Yeah, the girl you called me about."

"Oh, she left. I was going to call you, then Tina had to leave for a break and I got stuck back here. Sorry."

"You mean I came down here for nothing?" Angie couldn't believe it.

A hand circled around her arm. "It doesn't have to be for nothing, I can buy you a drink."

She couldn't believe that cowboy wouldn't take no for an answer. She spun around, ready to fight, and instead of the tall, drunk cowboy, the man from this afternoon stood in front of her. What was his name? Then it came to her: Evan. "Thanks anyway, I've got work tomorrow."

She tried to move around him, but he blocked her exit. "This has to be a sign. Twice in one day. Why don't you give in to fate that keeps throwing us together and let me buy you a drink?"

Angie stared at the guy. He was flirting. Time to shut this down, now. She was too tired to play games. "One, I don't believe in fate. Two, I already told you, I don't want a drink. And three, I have a boyfriend."

The smile came over his face again. "You have a boyfriend? Like you had pepper spray in your pocket?"

"No, I really do have a boyfriend. His name's Ian. Ask Barb if you don't believe me." She waved toward the bar. Then she paused, considering the guy. "And how did you know I didn't have pepper spray?"

"Your jeans were too tight. A canister of pepper spray would have made an impression." He turned to let Angie walk by. "I really would like to buy you a drink. Maybe some other time."

"I doubt we'll see each other again." Angie started walking out of the bar, then turned back. "What did the office tell you about the petroglyphs?"

He shook his head. "Sadly, they are not letting anyone inside the cave, not yet. I guess I made the trip for nothing."

"That's too bad." Angie spied the cowboy moving her way. "I've got to go."

She got outside without running into the cowboy again, then hurried to her car. Tonight was just getting weirder and weirder. She unlocked the car, climbed inside and, for the second time that day, locked the doors after her.

Time to go home. And when she got there, she'd do the one thing she'd forgotten to do earlier today. She'd find the University of Utah's website and see if Evan Morris really did work for them.

As she'd suspected, there was no listing of Evan in the professors list, but then again, the college only listed their tenured professors for each department. She tried to access last summer's schedule, but it was already off the page and next year's hadn't been posted yet. She sat with a cup of hot chocolate pondering the screen. Then she went through all the social media programs she was part of. No luck with Evan Morris, although Facebook did have about sixty screen names listed for the name or a version of the name.

Then she ran Daniel Monet through Facebook. Fewer matches and one hit. Daniel had used a shot of him teaching at the culinary school for his banner, and his portrait was the same professional shot he had on the college website. The account showed he'd been a member since August of that year. Maybe Facebook wasn't popular in the Canadian college crowd, but Angie thought the better answer was Daniel Monet only became a person when he moved to Boise. So who had he been before when he'd been that troubled teenager that Ian had known?

She racked her brain, trying to remember what Ian had called him that night. Arnie, but Arnie what? It had been close to Monet, but not quite.

A cold nose came up under her forearm, bringing her back to the present. Then Dom's head fell in her lap. He quietly whined. "Hey, buddy, what's the matter?"

She glanced at the clock. Almost midnight. She needed to get some sleep. And apparently, her dog thought the same thing. She stroked his wide head. "You don't like anyone messing with your bedtime, do you?"

His tail beat quietly on the floor.

"Okay, then. Let's hit the hay." She closed the laptop and checked the doors to make sure they were locked. Normally she wasn't this safety cautious, but something about Evan being everywhere tonight had kind of freaked her out.

Even though she was tired, it was long after she started hearing Dom's snores from his bed before her mind settled and she followed him off into sleep.

* * * *

Estebe was already in the kitchen when she arrived on Tuesday. "You're in early." She set a box down on the counter. "Can you get the rest out of the car? I'd like to get the soup on the stove to warm."

"Sure." He put down the knife he'd been using to chop vegetables. After he brought the box in, he refilled his coffee cup. "I didn't get a lot of sleep last night."

Now that Angie could relate to. "Worried about the class?"

He shook his head. "Worried about our Hope. That man has her in a bad spot."

"All we can do is be there for her. She's going to be okay. There's no way they will charge her in his death." Angie poured another cup of coffee for herself, although she'd drunk two cups more than usual at home. By the time the class was over she'd be wired from the caffeine and the adrenaline. She wouldn't sleep tonight. There was no doubt.

"You have more faith in the legal system than I do. My cousin, he's seen innocents broken by the process. Hope is such a sweet girl. She'll make an excellent chef one day." He sipped his coffee. "My stomach is going to revolt if I don't eat something soon."

"Let's just get through today." Angie put a hand on his shoulder. "We're doing everything we can for Hope. There's no use borrowing trouble from tomorrow."

He smiled at her. "My grandmother always used to say that when I'd go off on one of my tirades about the world and how unfair it was. She always knew how to calm me. I find you have the same effect on my mood, Angie Turner. Thank you for your steadiness."

"Neither one of us is going to be steady if we don't get these soups done. And we can't cook if we're hungry. Why don't I make us some sandwiches with the leftover spareribs we have from Saturday night? I'll get these together and then we can sit and talk about the class. I'll call Felicia and have her come down to eat too."

Food. It was the ultimate comfort. For the nerves they felt doing their first class. And also for the fear they were holding on to for Hope's future. They worked side by side in the quietness, each lost in their own thoughts. When she was ready to plate, he surprised her by handing her a salad to add to the dish.

"Broccoli, apples, and cabbage. Sprinkled with a few nuts and some feta." He handed her a bottle of vinaigrette. "Toss it with this just before you plate. I'll go see if Felica is out in the dining room."

Angie was always shocked at the way Estebe knew just what to add to a dish to make it pop. He'd taken several of her recipes that she'd thought were perfect, and with one small change, made them better. The guy had a spotty work record because of his temper, but his skills in the kitchen were unmatched. She was blessed that they worked so well together. She plated the food and walked two out to the table. Then she went and got the silverware and the last plate. The only thing missing when Felicia and Estebe came back into the kitchen was the drinks. "Water? Or something else?"

"Water for me. I'm off the coffee." Estebe moved toward the small fridge. "I'll get them. Felicia? Angie?"

"Water will be perfect." Felicia fell into a chair. "Taylor and I were working until late last night at the donation center."

"I thought you just did that?" Angie asked as she sat down.

"It seems like that's all we ever do now. If we're not helping to serve meals, we're sorting clothes. Seriously, I like his dedication, but I'd like a real date at least one night a week. I feel like I have two jobs." Felicia rubbed her shoulder. "I told him I couldn't see him until Sunday, as the restaurant needed me. Hopefully my lie won't turn out to be the truth. I'm dying for a long, hot bath tonight."

"I'll back up your story." Angie took a bite of the sandwich. The meat was so tender and flavorful, she almost groaned. She hadn't realized how hungry she really was.

"You should tell him the truth. A woman like you shouldn't be used as a workhorse, she should be courted. He should be taking you out, dancing, movies, long walks." Estebe waved his sandwich to make his point. "You should not be sorting used clothing for others."

"Why, Estebe, I didn't know you were a romantic." Felicia smiled at him and Angie could see the red flush on his neck. She set her own sandwich down and leaned back in her chair. "You're right, of course. I should tell him the truth. But at first, I really didn't mind. And I don't mind now, but why does it have to be a work session every time we see each other? I'd settle for a walk on the greenbelt talking about the falling leaves or last week's football games."

"I've never seen you not put your needs first in a relationship. You know you have to put on your own oxygen mask. So why aren't you doing that with Taylor?" Angie watched her pick at the salad.

"You're both right. I should. The guy is just so good. I wanted to prove that I was worthy." Felicia laughed and put up her hands. "Before you go all intervention on me, I get it. I am worthy. I'm good enough. And by God, people like me."

"Amen, sister." Angie held up a hand and the women high-fived.

Estebe stared at them. "I do not understand. Of course people like you, Felicia. You're a nice person."

"Sorry, it's a joke. But thank you for the vote of confidence. I'm going to call Taylor and tell him I'm not available for manual labor anymore. And the next time we go out, we need to actually go out." Felicia brightened at the thought. "If he breaks up with me, I get my life back."

The three ate in silence for a few minutes. Then Felicia glanced at her watch. "We're going to have guests in less than two hours. I take it you want them here, in the kitchen?"

"We'll move this table and a second long one from the dining room here." Angie pointed to an area in front of the expediting station. "Then

I'll work off the table in front. If we keep doing these, we'll need to add an island here that we can also expedite off, but for today, this will be okay."

They talked about the setup for the class for a few minutes with Estebe adding or adjusting the plan. When he excused himself to take a break, Felicia watched him leave. "He's really good at this."

"I've decided he's like seasoning. He makes everything better." Angie took the plates off the table. "I'll keep getting things prepped. You and Estebe set up the guest tables."

"Works for me." Felicia paused and leaned against the table. "You didn't come looking for me last night, did you? I thought I saw your car leaving the parking lot as I was coming back from Taylor's."

"No, I wasn't looking for you. Barb called me into town for a wild goose chase." Angie told Felicia about the phone call and how when she arrived, the girl had already left. "Then Evan tapped me on the shoulder and I talked to him for a while. Mostly I was trying to avoid the cowboy."

"Wait, who's Evan? And who's the cowboy?" Felicia looked totally confused.

Angie told her about meeting Evan out at the hiking trail, then finding him at the Red Eye when Barb had called her into town. "Weird thing is, I can't get him to pop on the faculty register for the university he claims to work for. Oh, and the cowboy, well, he just wanted to dance. I had to turn him down."

"Man, Ian goes out of town and not one but two guys hit on you. That boy better make his way back home before you get all gooey eyed over someone else."

Angie shook her head. "That's not going to happen. Besides, Ian is arriving sometime this afternoon. The sheriff is picking him up—probably because asking his girlfriend after disappearing for a week might just be a tad bit uncomfortable. For him."

"And with that uncomfortable image, it's time to get ready for our first County Seat class. Good luck, guys." Felicia left the kitchen for the dining room.

"I better follow her or she'll try to drag that table all by herself. She's a tad bit stubborn." Estebe smiled at the door that still shook after she'd pushed her way through to the dining room.

"I heard that." Felicia's cry came from the dining room.

Angie shooed him away with her hands. No need to poke the bear any more than it had already been poked. She glanced at the list of recipes they'd planned to demo and started setting up the *mise en place* for the first dish. Then she went back into the storage to grab bowls. This first class would be more of a demonstration of the dishes, then the participants would be eating the results. She had to think through a way that she could have unexperienced cooks working the line without getting in each other's way. Today's game plan was for her to demo a soup, then she and Felicia would serve the food, and Estebe would demo the bread to go with the soup. Five rounds of this, and then the participants would go home with a recipe booklet with all the dishes they'd demoed that day. She hoped the class would bring in more bookings at the restaurant. But at least they'd be able to pay the utilities and the remodel loan one more month based on the profits of this one class.

With the setup complete, Angie joined Estebe, who had returned to cooking after helping Felicia set up tables. She took a minute to let the smells of baking bread and the variety of winter soups fill her, making her mind flit from one memory to another. She started setting up for the next soup.

"This is nice. Cooking together." Estebe didn't look up. "This feels like home."

And because she agreed, she paused for a minute, looking around the kitchen that had so recently become that center stage for her crew. Her family. She met Estebe's gaze. "Exactly."

It was during the first tasting that Angie pinpointed Tanya Livingston. Barb had described her perfectly. The woman seemed to run the group of women around her. What Tanya said, went.

And when a woman sitting next to her spilled a drop of soup on Tanya's pantsuit, Angie got a full taste of the woman's rage.

"You idiot. Do you realize how much this outfit cost?" Tanya had gone from sunny socialite to screaming witch in less time than it took for the drop of soup to fall on her sleeve. The woman next to her paled.

"I'm so sorry." She grabbed a napkin and tried to wipe the offending spot clean.

Tanya jerked away. "The damage is done. I'll send a bill to your house. You better hope my cleaner can get out the stain, or you're going to be dead to me."

Chapter 12

Angie stepped between the two women. She took Tanya's hand and led her away from the table, motioning Felicia to come and deal with the other woman, whose breath was starting to hitch into what Angie assumed would be uncontrollable sobs. "Let's go get some club soda on that spot. There's nothing that a little TLC won't fix."

"That woman is a menace. I've talked to the social chairman several times about her. She just needs to be kicked out." Tanya leaned closer to Angie. "If her husband wasn't a dean over at the university, she would have never been allowed to join. The things that man has to put up with. I swear, he's always complaining about how inadequate the woman is."

Angie had to bite her tongue to keep from telling Tanya what she really felt. As she grabbed a bottle of club soda off the bar with a white linen towel, she kept her back to the woman so she wouldn't be able to read the disgust on her face. "Some people are just clumsy. You say her husband works for the college? Wasn't that awful about the professor who was killed last week?"

"Daniel's death is a real tragedy to the school and the community." Now Tanya teared up.

Interesting. Angie put the club soda on the towel and started to dab at the almost undetectable area where the splash had occurred. "I know. And from what I hear, he was dating some of the college girls. I might be old fashioned, but seriously, he had to be old enough to be their fathers. Eww."

"Daniel was not dating any of those tramps. And if they say differently, they just want the attention." Tanya pointed toward the bar. "Would you be a dear and pour me a shot of Jameson. I like a more mature Scotch whiskey, but it looks like you're only stocking the cheap stuff."

Yeah, not like the Red Eye, where you liked to drink with your friend.
Angie kept that tidbit of information to herself. No use poking the bear
before you find the honey pot. "Sure. Sorry about the brands, my partner
handles all the bar ordering. We probably could get something in here if
you're going to be a customer. Do you and your husband like to dine out?"

Angie saw the flinch on the woman's face before it went back to its
frozen state. "We've been considering coming by. He also works at the
college, so there's a lot of social engagements we're committed to just
because of his job." She threw down the shot like a professional and then
considered the glass. "Anyway, Daniel didn't deserve to die, no matter
what they're saying about him."

"You sound like you knew him." Angie's eyes widened in fake shock.
She leaned closer. "Don't tell me you were having a thing with the guy. I
mean, I saw the picture they had in the paper. That man was fine. I wouldn't
blame you for going after some of that."

"Daniel and I were friends."

Angie could see the whiskey loosening the edges of Tanya's hard-angled
face. She poured another shot. She'd make sure one of the club drove this
woman home, but right now, she wanted some answers. "That's the way
the best romances happen. Friends to lovers. Tell me more."

Tanya drank the second shot just as fast. "He was a lovely man. That
English accent that used to come out when he'd been drinking, well, it just
turned me on. Of course, my husband, well, he wouldn't understand. The
man's a pig in the sack. But Daniel was so gentle and caring." She turned
her eyes on Angie. "We made love. It wasn't sex. Then he broke it off a
couple of weeks ago. I tried to reason with him, but he was done with me."

Angie watched as Tanya rubbed at imaginary lines in her face as she
stared at herself in the mirror. "Do you know what it's like to lose this
beauty? It gives you so much power when you're young, then it steals it
away from you."

"Why did Daniel break up with you?"

She glanced at Angie. "Of course you don't. You're cute in a unkempt
way."

"Daniel? Why did he break up with you?" Angie decided she could hate
the woman later. "Did he find someone younger?"

"No!" Tanya slammed her fist down on the bar. "He loved me. He said
there were people looking for him and it wasn't safe. He didn't want me
in danger. He said he'd deal with the issue and then we could be together.
All he needed was a little bit of money."

Angie felt sick. The woman had been taken as a fool and she was still in love with the guy. "So you gave him money? How much?"

"Not a lot. I had some from my inheritance. Fifty thousand." She wiped her tears. "I guess I should contact my lawyer and see if he can get the money back. Certainly he couldn't have spent that much in three days."

"You just gave him the money?"

"The transfer went through the Friday before his death." Tanya pulled out her phone. "I need to call my lawyer. I'll be back in for the demo in a few minutes."

Angie had been dismissed. She considered trying to listen in on the conversation with the attorney, but she figured she'd gotten as much information as she could from Tanya. Man, the woman was toxic. Why anyone would want to be in a social club with her didn't make any sense to Angie. Popularity at any cost. She'd thought that mind-set had died when they'd left high school. Apparently not.

Heads turned when she came back into the kitchen. The unfortunate woman who had spilled on Tanya had been moved to a different table and a new person sat by the empty seat. Eyes wide, the violator jumped up. "Oh, no, is Tanya all right? I didn't burn her or something, did I?"

Angie glanced at Felicia, who rolled her eyes. "No. Tanya's fine. She's making a personal call and will be right back in. Let's continue the demonstration. Estebe, do you want to explain the history behind sheepherder's bread?"

Felicia came to stand by her and they moved to the edge of the kitchen, still watching the group.

"You wouldn't believe how scared they all are of this Tanya chick. She's not in my yoga group, but everyone is frightened to death of getting on her bad side." Felicia shuddered. "I had visions of the mean girls from back when I was in school."

"I know, right?" Angie crossed her arms and watched the group watch Estebe. The women were starting to relax, which was a good thing. "Tanya admitted to the affair with Daniel. And she gave him a lot of money just before his death. That's who she's calling, her lawyer, to try to get it back."

"A lot of money?"

Angie nodded. "Fifty thousand. Now why did a culinary school professor in a small town like Boise need that kind of money? Maybe he was buying a house? But that doesn't make sense. He wasn't on permanently with the college. Why invest in a house?"

"This guy just gets weirder and weirder the more we know about him."

The door opened and Tanya made her entrance. Apologizing to Estebe for interrupting, she flounced to her chair and smiled at the woman who sat next to her. Apparently the call had gone her way.

"We need to keep an eye out for that one." Angie nodded at Tanya. "There's something she's not telling us about her relationship with Daniel."

"She *is* married. Maybe she's afraid he'll divorce her?" Felicia studied Tanya, who kept checking her phone. "What, does she think the lawyer's going to call right back with the good news?"

"She's looking for some type of message." Angie went back behind the stoves and started prepping for their last soup. Keeping a class entertained for two hours was hard. She didn't know yet if she liked this new venture. Estebe seemed to thrive in the role of teacher and had the ladies eating out of his hands.

Somehow she got through the rest of the class, and as Felicia moved the group away, Angie sank into a chair with a bottle of water.

"You're tired?" Estebe sat next to her. "I could cook for another three hours."

"You're good at it. The women like you. I think I'm going to turn all the classes over to you. I can play sous chef or we can bring in Nancy or Matt."

Estebe shook his head. "You are good too at this teaching thing. I think these women just liked me because I am a man."

"Yeah, I got that too." Angie grinned. "But I'm serious about you taking on a more leadership role in these. I don't have as much fun as you do in presenting."

"We'll talk. Right now, I need to clean the kitchen. And you need to go home. You look beat." He put his hand on her shoulder. "I think our first venture into the cooking class world was a success. Even though that one woman had a chip on her shoulder."

"You could see that too?" Angie always wondered what a man saw of a beautiful woman's actions. Tanya seemed to think she had all the power.

"She was not nice to that other woman. That makes her less, at least in my book. People should be nice to others. Like you and Felicia. You are both nice. Nice is good." He stood and looked around the kitchen. "I'll put the soup and extra bread in the freezer. Felicia can take it to her man, and that way they don't have to cook for the others."

Angie thought about arguing, but Estebe had called it. She was bone tired. Ian was coming in tonight. Hopefully he wouldn't want to see her because she had big plans tonight after she got home and fed the animals. She was going to put a pot of soup on to warm, make a sandwich with some of the leftover bread, and then sit in front of the television until she either fell asleep or finished eating.

She got as far as the soup being on the stove before her phone rang. Glancing at the display, she saw it was Ian. She sat at the table and put the phone on speaker. "Hey, are you back?"

"I am. Allen just dropped me off at my place. You want me to come over?"

Angie thought about saying yes, but then he spoke up again.

"That pause tells me the answer. You're not mad at me, are you?"

Was she mad? She should be mad. She definitely was mad. Her brain felt fuzzy. "Honestly, right now, I'm just so tired I could climb into bed and sleep for a week."

"Allen told me you taught a cooking class this afternoon. How did that go?"

She felt bad. He sounded so chipper, so excited to chat. And all she wanted was to go curl into a ball. "It was good. Hey, why don't you come over for breakfast tomorrow? We can talk then. Right now, I don't think I can form another coherent thought."

"That sounds great. I'll bring orange juice and donuts from the store. Is seven too early?" He sounded excited, hopeful.

"Let's make it eight. That way I can feed Precious and Mabel before you get here."

"Leave that to me. I've missed the zoo." He paused and Angie wondered if he'd hung up, but just before she responded, he continued, his voice low and comforting. "I've missed you too."

Well, don't go taking off without telling me, was the first response she considered. Then she took a breath. She was tired. No need to bring out the worst in herself just because she needed a nap. "I've missed you. See you in the morning."

This time she was the one who hung up first. And then she forced herself to pour a bowl of soup and made herself a sandwich. She ate at the kitchen table, looking at her phone. What had caused Ian to take off so abruptly? And the better question was, would he tell her? Leaving the dishes in the sink for tomorrow, she climbed the stairs to her bed and fell across it, not even changing into pajamas. Dreams didn't come when she fell into sleep.

* * * *

The next morning, she woke without an alarm. She had thirty minutes before Ian would be here, and typically, the boy was early. She headed to the shower to get ready and within twenty minutes was downstairs making coffee when his car pulled into the drive. True to his word, he first went out to the barn, which gave Angie time to pull out the bacon and eggs she'd planned on making for breakfast. By the time he let himself in the kitchen, she was sitting at the table, reading the morning news on her tablet and drinking her first cup of the day.

"Good morning, beautiful." He took off his coat and hung it up. Then he dropped a bag on the table. "I'll put that away as soon as I wash my hands. Precious wasn't having anything to do with me doing a quick feed and hello. The girl had a lot to tell me."

"Yeah, she's been a little clingy lately. Maybe it's because you were gone?" Angie used her cup to point to the coffeepot. "Grab a cup and sit down. We'll have the dessert part of breakfast first. Then I'll make a hash scramble for the main event."

"Sounds wonderful, but you don't have to feed me. It's bad enough I pushed my way into an invitation for this morning. Rather cheeky of me, don't you think?" He dried his hands, then poured the coffee, refilling her cup before he sat down.

"I really am glad you're back." She watched as he unpacked the donuts. "Do you want to tell me what the impromptu trip was all about?"

"I should have called you before I left. I realized that once I got on the plane from New York to London. I was selfish and rude. All I can do is say I'm sorry and explain why I had to leave."

When she didn't respond, he nodded.

"I don't blame you for being angry, but I went looking for my past." He handed her a maple bar and a napkin. "I hear you've been playing your version of Nancy Drew while I've been gone."

"Your uncle isn't happy with me." Angie shrugged. "But I can't help it if people just like to tell me things."

"When you go around asking questions…" Ian added to her statement. He waited for her to react. When she merely shrugged, he grinned. "Are you still tired? You usually put up more of a fight than that."

"I am tired. However, he's right. I am trying to figure out who would have had motive to kill Daniel. And honestly, there's a couple of people in line before Hope, which makes me relax a little. The girl doesn't need to be dealing with this. She should be going to football games and dances and hanging out at the quad. You know, like a normal college kid. Instead, she's working as many hours as she can get, carrying a full load of classes, and I believe she volunteers with her church group. The kid's a saint."

"Then there's no way she's going to be charged with killing Arnie." Ian reached over and took her hand. "You don't have to carry the weight of the world on your shoulders. You can let others solve some of the problems."

"I don't take all the world's problems." She squeezed his hand, thankful he was around. "I haven't gone out of our little world here in River Vista."

"Yet." He smiled and they ate their donuts. Then she frowned.

"Wait, you called him Arnie again. You called him that the night we met him. Did you know the guy?"

"And that's the story I came to tell. Can I help you make breakfast while we talk? It would help me to keep my hands busy during this discussion. I'm not quite sure how you're going to handle what I'm going to say." He nodded to the sink. "I'm a pretty good potato peeler."

She laughed, remembering Estebe's request. "That's a good thing because after you talk, I have to ask another favor of you."

"Now, this is getting interesting." They stood and she handed him the potatoes to wash and peel as she chopped onions and bacon.

"I'm not sure where to start with this, so I'm going to start at the beginning. I didn't fit in in England. The kids all called me Yank and I got in more than my share of fights about my heritage and my lack of a father." He didn't look at her, just focused on the potatoes. "I told you when my mom got pregnant, she left the States and set up her future in London. Well, it worked out great for her, she got a great job and loved living there. I always felt like an outsider."

Angie's heart ached for the little boy who was just trying to find his way in the world.

"One day in middle school, I was in the middle of a fight and losing. It was three against one, but I was giving as good as I got. All of a sudden, I felt someone at my back. It was Arnie, and he was fighting off one of the bullies." He smiled at the memory.

"That must have surprised you."

"Definitely. Arnie was the new kid, and being from Canada, he wasn't fitting in well, either. So after that day, we were best friends and thick as thieves. Arnie's folks lived on the shady side of the street, but no one was ever home at my house. So we hung out there a lot." He put the last peeled potato on the cutting board. "Do you want these peels in a compost heap?"

"I'll take them out later." She quickly chopped the potatoes and put them in the large cast iron skillet with the onions and bacon. "So if you were friends, why didn't he recognize you?"

"He did. The problem is we didn't stay friends." He put the peelings into a plastic bag, then ran water over the dishrag and rinsed out the sink. "We were in high school and my mom was taking me to Paris for a weekend trip. She wanted to have the college talk with me, and getting me away from Arnie was a bonus."

"I think I like your mom."

"I think you will. Anyway, Arnie said he had something big going on and I should stay home and hang with him. My mom laid down the law, and I went with her. When I came back, Arnie was in juvenile, charged with grand theft auto. Someone died during the job. I don't know what happened, but there were rumors all over school the next week. I never saw him again until last week."

"You would have been with him if your mom hadn't taken you out of town." She poured more coffee into her cup and refilled Ian's as well. "You must have felt lucky."

"I felt guilty. Like maybe I could have talked him out of it." Ian joined her at the table and sipped his coffee. "So when he told me I was wrong, that he wasn't Arnold Manner, I went back home to see if I was crazy. If I could find out what had happened to my old friend. Mom has been on me to visit, so I took her up on her offer and went. I found that article I sent you, then nothing. I thought if I was there in person, I might find something in the records, but no, it was a dead end. I talked to everyone we'd known as kids. Even took the train to Paris one day to track down a guy who had run the gang Arnie was part of. No one had seen him since he went to jail. His folks had died years ago. When I didn't find anything, I came home."

"But you still think Daniel Monet was your friend, Arnie Manner."

He nodded. "I know it was him. I just don't know why he didn't want to acknowledge me."

"Maybe he didn't recognize you. Or maybe he was scared you'd out him when he'd turned his life around." She opened her notebook. "Do you want to know the weird thing about 'Daniel Monet'? I can't find him on the web. Anywhere. No mention of this guy who supposedly is a visiting professor from this culinary school in Toronto. I even called the school and asked for him, but no one knew any one by that name."

"Arnold Manner disappears and years later, Daniel Monet appears." He picked up a pen and drew a line down the middle. On the right side, he wrote *Arnie Manner—England*. "What date was that article I sent you?"

Angie checked her email. "Two thousand three."

"So we know he was in England then and would have been about eighteen." He finished his chart listing out years and ending with *2017* and the name *Daniel Monet.* "Now we just need to find out where he was and, possibly, who he was for those missing years."

He took Angie's hand and squeezed it. "I'm sorry for not keeping you in the loop. I'll never do that again."

Angie squeezed his hand back, but inside she wondered if that was a promise Ian shouldn't have made.

Chapter 13

By the time Ian left, they'd been able to fill in three more years, two at the top with Arnie in England and one at the bottom where the Boise school had announced Daniel Monet's upcoming visit. The other twelve years were still a blank.

"At least it's something." Ian kissed her at the door. "Thank you for breakfast."

"Thank you for playing Clue with me." She pushed his hair out of his eyes. "Your uncle is going to tell you I'm a bad influence."

"He's already mentioned that fact a few times." He hesitated. "I hate to bring this up, but Allen told me one more thing about Daniel's death. The guy was naked when they found him. Hope didn't say he'd tried to force her into anything, did she?"

"She hasn't said anything like that to me." Angie pondered the idea. Could Hope be minimizing what happened because she was embarrassed?

"You might want to let her know if he did, she wasn't to blame. The guy was always pushy with what he wanted, even back when we were kids. Anyway, speaking of Allen and Maggie, we're going over there on Sunday for dinner. Do you want me to pick you up before or after I go to church?"

"If I'm meeting the pseudoparents, I guess I should play the whole game. Pick me up before. I have a dress I haven't worn in years. I hope it still fits." She leaned into his neck. "Or we could just stay here and I could cook."

"They're not bad people, really. Maggie already thinks you're a peach because you stood up to Allen. She says the family needs more strong females to keep the men in line."

"I don't know about that." She stared at him. "You took off without even mentioning you were leaving."

"Now, see, I knew you were mad." He leaned against the doorframe. "What can I do to make it up to you?"

"Not make me go to dinner with Allen and Maggie?" She tried for a pleading look, but apparently, it just looked funny because he broke out laughing.

He stepped out onto the porch. "Save me a spot at dinner Thursday. I don't have anything in my fridge and I don't have time to shop."

"There's always room at the bar," she called after him. She watched him get into his truck and back out of the driveway. Grabbing the sack off the sink, she went to drop off the peelings into the compost pile. Next year, her garden was going to be amazing. Back in the house, she finished putting away things from breakfast, then sank into the chair, glancing at her notebook. Right now the only suspects she had in Daniel's death were people she didn't think would kill the guy. One was Hope, who had left physical evidence at the scene. Then there was Meg, the over-the-top student he'd been sleeping with. And finally, there was Tanya or Tanya's jealous husband. Tanya in her weird way had loved Daniel, so if their affair was the reason Daniel was dead, then the husband had killed him.

Then you had the fact that Daniel Monet was an alias. Normal people didn't change their name and start a new life. Wait, he could have been in the witness protection program. Did Canada even have something like that? And if so, wouldn't his murder have been covered up? Angie decided she'd been watching way too many cop shows. She looked up the address where Daniel had been living on Google. A link to Zillow showed her the house had been up for sale and just taken off the market last week. After Daniel's murder. She flipped through the staged pictures of the rooms, landing on the game room where he'd been strangled and left on the top of the pool table.

The newspapers had given her the how and where, but Ian had added in the other piece. Daniel had been naked. She picked up her phone and called the one person she knew in real estate. Reana probably wouldn't be happy to hear from her, especially after what had happened earlier this year. But a Realtor never breaks bonds with a potential client.

She got voice mail. "Hey, Reana. I was wondering if you could get me a look at this house?" She rattled off the street address. Maybe she'd get lucky and the realtor would be unaware of the murder. Of course, she would have had to be out of state not to hear the details of Daniel's death. Anyway, it was worth a shot. "Call me when you can get me inside."

She spent the rest of the morning cleaning the house, getting more information on Tanya, and trying to identify the mystery student. When she was about ready to drive into Boise and check out Daniel's office again, her phone rang.

"You know I shouldn't be getting you in there." Reana was direct and to the point, a quality Angie had admired when she was looking for the County Seat.

"Come on, Reana. I've got dinner reservations for two at the restaurant on Saturday night if you can."

"How can you pull that off? I just called to get a client in for his anniversary and you're booked for over a month."

Angie smiled. She had Reana right where she wanted her. "I have my ways. You name the date you need a table and I'll get it set up. And their meal's on me too."

"It better be. I had to sweet-talk my way into the house. The owner really wants to sell now, but the police tape is scaring away potential buyers."

Angie heard a doorbell ring, and Reana called to someone that she'd be right there. Then she dropped her voice. "Look, I'm alone in the office until Merry gets back from lunch. Meet me at the house in an hour. The police have released it back to the owner, and his Realtor is getting ready to have a crime scene cleaner go through the place. I don't know why, everyone is going to know what happened. The place will never sell now."

"Thank you. I'll be there in an hour." She hung up the phone and looked at the photos again. She'd look at the game room first, then she'd go directly to Daniel's home office. If he was a ghost, no one would be showing up to claim his belongings. Maybe she could find out where he'd been before Boise. She tucked her notebook into her tote bag and grabbed her jacket and keys. Dom wagged his tail, hitting the floor.

"Sorry, guy, I don't know when I'll be back." She checked his water dish just in case her errand took longer than she planned, then she locked up the house.

It took forty-five minutes for her to get to the north end of Boise. A lot of these houses were over a hundred years old and built to be mini-mansions of the day. She drove slowly to the road that would take her to the house and wasn't surprised to see Reana's compact parked in front of the house.

She climbed out of her SUV, hit the remote lock, and then went to knock on Reana's window. The woman jumped in her seat, dropping the phone she'd been texting on to the floor of the car. She fumbled to retrieve it, then climbed out of the car.

"You scared me." She smoothed the skirt to her suit and adjusted her matching jacket.

"Sorry. I thought you knew I was coming."

"Let's just get this over with. I don't want the cops showing up while we're inside." She locked her car and power walked as fast as she could toward the house in her three-inch stilettos. "And I need a reservation for this Saturday. For John and Carol Huffington. Seven p.m. okay?"

Angie keyed the information into her phone. "It's done. I pay my debts."

"I know. I'm just a little wigged out about going inside. You know these old houses hold spirits. I wouldn't be surprised if this one has more than one ghost." She keyed a code into the lock box and the key dropped out. She glanced back at Angie. "Are you sure about this?"

"We're not going to run into a ghost." Angie put her hand on Reana's shoulder. "But if you want to stay out here?"

"No. I'm a professional. I should be with you when you tour the house." She opened the door to a huge foyer. "What exactly are you looking for?"

"I guess I'll know it if I find it." She nodded toward the right. "The game room's that way, right?"

"Go ahead, I'm not in charge of this fool's errand." Reana shut the door behind them and flipped on the hallway lights. "I can't believe how dark it is in here. They're never going to sell it until they lighten the place up."

Angie walked through the hallway toward the game room. At the end of the hallway was a set of double doors. She knew in her heart this was the room. She opened the doors, somewhat expecting to see Daniel standing behind them. Instead, the room was dark. Reana reached over and flipped on more lights. Fingerprinting powder covered every surface, including the pool table. Blood or some type of dark fluid had stained the green felt. "That's going to have to be replaced."

"Definitely." Reana shuddered. "I don't see anything in the room that tells us anything about the killer, do you?"

"I didn't think the clues would be here. Do you know where he set up his office?" She glanced at Reana.

"What, you think I'm his secretary? This is the first time I've been in the place too. Give me a break."

They stepped into the hallway, and that's when they heard the bang from upstairs. "We're not the only ones here," Angie whispered.

"We should get out of here," Reana said at the same time.

Angie shook her head. "Let's see if we can find out what made the sound." She grabbed a baseball bat that had been tucked in a corner of the game room. Probably just a prop, but it would do if she needed it. She glanced back at Reana as she started up the stairs. "Get your phone out and get ready to call 911 if we need to."

"I think we need to now." Reana rolled her eyes when Angie shook her head. "Fine, let's go see what's in the basement like the too-stupid-to-live girls always do in the movies."

Angie pressed her lips together to make sure she didn't laugh at Reana's descriptor. When she got to the second-floor landing, she paused, pointing toward the pool of light pouring out of one of the rooms at the top of the stairs. She inched toward the doorway, then clutching the bat tight, made a quick peek into the room.

Then she did a second take. She set the bat down and stepped into the room. "Tanya, what are you doing here?"

The woman was sitting on a round bed covered in a red satin cover and crying. Tissues covered the bed like snow on the red background. She looked at Angie and sniffed. "I just miss him so much. We were going to be together. I was going to divorce Steve and we were going to be together. And now he's dead."

The tears started up again, and Reana stepped into the room and snapped a photo of the crying woman.

"What are you doing?" Angie turned her head and stared at Reana.

Reana's face flushed. "If she kills us, there will be evidence on my cloud account. I'm not stupid."

"I'm not going to kill you. Someone killed my Danny. Why would someone kill such a gentle man?"

The over-the-top grief Tanya was showing seemed to be diminishing as she followed her statement with only two sobs this time. Then she glanced at her watch.

"I've got to go. I'm expected at a cocktail party this evening." She wiped her face with the tissue, then opened her purse.

Angie could feel Reana stiffen, but then she relaxed when Tanya pulled out a compact.

"My eye makeup is ruined. I need to be home before Steve or he'll see me like this." She dabbed on some power, then shoved the compact into her purse.

"How did you get in?"

Tanya glanced around the room, probably making sure she hadn't left anything except the tissues. "Daniel gave me a key."

"Oh." Angie watched as Tanya made her way out of the room, then paused at the doorway.

"So how did you two get inside?"

"I'm a Realtor." Reana held out a hand to shake, then thought better of it and let it drop.

Seemingly satisfied with the answer, Tanya made her way downstairs. Angie leaned over the banister. "Hey, did Daniel have an office here in the house?"

Tanya turned and looked at her. Curiosity filled her face. "Of course. It's the next room over from the bedroom. What are you looking for?"

"Honestly? I have no idea."

Tanya nodded, then strolled toward the door. When Angie heard the door close, she turned toward Reana. "Office is the next room."

"What if she calls the cops?" Reana took a few steps toward the stairs. "We should leave."

"She's not going to call anyone. We found her here, and she doesn't want anyone to know about her and Daniel." Angie smiled. "Mutual assured destruction. She rats us out, we let her husband know about the affair. And besides, you have a slightly legitimate reason to be here. You're showing a house to a potential client."

"You're devious. I didn't realize this about you." Reana followed Angie down the hall. "If someone kills me, I want you to find the killer. You're good at this stuff."

"I just keep asking questions. Like why would a chef have an office on the second floor when the kitchen is on the main floor?"

Reana studied her. "Where's your office?"

"At home it's in the kitchen. I made room for a desk I can work at if I don't want to work at the table. Which is where you typically find me working on recipes and stuff." Angie opened the door to find an over-the-top office more suited for a country gentleman than a working professor. The desk was almost totally empty. A pen and pencil set sat in the middle on top of a green blotter that reminded Angie just a little too much of the pool table downstairs.

She sat at the desk and started to pull out drawers. Pens, pencils, a stapler sat in one. In another was empty files. In another, blank paper. And in the last one, a tablet. She pulled it onto the desk and sat down, hoping Daniel hadn't used a password.

The blinking screen disappointed her immediately when she booted the computer. Enter password. She went through the drawers again, trying to find a place where he'd written down a password, but nothing. She stared at the blinking curser, then typed TopChef.

"Why would that be his password?" Reana peered over her shoulder. When the main page came on, she whistled. "Wow, you're good at this."

"I'm thinking Daniel's actual culinary schooling wasn't at an accredited school. According to Hope, the guy liked the students to experiment on a

theme he'd give them. It just reminded me of the challenges on the show."
She went straight to the computer's history. When it booted up, her guess
was confirmed. The guy had watched a lot of the old *Top Chef* and other
cooking shows within the last six months. He'd also checked in with a
local newspaper in Fort McMurray, Alberta. She pointed to the newsletter's
masthead. "Maybe this was where he came from, not Toronto."

"Seems logical. But why would he lie?"

"That's the question, right?" She flipped through the rest of the programs
and email accounts available on the tablet. He'd set up his work email to
come to the tablet, so a lot of the emails that had arrived in the last week
were letters of goodbye. She saw one from Tanya and clicked it open. As
she'd suspected, it was filled with longing and graphic descriptors of what
they'd done to each other. None of the other new emails indicated such
an intimate relationship, but Angie knew there was at least one more, if
the rumors were true.

She was just about to close the program when the subject on one email
caught her attention: *One last warning.*

"Open it."

When Angie did, there was only one line. She read it aloud. "'We've
found you.'"

"That's it?" Reana inched closer to read it herself. "Is there anything
else from that sender?"

Angie sorted the emails by sender name. "Only this one. And it was a
week before Daniel was killed. It could have been a joke."

"We both know that's not true. But why wouldn't they tell him how
to fix the problem? Like, isn't that the way criminals act in the movies?
Shouldn't they have said something like 'we found you, drop our money
off at the Ice Cream Palace on Sunday in a duffel with unmarked bills'?"
Reana shivered, then looked around the room, rubbing the top of her arms.
"Do you think it's cold in here?"

"The landlord probably turned down the heat after they took Daniel
out. You know these houses eat up heat." She turned off the computer and
slipped it back into the desk. "I don't think we're going to find anything
else here."

"Thank goodness. I'm getting freaked out being here." Reana headed
to the door.

On the way out of the study, Angie noticed a coffee table book on
London on the shelf. The book was well worn, like its owner had gone
through the pages time and time again. Another clue that Daniel Monet
was Ian's Arnie. But like everything else, it was just a hint, not fact. She

caught up with Reana. "Let's just walk through the other rooms and then we'll be done."

"Promise?"

Angie nodded. "Definitely."

They made their rounds in all of the rooms, and in each of them, as she had in the office, bedroom, and game room, Angie took several pictures. A brief flicker of doubt made her pause when she thought about what Sheriff Brown might say if he saw her camera roll, but she pressed on. Something might look off when she looked at it later. But as far as she could see, it looked like a house where a single man lived.

A single man who was posing as a culinary instructor. And who'd been killed for some reason. A reason she thought was right there, but she just couldn't put her finger on it.

Chapter 14

Angie had spent the evening glancing at the pictures time and time again, alternating with scanning the Alberta newsletter, but by the time she'd gone to bed, all she succeeded in doing was building up to a headache.

Thursday morning, she did her chores and decided to put Daniel's death on the back burner. More talented investigators than her were looking into the issue. She needed to focus on the upcoming service that night and the rest of the weekend. She also wanted to know what the response from the cooking class had been. Felicia should have had a yoga class with the women by now.

Angie spent the morning working on a recipe for Nona's cookbook. At this rate, she should have something ready to show an agent by next spring. She could see the cover, a shot of Nona's garden. Or maybe the County Seat. Something warm and comforting and inviting. Or, she thought as she stirred the potato soup she'd made that morning, finalizing the touches she'd added for the class, maybe just a pot of soup. There wasn't anything more comforting than creamy potato soup. This was probably the one dish her Nona had made that to Angie said home. And love. She glanced over at Mrs. Potter's empty house. Typically, she would have taken a batch over to her, but the woman and her granddaughter were still out of town. As the days passed, Angie wondered if she could stay in the warm, sunny climate of California where her son lived.

As the soup cooled, she dished up some for lunch, then added a turkey sandwich. The good thing about being a chef was she always had food around. The bad thing was she always had food around. She opened her laptop and scanned her emails. She had one from Reana basically telling her not to forget their deal.

One from Felicia that outlined the staff changes for the week's schedule. Her kitchen staff rarely missed a shift, mostly because it was only part-time hours for most of them. Felicia also outlined the three new classes they'd already booked for the next month, including a mommy and me cookie class. She'd ask Nancy to work with her on that one. Nancy was trained as a pastry chef and loved desserts. She quickly emailed an outline to Nancy and one to Estebe on which classes she'd like them to take on.

With that done, she scanned her emails for anything else she needed to deal with. One stood out as total spam.

The subject line said *Hi Angie.*

She opened it, just in case it was someone who wasn't used to email protocol. Like Mrs. Potter.

She read it aloud. "'I really enjoyed our chance meetings, not once but twice. I know you said you are involved, but I'd love to meet for coffee. No strings. I'm leaving town in a few days, and would love to talk about what you saw in the cave. Yes, I looked you up when the park employees told me your story about finding the petroglyphs. No funny stuff, I promise. I'm just curious. Evan Morris.'"

Angie looked at the email address. It wasn't from the university. Those typically had an .edu extension. No, this was a Gmail account. If this guy was on the level, why wasn't he using his work email to reach out? On the other hand, she knew a lot of people who didn't use their work email except when they were at work. Except this guy should be different, especially since he was supposedly on assignment to find out more about the recently discovered Native American drawings.

She went to refill her coffee cup. Maybe she was just seeing issues with everything. She reread the email. Now that Ian was back, it didn't feel as much of an issue for her to meet this guy. What could coffee hurt? If he was who he said, she wanted to know what the university was planning on doing with the information. She'd hate to have her favorite hiking spot turned into a tourist trap. But if, as she thought, there was more to Evan than met the eye, this would be a great time to see what else she could find out about him.

She didn't have to be at work until three. If Evan read his email, maybe they could set up a time today. She responded, telling him she'd meet him today at two at the Library. It was a coffee shop in Meridian and should be far enough away from the small-town gossips who liked to report all her actions to Ian.

Not only did Evan read his email, he had to be online now, because he answered within minutes of her sending the response.

Just to make sure Ian wasn't in the dark with this, she sent him a quick text. *Meeting a university professor for coffee about the cave at two. Will call you on the way home.* That way, if something happened to her, at least someone would know to go looking.

Have fun. The response was quick.

Sure, you can text me now but you couldn't have sent me one before you stepped onto that plane last week? Angie was still mad at his abrupt disappearance.

Feeling like she'd covered the bases, she got ready for work. By the time she stopped for coffee and drove back to River Vista, it would be almost time for her to start prep. Besides, she needed some planning time to outline these new classes Felicia had set up. The first time would be the most work. Then they could just rotate the classes through the year, adding one or two new ones for each season.

She went out to the barn and did the evening feeding early. Precious was out in the pasture and didn't even look up when Angie filled her food dish. Mabel was out of the barn as well, looking for insects in the farm yard. At least when they returned for the night to their sleeping areas, they would have food available.

With the outside animals fed, she checked on Dom's food and water. He watched her with mournful eyes as she put her notebook into her tote and grabbed her keys. Angie walked over and crouched down to give him some love. "Sorry, guy. It's go-to-work day. Thursday, Friday, and Saturday. You know the drill. I'll be home late but we'll eat ice cream and watch a movie when I get back."

Dom snorted and closed his eyes, pretending to go to sleep. She knew he'd walk the house a few times while she was gone. She'd started locking her bedroom door because she had a feeling, proven by an increase in dog hair on her comforter, that he was taking advantage of her absence to sleep on her bed.

She kissed him on his broad forehead and locked the house. She loved the company of having the guy around while she was home, but she felt bad every time she left him to go to work. What would she do if she ever had kids? Of course, they wouldn't be left alone. They'd be left with a babysitter or at a day care. She wasn't sure what was worse. But she knew the leaving would break her heart every time.

Driving into town, Felicia called. Angie picked up the call on her Bluetooth. "What's going on?"

"Just letting you know that I'm pulling in a temp bartender tonight. Jeorge caught some type of cold or flu and doesn't want to leave the house."

"That's too bad. Maybe we should send him over some of that chicken soup we had left over from the class."

"That's a great idea. I'll send one of the staff over as soon as I get a server here. You're just full of good ideas lately. Why do you sound like you're in the car? You don't have to be here for a couple of hours."

Angie told her about meeting with the guy from Utah.

"But you think there's something hinky about him?" Felicia sounded worried. "So why are you meeting him?"

"Because maybe it's just my imagination. Besides, I'd like to be part of documenting the new find if I can help." Angie paused, trying to put her feelings into words. "I just think there's something more to this Evan guy, and I want to figure out what it is. I sure haven't been able to help Hope's lawyers find out who really killed Daniel."

"I'm sure I've said this before but, Angie, you're a chef, not a private investigator or a law enforcement professional. You should be worrying about what you're going to cook tonight, not why people are killed."

"Why can't I be the perfect superwoman?"

Felicia laughed. "And you think I'm a perfectionist. Just keep your phone handy and stay out of alleyways. Where are you meeting in case you don't show up and I have somewhere to send the police to start looking for you?"

After Angie hung up with Felicia, she wondered if this was stupid. One, if the guy was just looking for female companionship, she was dating Ian and off the market. But she had told him that and he still wanted to meet. He was looking for something more than just information on the caves. Now all Angie had to do was figure it out.

She parked in front of the building on the street. The owners of the Library had taken an old house just off Main Street and turned its rooms into book-filled heaven. The coffee bar was in what had been the kitchen, and all the other rooms were filled with homey furniture, bookshelves stuffed with books, and places to sit and get lost in a story for a while. Books were on a loan system. You bring one, you take one, it didn't matter. She'd found this place just after she'd moved back and had spent a lot of time just sitting and dreaming while she and Felicia developed the concept for the County Seat.

"Hey, Chris," she called out to the morning barista. "Large hazelnut with one of your peanut butter cookies, please."

The woman looked up from what she was doing behind the bar. "Hey, Angie! I haven't seen you in here for weeks. I hear the County Seat is rocking. Everyone's talking about it."

"You haven't stopped in?" She pulled out money to pay along with a business card. "Call Felicia and we'll get you a reservation."

Chris took the money and the card. "I just broke up with the most recent loser, but I bet my sister would love this. I'll set up a date soon."

"Thanks." Angie glanced around the almost empty coffee shop. "You haven't seen a guy in here waiting for me, have you?"

"Ian?" Chris looked confused. "No, he's not here."

Angie smiled. Small towns. "Not Ian, I've got a meeting with a professor about the find out at Celebration Park."

"You're the first customer I've had since the pre-work rush."

Angie glanced at her watch. She was early. "I'll be in by the fireplace if he shows. I'll give him a few minutes."

She got settled on the couch and found a new Robyn Carr book she hadn't read. She was just finishing up the first chapter when she heard a man's voice in the coffee bar area. She kept reading, but when she saw the shadow cross over her, she put a bookmark in her place and slipped the book in her purse.

"This place is great. I wish they had one at home. I would spend all my time here." He sat across from her and pushed a plate of cookies toward her. "I couldn't decide which one I wanted, so I got one of each. Take one."

Angie grabbed a second cookie, this time a fudge and vanilla striped sugar. It was her second favorite. "So, what do you want to know about the caves?"

"Right down to business, huh?" Evan sipped his coffee and took out a notebook. "So how long have you lived here?"

"What does that have to do with the petroglyphs?" She studied him closely. His clothes looked way too put together to be a researching professor. And he was wearing brand-new tennis shoes. Now, how did he go hiking and cataloging remote sites and not get his feet dirty? "When did you buy your shoes?"

He frowned and looked down at the sneakers. "I just picked them up at the mall here. My old ones were falling apart."

Okay, that was logical. Or at least plausible. She leaned back and waited for the next question.

"I was asking about your residence time here to get a feel for your historical knowledge of the area. I'd heard you just opened your restaurant this year." He glanced back down at his shoes, apparently jolted by the question. "I'll just go on. Had you ever heard of petroglyphs in the area?"

That wasn't what he planned to ask as his second question. Angie was sure of that. "My grandmother told me stories of the people who used to roam the area. But it was all about how they were the original owners of the land and how we could learn a lot by studying their culture. When did you hear about the cave?"

This time, her question didn't take him by surprise. He was finding his rhythm with her tactics. "I thought I told you that. We got a call from the local university about authenticating the site. I'm here for the pre-work."

"Oh." Angie sipped her coffee, letting the silence fill the space between them. He broke first.

"I hear your restaurant is something else. It must take a big team to run it. Where did you get qualified help?"

She broke another cookie in half. "Now we're talking about my hiring process? I'm really confused." She waved the half a cookie at him. "Do you want to stop the dance and tell me why you're really here and what you're looking for? Are you investigating Daniel Monet's death?"

A flash of anger filled his eyes but was gone before Angie could even confirm the emotion. It could have been surprise. Either way, she'd hit him full in the secret mission status of his interview.

"Daniel Monet? Oh, he was that professor that was killed. I don't know why you think I'm some sort of investigator. I study Native American art."

And I'm an expert on the Queen of England's wardrobe choices. She finished the cookie. "Seems strange that you just showed up right after his death."

"Boise is not that small. I could have been here for a number of reasons." He studied her and the focus made her uncomfortable. "Besides, if you think I'm involved in this, how do you know I didn't kill the guy?"

"I don't." She didn't feel as strong as her voice sounded. "But if you had killed him, you wouldn't have stayed around, making it easy for the police to find you."

"Good point." He glanced at his watch. "I really do need to be working on the survey for the cave, so if we're done playing what's my line, I guess I'll go find people who want to talk to me."

She watched him take his coffee and step toward the door. "Hold up, Evan."

He turned toward her, hope filling his face. "Yeah?"

"You forgot your cookies." She pointed to the plate. "Chris will probably put those in a bag for you."

"You take them." He spun back around and out the side door.

Chris came and stood by Angie as they watched him pull out his phone and then get into a black SUV parked on the street. "Man, that guy is razor-edge focused. You seemed to get under his skin, though. You sure you're not looking to replace your English fella?"

"I'm sure, but I don't think Evan was here looking for a date or information about old Native American artwork." She thought about what Evan might have really wanted as he drove away. At least with him gone, she wouldn't have to worry about someone attacking her before she got in the car. It was just Meridian, for goodness sake.

Chris went back to the cash drawer and pulled out a receipt. She held out the paper to Angie. "You might want to take a picture of this. I don't know if you can trace it. I heard you call him Evan, but his credit card says Robert."

Chapter 15

Felicia meet her at the kitchen door when she arrived at the County Seat. "I've been worried about you. It's been an hour since you texted that you were leaving Meridian. Where did you go?"

"I stopped by the police station and told Sheriff Brown about Evan or Robert or whatever his name was." Angie glanced around the still-empty kitchen. "Come into the office and I'll tell you all about how stupid our sheriff thinks I am."

Felicia followed her into the office and shut the door. "Don't tell me he didn't think the guy was weird."

"He thought it served me right for trying to be an investigator. Seriously, he's all up in my face about meeting strangers to talk about things that aren't any of my business." Angie opened a desk drawer and dumped her purse inside. "I think he was hiding something. Did you ever notice that guys get defensive when they're hiding something?"

"I haven't noticed that with all guys. Todd, yes, he used to rip my head off anytime I brought up a subject he didn't want to talk about. Like money." Felicia sank into a chair. "Maybe you're just seeing the red car."

Angie grabbed two bottles of water out of the mini-fridge in her office. She held one out to Felicia. "The red car?"

"Yeah, it's some psychobabble about how when you're focusing on something, like buying a red car, that's all you see. So since you think all men get defensive when they're hiding something…"

"That's all I see." Angie sank into her chair. "You might be right. Did I tell you that I'm having dinner with Sheriff Brown, his wife, and Ian on Sunday? Shoot me now."

"That might be the other reason you're seeing red cars. It's a known fact that when you're stressed about things, you don't see reality, you see what you want to see." Felicia opened the water and drank half of it. "I really should hydrate more."

"You're just full of all of these theories today. What exactly have you been reading lately?" Angie eyed her partner suspiciously. "Don't tell me you're going back to school to become a counselor."

"No. I hated school the last time I attended. There's no way I'm going back." Felicia wouldn't meet Angie's gaze.

"So where's all the psychology fun facts coming from?" Although Angie thought she knew the answer.

"I'm helping Taylor study for his master's. He has a really hard time getting into the books they're assigning, so I'm reading them too and then we discuss." Felicia studied her nails. "It's not like I'm taking his tests or anything. I'm just helping."

Angie studied her friend. Felicia was hot or cold with men. Either she was just casually dating, usually in a group, or she was all in. Like she was with Taylor. Working at his shelter, helping him study, reading his textbooks. "Let me ask a question, and you don't have to answer, just think about it. When was the last time Taylor did anything just for you?"

Felicia opened her mouth to respond, then closed it again. Then she shook her head. "It's not like that. Taylor's very busy. He's got people who depend on him."

Holding up a hand to ward off the excuses, Angie shook her head. "I told you, I don't need the answer. But I think you do."

They sat in silence for a minute as they finished their water. "I do think you're stressed about meeting Ian's parental figures."

"And I wouldn't disagree with you there. I'm going to have to figure out what to bring. Nona always said never come to someone's home empty-handed. But if I make a dessert and she's already made one, I look like I think I'm a better baker than she is."

"You probably are." Felicia shrugged. "What? We run a restaurant. She's probably afraid that you're going to criticize her food. Why don't you just call her and see what she'd like you to bring? That way, she's forewarned and you don't step on toes."

"Why do you always think of the simplest solution to everything?" Angie threw her bottle in the trash. "And the best solution."

Angie opened her computer and saw the email from Reana. "Oh, and I told someone they could get a reservation no matter what. I'm going to send you this email and can you see if you can fit them in?"

"You're wanting a miracle. We're booked for six solid weeks." Felicia checked the reservation calendar on her tablet. "What day?"

Angie recited off the day and preferred time. Reana's instructions were detailed down to the letter. "Maybe if we have to, we could set up a chef's table here in the kitchen?"

"Are you sure? You really don't like people watching you cook."

"It's going to happen sometime. And maybe I'll get as pumped as Estebe does during the cooking school classes." She shrugged and laughed at the look on Felicia's face. "It could happen."

"Doubtful." She glanced at her watch. "Anyway, I need to get going. Anything else I need to know about tonight's service? Did you invite the local football team to come sit at the bar?"

"No." Angie was lost in the list of dishes they had to prep for. "But maybe we should have a Feed a Teacher table when it slows down. That could be our own form of community service."

She could feel Felicia's stare before she even looked up. "What? Did I say something wrong?"

"Actually, no, it's a great idea. I'm always just shocked when you come up with these on the fly." Felicia made a note on her tablet. "I'll put it on next week's planning meeting and I'll start blocking off a table."

"I said when we slow down." Angie turned and stared at her. "And why are you shocked if I have a good idea?"

"Marketing isn't your strong suit. A lot of teachers would think we're out of their price line, but if we get them in here, they'll be hooked on the food and won't worry about the price, at least for special occasions."

"Marketing using the old drug dealer mantra, 'first one's on me'?" Angie scribbled her last note and stood with the notebook.

"Model what works, I've always believed." Felicia paused at the door. "Have you seen Hope since last weekend?"

"No, and I'm getting more and more worried about her. I'm not sure the police are really looking for another suspect. Hope fits their theory. She killed him in a fit of rage because Daniel wasn't ready for a full-time commitment. But if that's the motive, Hope's not the only potential suspect they should be looking at."

"Besides, I don't think the girl knows rage. She's a mini version of Mary Poppins. All sunshine and light."

But Hope wasn't exhibiting the sunshine and light as she came into the kitchen later that day. "Sorry I'm late."

Estebe caught Angie's gaze. They were both worried about her. He put down his knife and went over to talk to the new arrival.

When they were done, Angie told Hope she needed to work with Estebe as they were doing some new recipes today. She tried to sound casual, but even she heard the hesitation in her words. "I'd like your opinion on how these recipes worked for us tonight. Are they too time-consuming to prep? Or is this better than something we have on our standing rotation? I need to hear your comments. This kitchen isn't just me telling you what to do."

"Well, it kind of is." Matt paused in his chopping when everyone stopped and looked at him. "You made the recipes, right?"

"Matt," Estebe warned, but Angie cut him off.

"You know what, you're right. So from now on, each of you is responsible for bringing one new recipe to our monthly family meal. Rotate the responsibility. Hope, would you bring something for our next meal?"

Hope dropped the pan she'd been setting up on the cook line. "Wait, you want me to present a recipe too? Just like the chefs?"

"You are part of our team, right?" She waited for Hope to smile and was surprised when the girl started crying. "Oh, no, did you hurt yourself?"

"No." Hope sobbed as everyone gathered around her.

Angie looked at Estebe, who was staring at Hope, wide eyed. He shook his head indicating he didn't know what was wrong either. She put a hand on Hope's shoulder. "What's wrong?"

"You've just been so nice. Even with this whole murder investigation thing going on, you just treat me like I'm one of the team." She glanced around at the four others. "Thank you."

"You are part of the team. And I don't believe you could have killed Daniel or anyone else." Nancy hugged Hope quickly. "Buck up, girl, things will get better."

"Yes, listen to Nancy." Estebe patted Hope's arm. "You are a good girl."

"So, it's settled. We'll start this up at the next family meal. You have three weeks to figure out what you'd put on the menu if you were head chef. And just to keep it fair, it has to be seasonal and something the County Seat could add to the menu. Which means the majority of the ingredients need to be local." Angie thought that about covered the rules.

"I know exactly what I'm going to present." Matt grinned and returned to his work. "Can I go next?"

"That's up to Estebe." When he looked at Angie, the fear on his face made her laugh.

"I don't understand." Estebe stepped away from the group, looking for a way to escape.

"Don't worry, I just want you to head up this project. Would you handle the scheduling? I'd like to do at least two rounds before we reevaluate the process." Angie picked up the pot that Hope had dropped on the floor and put it on the dishwasher station. "Now that we've got that settled, let's get ready for service. What else needs to be done?"

When they broke for a quick meal before service, Estebe sat next to her at the kitchen table. The rest of the group were still milling around, getting their food finished. Matt was grilling burgers for the women and entertaining them with tales from his past.

"You did a good thing. Thinking about the recipe will keep her mind occupied during this trial. You are a good person, Angie Turner." He handed her the plate he'd made for her and then sat next to her to eat.

"I worry about her. She's usually so tough. This has her questioning everything about herself." Angie dug into the chicken dish that Estebe had made for their dinner. "They need to close this case, and soon. Before she totally freaks out."

"The justice system takes time to do the job right. You wouldn't want someone to rush to a decision here. The longer it takes, the better it is for our Hope. At least that's what my cousin says. He said if they had anything solid, they would have already arrested her for the murder."

The other three moved toward the table and Angie glanced over toward them, hoping that Estebe had heard them coming as well. She didn't have to worry. He nodded at her, understanding the conversation was over. He stood as the other three sat. "I'm getting water bottles. Who wants one?"

The rest of the evening, the kitchen almost felt back to normal. The service was flowing with everyone working closely together. After the last plate was delivered, Estebe took over closing down the kitchen. She'd never asked him to take on this assignment, but somehow, it had become his time in charge of the kitchen. And honestly, she was too tired to give the process the attention it needed.

She'd been going over the night's evaluations when Estebe sat down, this time with two beers in his hand. He opened one and set it in front of her. She wanted the drink. Honestly, she wanted more than one. But she'd never get home if she did, and the zoo needed her. She picked it up and took a long sip. "Thanks."

"You are welcome. You looked like you needed something. Is everything all right? Well, besides Hope's troubles." He fumbled with the label on the bottle. "Are you and Ian still a couple?"

Angie nodded. "Ian and I are fine. I guess I didn't realize how worried I've been about the murder. I think I'm taking this investigating thing too far. I accused a professor of being some kind of law enforcement investigating the murder. Felicia thinks I'm seeing everything through a bad lens. I'm beginning to agree with her."

"I've never known your perception about anything to be off. Maybe you are just tired." He glanced around the empty kitchen. "If you need me to drive you home, I can."

"I'm beat. But I can get home." Angie yawned. She took one last sip from the beer and then walked over to the sink and dumped the rest down the drain. "I *am* going to fill my travel mug with coffee."

"I left it on just in case. I will fill mine as well." He joined her at the coffeemaker. "We make a good team. I wasn't sure what it would be like to work for a woman."

"And I wasn't sure what you'd be like. Your references were a little sketchy. But like you said, we work well together. I'm glad for that." She took the mug. "I'm heading out as soon as I grab my purse from the office and say good night to Felicia."

"I will wait and walk you to the car." He filled his cup, then took the carafe to the sink to wash it out.

"I can get to the car by myself." She headed to the office.

He turned on the water. "I will walk you to the car."

As she grabbed her things, she thought about how steadfast Estebe was. He was a big part of why the County Seat was so successful. He had a knack to twist a recipe just enough to make it sing. She just hoped he wasn't harboring some hope that she might break up with Ian and be free to date. She'd have to talk to Felicia about her impressions tomorrow.

Tonight, she just wanted to get home and snuggle with Dom. The St. Bernard was becoming her touchstone when she needed comfort.

Her phone rang when she was in the car heading out of town. "I saw your car just leave the restaurant. Long day?"

"Ian. Weren't you coming in for dinner? Don't tell me you were there and I didn't even know." She turned up the heater.

"I didn't make it. I've been playing catch-up on work since I got back from England." He sounded as tired as she felt.

"So you made ramen for dinner? You should have just called in an order. I've got connections, we would have found someone to bring you food." She missed him. The thought surprised her, especially since she'd just seen him a few days ago.

"Worse, peanut butter and crackers. And a can of those circle noodles."

She couldn't help it, she laughed. "SpaghettiOs? Do they even sell those anymore?"

"I have five more cans in my cupboard. You could come for dinner some night and I'll cook."

"I'll pass. But I'll make dinner next week. What day don't you have something going?" She knew her schedule was unusual, but he tended to work a lot of evenings during the week. Sometimes breakfast was a better option for both of them.

"You remember we're having dinner with Allen and Maggie on Sunday, right?"

She inwardly groaned. At least she hoped she kept her reaction silent. "Yes, but I was thinking a dinner with just the two of us. I'm going to call Maggie tomorrow and see what I should bring."

"You don't have to bring anything."

She heard the tiredness in his voice. "I know I don't have to. I want to. Besides, it will give me and her some time to talk before the main event. It's a game that women play. And I want to do everything right in this case."

"She already loves you. What else can you do?"

Screw it up? She didn't say the words, but she wondered if he read the answer in her silence.

"Look, I'm almost at the house. Go to bed. I'll talk to you in the morning." She turned the car into the driveway.

"Sleep well." He hung up.

Angie let Dom out of the house and grabbed a flashlight. The two of them went to the barn to check on Precious and Mabel. She felt bad disturbing their sleep, but she wanted the comfort of knowing they were safe and warm and fed.

With that done, Angie went into the house and reheated a cup of hot chocolate. Adding whipped cream on the top, she took the cup and her book and curled up on the couch with Dom to wind down.

But thoughts of Daniel kept running through her head. Who was the culinary professor really? And what secret did he hold that would have gotten him killed? She decided to go back to the college tomorrow and see if she could talk to some of his peers. Maybe they had some insight into Daniel Monet. If she could figure him out, she could figure out why and get Hope off the hot seat.

Chapter 16

Friday morning, she dialed the direct line to the dean. When she got the front desk clerk, she checked her calendar. No, it wasn't a holiday. "Good morning, I was wondering if I could talk to Dean Schwartz."

"I'm sorry, everyone is out today. They're going to the memorial." The woman sounded bored to the tenth power. "I'm here answering phones until five."

"Daniel Monet's memorial? Do you know where it's being held?" Angie held her breath. This would be the perfect place to interview some of the faculty. They'd want to talk about Daniel.

"Yeah, hold on. They left an address in case one of the students lost the information. They're always losing something. You wouldn't believe the number of ID cards I have to replace every week."

Angie waited as she heard drawers being opened and closed. Finally the woman came back on the line. Apparently the students weren't the only ones who misplaced things.

"Here it is." She took in a long breath. "That's some fancy place."

"Where is it?"

"The Owyhee Hotel, downtown. This says the memorial service will run from noon to one with a small wake to be held afterward in the ballroom. They're having a cash bar." She snorted. "Sounds like an excuse to get drunk to me."

"Thanks, I appreciate you looking that up for me." Angie paused. Sometimes the office staff were the best ones to ask questions. They saw everything. "Did you know Daniel?"

"Kind of. He'd come in here every morning with a bright smile and a good morning, but I could tell he didn't really mean it. You can tell that with some folks, you know? My ma always said that a sharp dressed man was something to stay away from, and with Professor Monet that was certainly the case."

"Did you see him with any women?"

"Ha. Half the faculty and most of the students tried to get time with him. I handle the professors' office hour appointments too. I don't know of one male student who even tried to get time on his schedule." She sighed. "It is a shame. He was a good-looking man."

"Did he ever fight with anyone?" Angie thought her questions were getting direct, but at least she wasn't standing in front of the woman. She could pull off a casual interest over the phone. In person? Maybe not.

"Not that I saw. You're the second person to ask me about Professor Monet today. The man said he was with the FBI. Why in the world would the FBI be interested in a death in such a small town like Boise?" The woman paused. "Who did you say you were again?"

"I appreciate your time. Have a great day." Angie hung up before she could trip over some question and spill her identity. She'd never talked to the woman before, so she wouldn't be able to recognize her voice. She wondered about the FBI agent, though. There was no reason for the Bureau to be involved in a local murder. Unless Daniel was more than he seemed.

Time to go upstairs to find her black dress and get ready. She was going to a memorial service. She grabbed her phone and dialed. "Hey, can you do me a favor?"

Felicia was waiting outside the restaurant when she pulled up. She got into the car and clicked on her seat belt. "I can't believe we're doing this."

"What? We should pay our respects."

"We didn't even know the guy." Felicia gave her a pointed look. "All you want to do is go snoop around."

"Seems like a good place to do it." Angie pulled the car out onto the street. "Come on. It will be fine. We can meet some of Hope's instructors, and you've wanted to make better connections at the school. This way, we'll look like caring people."

"Versus the rotten, horrible person I feel like right now for crashing the service?" She checked her makeup in the vanity mirror and then flipped it back into place. "Don't mind me. I'm a little put out with Taylor. I called him last night just to talk and he blew me off. He said he was too busy to waste time chatting on the phone. I'm sorry, aren't we in a relationship here?"

"I probably shouldn't say this, but Ian called me on the way home just to make sure I wasn't too tired to drive." Angie turned onto the highway that would take them to the freeway and into Boise. "Maybe he was just tired."

"I guess. I get grumpy when I'm tired. I'll try again tonight, but if I feel like I'm bothering him again, that's it. We're done." She opened the glove box. "Where's the almonds? All I see is candy in here."

"I decided to change to sugar in case I'm out somewhere and need a fix." Angie turned her head and met Felicia's gaze. "It's a safety thing. You could die without food."

"Almonds might just keep you alive while you wait to be rescued. Anyway, you're going to have to restock, because I'm stealing them. I'm starving." She opened the bag and poured out a handful of colorful candies. "You want some?"

"Of course." She let Felicia pour a pile into the palm of her hand and then threw some into her mouth. After a few minutes, she continued the conversation. "You're going to dump Taylor because he doesn't want to talk to you on the phone?"

"No, I'm going to have a long, adult, heart-to-heart conversation about what he sees in our relationship, and then if I don't like the answers, I'm dumping him." She dumped the rest of the bag into her hand. "They don't put a lot of candies in here."

"Normal-size bag. Maybe you were just hungry."

Felicia shook her head. "Don't know how. I ate a three-egg omelet for breakfast, then I went down and raided the fridge for any leftover desserts from last night. And I just got back from grabbing a burger and fries at the drive-in." She shrugged. "I didn't know if we'd have time to each lunch before we drove back."

"I was planning on stopping and getting something after the memorial." Angie turned the car onto the freeway. "Man, traffic's heavy today."

"We can still stop. I'll be hungry by then anyway." She stared out the window. "I don't want to think about Taylor anymore. Tell me what you're looking for at the thing and maybe I can help you talk to people."

"I think it's one of those things where you'll know it when you hear it." Angie navigated around a slow-moving Cadillac. "Just keep people talking about Daniel. I'd like to know their impressions of the guy."

"I'll wander around and be the social butterfly." She grinned at Angie. "It's why I'm front of the house. It's a gift."

When they arrived at the hotel, they found parking on the street. Angie fed the meter and set an alarm on her watch. "We're probably going to have to come out during the wake and feed this thing. It only goes for two hours."

They started walking toward the hotel when she noticed a black SUV on the side of the road. She angled over to the edge of the sidewalk and looked inside.

"Angie." Felicia pulled her away from the car windows. "You look like you're about to break into the vehicle and steal it."

"Yeah, in my little black dress." But she followed her toward the hotel. There had to be a lot of that specific model in black hanging around Boise, but something in her gut told her it was the car Evan had been driving.

The doorman held the door open for them as they walked toward the entrance. "Fancy digs for a funeral." Angie glanced around the opulent lobby.

"Here." Felicia shoved a pile of business cards at her. "Give these out."

Angie stared at the tastefully done County Seat card. "Don't you think this is a bit tacky?"

"Not at all. People are always curious about others. This gives them our details right up front. And if they decide to try out the restaurant, so much the better." She adjusted her dress and looked around the large room. "Do we know where we're going?"

Angie checked the event board that was set up by the side of the lobby. "Looks like the memorial service is in Grand Suite Ballroom A and the wake afterward is in Grand Suite Ballroom E."

They started toward the conference rooms. It was almost noon, so most of the mourners had already taken seats when they went in through the doors of the ballroom. A woman standing by a guest book offered them a flyer. Daniel's school photo, the same one he had on his Facebook page, smiled out at them.

"Would you like to sign the book?" The woman motioned toward the table. "That way the family can know how many friends and coworkers attended and send thank-you notes."

"The family? Daniel had family?" She shot Felicia a look that clearly said, *see, I'm already finding out new things.*

The woman shook her head. "No, I'm sorry, I spoke out of habit. I believe the university is putting on this service, not his family. But the platitude still stands. Someone is going to go through that book, page by page, and remember this day."

That might be true, Angie thought, *but it won't be because they want to remember the day. It's all about the visitors.* Which was why she was there. She passed on signing, mostly because the woman annoyed her.

They sat in the next to last row of chairs. Angie nodded to a weeping woman a few rows in front of them. "Isn't that your yoga buddy, Tanya?"

"She's not my yoga buddy, but yes, it most certainly is. I wonder if her husband came along with her to mourn her dead lover," Felicia deadpanned.

Angie's lips twitched and she pressed them together to keep the inappropriate grin away. "Again, not the best opening."

Felicia shot Angie a wicked look. "You're killing all my best lines."

The music increased in volume and the lights dimmed. At the front of the room, curtains pulled back to reveal a picture of Daniel, the same picture they'd put on the flyers. This wouldn't be a service with a ton of pictures from baby to time of death flashed on the screen behind the speakers, mostly because the man hadn't been in Boise long enough to make his own path. The school had been everything he'd been from the day he'd moved here. Or at least that's what Dean Schwartz had just said at the platform.

Tanya's sobs increased in volume, and a stoic man at her side handed her a tissue. Was this the famous Steve Livingston? Had she really brought him as her date for the event? What a loser. Angie watched the other mourners, and when she recognized someone, she wrote down their name on the back of the flyer. There was a lot of empty space, as Daniel's life seemed as much of a mystery to the flyer author. She should be able to talk to at least some of these people. The other ones, she'd give to Felicia.

As the crowd was moving out, Angie spotted Evan Morris on the other side of the room. His gaze found hers and he cocked his head. She could hear the question from him. *And what are you doing here?* She decided she was going to ask him the same thing. It had been his car she'd seen on the street.

"You ready?" Felicia stood, watching her.

Angie nodded. "See that guy over there?" She started to point toward Evan but he was gone. She scanned the area. There was no way, with this crowd, that he'd gotten out of the ballroom. Then she saw the side wall door slowly closing after him. He must have slipped through that.

"What guy?" Felicia tried to follow her directions, but the people were moving too fast.

Angie moved toward the line of people exiting. "Evan Morris was right over there. Why would an archeology professor from Utah be at a memorial service for a culinary instructor? I know there's more to him than he's willing to admit."

"You told Sheriff Brown about him. What more can you do?"

"Yeah, and he blew me off. But I'm texting him as soon as we get out of here. Something's off with this guy." They stepped outside the ballroom into the hallway, which wasn't quite so crowded, and followed the milling people to the room with the cash bar.

"You point him out and I'll go talk to him. I'm good at sizing people up in a hurry." Felicia grimaced. "Unless I'm dating them."

As they walked into the second ballroom, Dean Schwartz came up and gave them both a hug. "I'm so glad you could come today."

"It's such a shock." Felicia moved closer. "Angie and I were just about to invite him to the restaurant. You know Hope Anderson works with us on a part-time basis while she's getting her degree."

"I'm not sure I've met the young woman." He squeezed Angie's arm. "You two are making our program shine. I'm always being asked about successful graduates, and your names are always on the top of my list."

"That's so sweet of you." Felicia pulled out a few business cards. "Make sure you give them our card. If they happen to be at the restaurant, we'd be glad to talk to the families about the program and what it meant to us."

He took the cards and, without looking at them, tucked them away in his suit pocket. "What a great idea. I'll do that. My wife and I have been meaning to drive out, but it seems like you're always booked out so far."

"The price of success. We're always working. Now that we've added Thursday to our hours, we'll probably be able to fit you in. Don't you think, Felicia?" Angie smiled at her, putting her on the hot seat. "Oh, there's someone I really must talk to. Will you excuse me?"

She didn't wait for an answer, but the look on Felicia's face told her there would be words later about leaving her alone with the dean. The guy was full of himself and loved to talk. But maybe Felicia could get some information about Daniel from the guy. Angie beelined through the crowd and stopped in front of Evan, who was getting a drink at the bar. "You show up at the strangest places."

"As do you." He nodded toward the bottles lined up. "Can I buy you a drink?"

"Sure. White wine." She waited as the bartender poured her wine and gave Evan something golden on the rocks. When he turned toward her, she nodded to a table. "Can we chat?"

"I'm not sure I have any answers for you, but sure." He took her elbow and led her to the table. "You look lovely today."

"Hitting on people at a funeral is a little tacky." She sipped her wine and watched him.

He smiled and shrugged. "A lot of relationships start at events like this. Weddings and funerals are life's milestones. It makes the participants want to experience more in life."

"You sound more like a philosophy professor." She set her glass on the table. "Or is it sociology?"

"Studying human behavior doesn't change from studying the past or the present. Humans are fascinating creatures. They always show such a tendency to be curious, even when it puts them in danger."

"That sounds almost like a threat."

He laughed. "I'm probably the most unthreatening person in this room. But don't you worry that your presence here might put you in the spotlight? Why are you asking questions about the man's death? Is it to insert yourself into the case so you can watch your handiwork?"

"You can't seriously think I killed Daniel. What would be my motive?" Angie picked up the glass and sipped.

"I don't think that. I was just wondering what others thought." He watched her. "You're an interesting woman, Angie Turner. I wish I had more time to get to know you."

"I don't think we're on the same wavelength. And besides..." She paused as he held up his hand.

"Don't say it again. I know, you have a boyfriend. But where is he?" He glanced around the room, focusing on Tanya and her husband. "Most of the women here brought moral support. I guess Daniel had an effect on a lot of people."

"For someone who had only lived here a few months, I'd say he had a lot of friends, from the turnout." Angie ignored the barb at Ian. "Besides, my partner at the restaurant came with me."

"Oh, so you're not alone. But as far as Daniel having friends, well, faculty will do anything for a paid day of leave." He nodded to the doorway. "As soon as the dean moves away from the entrance, you'll see them escaping so they can get on with their life."

She glanced over and saw Felicia was talking with another professor now. She must have gotten away from the dean. "You're pretty cynical."

"I prefer to call it realistic." He glanced at his watch. "And I'm late. Thank you for the time, Ms. Turner."

"Thank you for the drink." She raised the glass and finished the wine.

He smiled at her. "Small-town people are all the same. Way too trusting."

Chapter 17

Felicia finished off her French fries as she listened to Angie's story. "So what do you think he meant about being too trusting?"

Angie took a bite of her burger as they sat in the parking lot of the Big Bun. She sipped the iced tea she'd ordered along with the mushroom burger and large fry. She shuddered, remembering the chill that his words had caused. "Honestly, I wondered if I was going to pass out from the drink. I think something else might have happened had I not mentioned you were there with me."

"You don't think he would have tried to drug you, do you?" Felicia's eyes were wide. "How would he have gotten you out of the ballroom?"

"He could have said I'd been overcome with grief. Tanya was. Man, I felt bad for her husband." Angie finished the burger. "Anyway, it was just a feeling. I'm probably imagining it all."

"I don't know…"

"I promise, I won't be alone with the guy again. He's creepy with a capital *C*." Angie put her trash into a paper bag. She held the bag open and out to Felicia. "Are you ready to head back to River Vista?"

Felicia wadded up her empty burger wrapper and grabbed the bag. "I'll take this to the trash. Don't steal my fries."

The fries were good, but she'd thrown away half of her own order. The drive-in was known for their generous portions, but honestly, it was just too much food for one person. She started the car and waited for Felicia to come back. She thought about Evan Morris. Every time she saw the guy, it just kept getting stranger. He seemed to know where she'd be and when. River Vista might be small, but Boise wasn't. And he'd never explained what he was doing at the memorial. No matter what Sheriff Brown thought, there was something going on with him. Well, at least she'd have some time with the sheriff on Sunday. Maybe she could get him alone and express her concerns. There was no way that guy was a professor. Too bad she didn't have some kind of facial recognition software like they did in all the crime shows.

"What are you thinking about? You should see the look on your face. Did you figure out the world peace problem?" Felicia slipped into the passenger seat and clicked on her seat belt.

"Actually, I decided to put Evan Morris out of my head, unless I happen to have some time for a private conversation with the sheriff." She pulled out of the parking lot and headed toward the road to home.

"You mean like on Sunday?"

Angie turned on her turn signal and eased the car out into traffic. "Why, I'd forgotten about Sunday. I guess I could bring up the subject then."

"You didn't forget, you're *planning* on ambushing him. Did you ever call Maggie?" Felicia checked her phone for messages.

"No. I'll call her when we get to the restaurant. Speaking of, Ian might come in for dinner. I gave him grief about what he ate the other night. I can't believe he's still alive considering how bad he eats."

"He needs the love of a good woman." Felicia side-eyed her.

"We're just dating. Not engaged. But we're...exclusive? Is that what we're calling it these days?" Angie took the ramp onto the freeway.

"I believe *exclusive* is the term." She sighed and put her phone away.

Angie thought she knew who Felicia was waiting for a message from. "Taylor might be busy with the shelter."

"Or he may be mad at me since I told him I wasn't folding clothes on my days off and how he needed to take me to a real dinner, one that we don't cook, and a film, one that isn't upstaged by a fight between the residents." She shrugged but Angie could see she worried over the consequences of her line in the sand.

"What did he say?"

Felicia closed her eyes. "He called me selfish."

"You? You're about the most unselfish person I know. Just because you want a little couple time doesn't make you selfish. How do you feel about this guy? Is he worth the work?" They were almost in River Vista, but Angie wanted to finish this conversation before Felicia had an opportunity to use getting ready for the evening's service as an excuse.

"I thought I loved him." Felicia shook her head. "I've never met someone who was so passionate about helping others. But I'm not willing to be his second-in-command for his cause. I have my own life, my own hopes and dreams. Which, by the way, we never talk about. When I bring up my plans for the future, he changes the subject to what a little more money would do for the shelter, or when I think the kitchen crew from the County Seat could come back and cook for the guys."

"You're kidding." Angie was beginning to think that she didn't like Taylor, not one bit. "Speaking of that, I told Estebe we'd help him with some holiday thing he cooks for over at the Basque Center. It's Christmas Eve, so people may have plans, but we'll need to bring it up with the crew at our next family meeting. I like doing different things as our community service events. It gets our name out there, you know?"

"Exactly. I told him that we needed to help other charities and causes and he went off on a rant about how no one cares about the homeless." Felicia started to reach for her phone but stilled her hand. "I've had a lot of time this week to think back on our relationship, and it's so one-sided. Taylor gets and does whatever he wants. I'm not sure I'm willing to sacrifice my life to his."

"You don't have to make the decision now." Angie slowed down to the in-town speed limit, which was way too slow in her mind. Especially today, when no one was on the road except her.

"I think I made my decision when I stood up for myself." She nodded toward her purse. "If he calls again, I'll be surprised. And if he does, it will only be because he needs something from me. That will be my sign from the universe that Taylor wasn't the man I thought he was. I should have realized that when I met him. Did you know he hasn't had one serious relationship? Well, except for with himself. The man is totally vain."

"If you need me to stay over or, better yet, why don't you come home with me after Saturday's service. We'll get drunk and watch *Top Chef* reruns and make fun of the contestants."

"That would be great, except you have to be at your boyfriend's family dinner the next day. Let's put it off for a few days. Maybe Monday or Tuesday night when neither one of us has something going." She closed her eyes. "Nope, Tuesday's out this week because we have family meal coming up on Wednesday, right?"

"Not this Wednesday. We have a couple of weeks. By the way, I have something to tell you. We're adding a contest to the agenda." Angie went through the idea the kitchen crew had developed. "Estebe is in charge, so get with him about the details. It shouldn't be that big a deal, but Hope's up first. I'm hoping it will lighten her mood and give her something to think about besides Daniel and the murder investigation."

"This is fun. I might ask Estebe to add me to the group. I've been meaning to work on a new dessert for the winter." Felicia's eyes softened as she thought about what she'd present. "Maybe change up the ordinary apple crumble recipe."

And this was exactly why Angie loved working in the food service industry and owning her own restaurant. Food healed. It wasn't a magic bullet, but cooking and eating and coming together over food was the best way to deal with any problem. At least in Angie's mind. "If we get enough great recipes, we could do one week a quarter where it's all staff-developed recipes."

"The patrons would love that. You don't know how many people come in because they know Matt or Nancy or Estebe. Even Hope has friends who show up and ask if she's working." Felicia glanced at the building that held the County Seat as Angie parked behind it. "We've made the restaurant almost into a home, a family."

"El pescado was great, but this feels different, doesn't it?" Angie turned off the car and glanced up at the brick building. "I'm so glad you agreed to come back to Idaho with me."

"I'm glad we told Todd he couldn't come with us. He would have messed this whole thing up." Felicia gave her a wicked grin and got out of the car.

Angie knew she was right. Todd had been a user. And now Felicia was dealing with a man who had the same huge ego. Maybe it was because chefs loved taking care of others with the food. Maybe that was why they were drawn into relationships where they took care of others. Either way, she knew she was done with that type of life. She hoped Felicia was too.

She hurried to catch up with her friend and get the work day started. The County Seat was what mattered, and that included the people who worked there. Her work family. No, not work family, her family. Angie stepped through the door and left behind all the worries she had been carrying. Now was about the food and the customers.

The kitchen staff came in in shifts after her. Estebe showed up first. His terse good afternoon at the door to her office brought her into the kitchen to help with prep. If he was surprised when she put on an apron and washed her hands, he didn't say anything. Matt showed up next, and then Hope and, finally, Nancy. She was still working at another restaurant for the morning shift to make sure her income covered her bills. Angie wasn't sure exactly how she'd gotten into such a financial hole, but she knew it was because of her divorce. Everyone had a story. Some of them you knew, others they kept close.

They were halfway through dinner service when Felicia came in. She pulled Angie aside. "Tanya Livingston is here and demanding to talk to you."

"Was there something wrong with her meal?" Angie stepped toward the expediter station and set up a tray for a waiting server. "Table fourteen."

"She's not a customer. She just came into the restaurant and demanded to talk to you. Carla was pretty shaken when she came to get me. She said Tanya seemed drunk and agitated. She was going to call the police but thought maybe you'd want to talk to her."

"That's weird." Angie motioned to Estebe. "Cover for me, I've got to handle something out front."

Estebe nodded and called Nancy over to take his station. They'd developed a pattern over the months for when Angie was called out into the dining room. This time, when he walked around, wiping his hands on a towel, he frowned at her. "You look upset. Is everything alright?"

Angie should have known that nothing would get past her second-in-command. "I think so. I'll be right back."

She moved her way through the dining room, stopping to greet a regular or two as she stepped through. She could see Tanya pacing in the lobby area and a worried Carla watching her. When the third diner stopped her to chat, Angie excused herself. "Sorry, I've got to deal with something."

The look on her face must have stopped others from reaching out to her or she just didn't see them. She was focused on the anger floating through the room, emanating from one person. Tanya. She nodded to Carla. "I've got this."

"It's about time. I've been waiting here forever." Tanya started, but Angie held up her hand.

"Outside. I don't want you disturbing our customers." Angie took Tanya by the arm and almost pushed her out the door. The woman was tiny, but she had some fight in her. Angie's grip tightened but then she released her as soon as they were outside. "What do you want?"

"I saw you talking to that man. Who is he?"

"At the memorial? Is that what you're talking about?" Angie sank onto the bench they'd set up outside the County Seat just in case they had waiting guests. So far, Felicia had done an excellent job of flipping tables and managing reservations, so they hadn't really used the outdoor area much. And most of the patrons liked to wait at the bar anyway.

"Of course that's what I'm talking about. Are you an idiot?" Tanya's face was beet red and Angie worried that if she'd been older, the high blood pressure might have had a bad influence on her heart.

"He says he's a professor from Utah." Angie watched as Tanya paced. "Do you know him?"

"That's just it. I think I saw him the last time Daniel and I were out. We had gone to the Crow's Inn out in the middle of nowhere, and we were drinking and talking. Then this guy walks in and Daniel goes all white. He grabs me, throws a twenty on the table for the drinks we'd just ordered, and drags me out." Tanya sank next to Angie on the bench. "But if he's just another professor, maybe Daniel was worried that this guy would tell my husband about the affair. That has to be the answer."

"You were wondering if he was the guy who killed Daniel."

Tears fell from Tanya's eyes and she dug in her purse for a tissue. "I've been crying all day but then when I saw that guy, I thought maybe, just maybe I could do something for Daniel. The police have been total idiots. All they've done is interview me and the tramps who said they were sleeping with him."

Angie didn't want to point out that Tanya might not have been the only one Daniel was doing the horizontal mambo with, upset as the woman tended to get.

"And before you say anything, my husband has told me all the rumors of Daniel and his students." She sighed, dabbing a tissue on her face to sop up the tears. "Steve has been a rock in this whole thing. I told him everything and he's forgiven me. I can't believe he's been so understanding. If he'd been the one having the affair, I would have done some damage to both of them before I decided to take him back again."

Angie wondered if Steve Livingston hadn't actually gotten his revenge and his wife didn't know it. "Where was your husband the night Daniel was killed?"

"He was at a conference in Seattle. That was why Daniel and I were supposed to get together after I put him on the plane. But the plane was delayed, so Steve and I had dinner at the Olive Garden on Franklin since it was close to the airport." Tanya sniffed and checked her makeup in the compact she'd pulled out of her purse. "I know what you're thinking."

"What am I thinking?"

Tanya shot her a flat stare. "That my husband took care of his competition and that's why Daniel is dead. Honestly, that's the most ridiculous theory. One, I saw him leave through the security gates that night to go to the conference. And two, my husband would never kill another soul. He doesn't have an ounce of violence in his body."

Angie watched as Tanya got up and tucked her compact back into her purse. "Well, I had to ask about that man. I guess it's just a coincidence.

Daniel must have been right, he was another professor. There's nothing more than professors like to do than gossip."

Being a professor would explain why Evan had been at the memorial. Angie just didn't believe it. There was something going on with that guy, and now she had one more piece of the puzzle to try to fit into the pattern. The problem was there were too many pieces still missing for her to see the picture clearly.

Angie stayed outside long after Tanya had left. Finally, Felicia poked her head out of the entrance door. "Oh, good, you're all right."

"What, you thought Tanya attacked me?" Angie stood from the bench.

Felicia held the door open for her. "I would have bet on you to win, but yeah, the woman is determined to get what she wants."

"Except now her lover is dead and she's stuck with the boring, but supportive husband." Angie shook her head. "But why would she be looking for Daniel's killer if she was actually the killer herself? It doesn't make sense."

"Unless it does." Felicia pulled her back toward the coat room. "What if she's just trying to put the blame somewhere else?"

"Is she that smart?" Angie thought about Tanya and her life. "I don't see it. She'd be further ahead if she blamed her husband rather than being his alibi."

Felicia nodded to the couple who'd just walked inside the restaurant. "Alibis can be broken."

Chapter 18

After service, Felicia was finishing with the accounting in the office and paying out the last server's tips when Angie came in and flopped into the visitor chair. When they were alone, she leaned forward and asked, "Do you really think Tanya could have killed Daniel?"

Felicia shrugged as she put the cash bag back into the safe. "I don't know about that woman. She's so manipulative. Did she come here to ask you about Evan? Or did she come here to move suspicion off herself? It's a crapshoot either way."

"How does she know I'm even involved in the investigation?" Angie stood and grabbed two bottles of water from the mini-fridge. She handed one to Felicia.

"You're kidding, right?" Felicia took the water and cracked open the bottle. "You're the talk of the yoga class. Everyone knows how you like solving cases."

"I don't think everyone knows that." Angie frowned. "Seriously? People are talking about me?"

"Small towns. I figured you already knew. Besides, they see you as some sort of cool superhero, which makes me cool because we're friends." Felicia rolled her shoulders. "I'm heading to bed unless you need to talk. Oh, Ian didn't come in for dinner tonight. I thought you said he would be in?"

"I thought he was going to show. Maybe he's still swamped at work." Angie grabbed her tote and switched off her chef jacket for a warmer one. "I'll give him a call tonight on my way home. I hope he at least went to the store today."

"Yeah, it would look bad if your boyfriend starved to death. I can see the headline now."

Angie laughed. "He's a big boy, he knows how to feed himself."

"Are you sure about that?" Felicia followed her to the kitchen door. "I'll watch until you get into the car."

"You know nothing's going to happen." They'd started making sure no one left alone. Typically, Estebe stayed and walked everyone out, but he'd had to leave as he was meeting a friend tonight.

"It takes a second. And besides, there's a killer on the loose, again. I swear, when you told me we were setting up our new restaurant in a small town in Idaho, murderers were the last thing on my worry list." Felicia leaned against the doorframe and watched her walk down the stairs.

"The area is more interesting than I'd remembered." Angie waved as she unlocked the car and then started the engine. She turned onto the road, then using her Bluetooth, she called Ian. The ringing went right to voice mail. "Hey, you didn't come in and eat at the restaurant tonight. If I don't hear from you tomorrow, I'll send your uncle over to do a welfare check because you must have starved to death. Anyway, talk to you soon."

She hung up and headed home to complete her own list of chores before she sank into bed and closed her eyes.

* * * *

Saturday morning, she was sitting at the table, drinking coffee and working on the cookbook she planned to publish in a few months, when she heard a truck pull into her driveway. Dom immediately woke from his nap and walked over to the door and sat, waiting impatiently as he wagged his tail over the kitchen floor. "You know who's here, don't you?"

She got up, poured a second cup of coffee, and set it on the table seconds before Ian came inside, carrying a bag of donuts. Dom whimpered a fast good morning as Ian leaned over to give him a rub on the top of his head.

"Hey, beautiful. I figured I should come by and let you know I'm not dead." He held up the bag. "And to prove I have foraging skills of my own."

"Did you get me a maple bar?" She grabbed napkins from the counter. He laughed as he handed her the bag. "I wouldn't show up without one."

As they enjoyed the sugary treat, she studied him. "You look like you haven't gotten much sleep. What's going on in the world of produce that has you in such a state?"

He sat his donut down. "There's some issues with the farmers market. Some of the farmers are saying the booth rentals are too high. They're threatening to leave and set up their own event in Nampa."

"Do they realize what it costs for overhead?" She didn't want to think about what would happen if the River Vista event closed down. Not only would Ian have to find another job, but she'd be back to trying to source local products from a ton of different vendors. She'd spend all week getting everything she needed.

"Apparently, they are questioning my salary." He sipped his coffee. "Will you still love me if I'm unemployed?"

"Your salary? You make nothing." She shook her head. "Seriously, what are they thinking?"

"Someone wanted to know how I afforded the plane tickets for my England trip last week. I guess they've never heard of credit cards." He pushed the donut away and leaned back into his chair. "As it is, I'll be paying that off for the next year. At least I will be if I keep my job."

"You should show them a comparison of the costs here and what it would cost going out on their own." Angie could feel the anger over the unfairness of the situation seeping into herself.

"And that's what I've been working on. You're pretty intuitive on these types of things. Maybe you could look it over before my presentation to the board next week?"

"Of course." She finished her donut and looked in the bag for what was left. "You want the apple cruller or the one with sprinkles?"

"Take what you want." He picked up his phone and read the incoming text. "Oh, Maggie wants to know if you eat pork."

"Yes." She stared at him. "That's a strange question. Why would she ask that?"

"I guess she's doing a crown roast of pork and wanted to make sure it wasn't against your dietary restrictions. Honestly, I think it's my fault. I was dating a vegetarian a few years ago. She's probably figured your tastes fall in that vein."

"Just don't let her eat at the restaurant. All her theories will be destroyed." Angie could feel her shoulders tightening. "Maybe this dinner thing isn't a good idea. You've got a lot on your plate. Your uncle has a lot on his plate. I'm busy with the restaurant. Maybe we should put it off."

"No way. We're going over there tomorrow come hell or high water, as my mum used to say. Sunday dinner is served at one p.m. sharp. The only question I have is are you sure you want me to get you before church service? We can do this either way."

"I know I said before, but since we've got a full house at the restaurant tonight, after would be lovely. I'm not going to be able to get into bed much before midnight."

"Works for me. That's an hour later I get to sleep in as well." He picked up his donut and finished it. "What's going on with the murder investigation? Have you figured out who killed Daniel yet?"

"No. But I'm leaning toward this Evan guy." She walked Ian through the times she'd met Evan and what had happened.

"So you think because he's hitting on you, he must be the killer?" Ian refilled their coffee cups.

"Wait, what? You think he's hitting on me?" She tried to replay the interactions she'd had with the guy. "I didn't get that vibe at all. Especially not at the memorial. He's intense but his focus keeps changing. First, he's all about the cave, then he wonders why I'm looking into Daniel's death."

Angie paused, thinking back. Had she been the one to bring up Daniel, or had he? "I feel like I'm just spinning my wheels here. Your uncle is right. I need to stick to running the restaurant and leave the investigating to the professionals."

Ian put her coffee in front of her and set down his own cup. He rubbed her shoulders. "Now, who would you be if you weren't sticking your nose into things that don't involve you?"

"Thank you, I think." She really would have punched him for saying that but his hands were doing magic on her tense muscles. "Anyway, this does involve me if it still involves Hope."

"According to Allen, the investigation isn't going toward Hope. But they're stalled on motive. The guy liked juggling his women. And Hope's lucky she didn't become one of his harem. If she had, she would still be on the top of the list for the primary." He kissed the top of her head and grabbed his coffee, sitting down. "What did you say this Evan was driving when he met you for your date?"

"It wasn't a date." Angie saw the smile and knew she was being teased. "The first time I saw him at the trails, he was driving a small sedan. I assumed it was a rental. This time, he drove a black SUV. I couldn't tell what make. Is that important?"

"I've been thinking about that night a lot lately. And one memory keeps coming back. I saw a black SUV at the mission that night as we were leaving." He rubbed his finger around the top of the cup as if he were trying to pull back the memory.

"Are you sure?" She hadn't noticed any specific car parked near them or on the road.

"Daniel came out of the building. I was watching him closely. I guess even then, I knew it was my old friend, no matter what he tried to say." Ian ran a hand through his hair. "Anyway, he came out, saw me, and turned the other way. Then he looked out toward the road and changed his mind, coming back toward us. I thought it was weird, so I glanced toward the road to see what he'd wanted to avoid more than talking to me. A black SUV was driving by slowly."

"If it's the same vehicle, that puts Evan in Boise on the night of the murder. I wonder if your uncle knows this." She reached for her phone.

"Hold on, don't jump so fast. We don't even know if it was Evan's car, just that it was a black SUV. I'll stop by the station today on my way back to the apartment and tell him this. Maybe there's a good reason Evan's hanging around." He ran one finger around the lip of his cup. "You've already told Allen about Evan and your encounters?"

"Yes. Well, except the last one. I didn't tell him about seeing him at the memorial. He didn't believe me when I told him about the other weird stuff."

"Sometimes you don't know what Allen believes or feels. He's got a pretty solid poker face." He finished off his coffee. "I'll ask him to talk to you tomorrow at this dinner thing. Maggie doesn't like shop talk on Sunday, so we'll have to make some excuse to get the two of you alone, but I'm sure he'll ease your mind about this guy."

She watched as he got ready to go. "Are you coming to the restaurant or should I just send over a delivery order?"

He chuckled. "You know I can feed myself."

"I know what you eat when you feed yourself." She smiled, thinking about his love of processed and junk food. "Besides, I'd love to see you for a few minutes."

"You're always so busy at the restaurant, I hate to take up your time." He leaned down and kissed her. "But if it will make you stop mother henning me about food, I'll come in and eat. See you tonight."

After Ian left, Angie sat at the table thinking about Daniel. They'd established he had been a kid in trouble. Maybe he'd kept up his troubled ways and gotten himself involved with a bad bunch. That would explain the name change. Had she looked further into Arnold Manner? Where had he been during the missing years? She pulled out her notebook and looked at the chart they'd made.

"Where have you been hiding, Danny Boy?" She opened her laptop and started searching again.

Two hours later, with a wicked headache, she closed the laptop and went to get ready for work. Cooking she could do, no problem. Looking into Daniel Monet's history, that was like finding a needle in a haystack. She needed to give up and focus on her strengths. As long as Hope wasn't in danger of being charged, she'd have to let the professionals figure out the why and who killed the Casanova Professor.

* * * *

Estebe came into her office around four that afternoon, worry carved into his face. "We have a problem."

"What's wrong?" She glanced at the clock. Service would start promptly at six. If she needed to restart something, they might just need to take it off the menu for the evening. "Did we run out of something?"

"No, the food is fine." He glanced at the pile of papers on Angie's desk. "I do not mean to bother you, but Hope's not here. She called me about two and said she had a meeting with one of her professors and would be in no later than three. I tried to call her at three thirty, but no one answered. I am worried."

Angie thought about the drive from the school to here. Even with traffic, it shouldn't take more than forty-five minutes. She stood and grabbed her tote and keys. "I'll go see if I can find her on the route."

"I will go with you." He followed her out of the office.

"What about prep?" They walked through the kitchen where an equally worried looking Matt and Nancy stood, watching them.

"We can finish prep. Just go and find her. Maybe she's broken down somewhere." Nancy glanced at her phone. "I've called, but it keeps just going to voice mail."

"Let Felicia know where we've gone. We'll be back before five." With or without Hope. Angie didn't add the second part of the sentence, as she was too worried that they would return empty-handed. Then they would have to just call the police and see if they would even start looking for her. Which they probably wouldn't, not for forty-eight hours. "Stupid rules," she muttered as she headed toward her car.

"I'll drive." Estebe took her arm and led her to his Hummer.

He unlocked the door and Angie scurried up into the passenger seat. When he joined her, she clicked on her seat belt. "Are you afraid to ride with me?"

"I am a faster driver." He glanced over at her. "I'm not afraid to get a ticket. Besides, if we have the police's attention, it will be easier if something is wrong when we finally find our lost girl."

"You really like her, don't you?"

"She is part of us. Like a little sister I've never had. She doesn't deserve these bad things to keep happening to her. If I could go back to that night outside the mission and stop her from driving that man home, none of this would be happening now."

"We'd all like a few do-overs in life." Angie leaned back into the leather seats. "I'm not sure that one would have kept Daniel Monet alive."

"But Hope wouldn't have been questioned in his death. It is not Daniel who I want to protect, but Hope." He floored the car and they went through town quickly. Then when he was on the highway, he really hit the gas. "Keep on a lookout for her car."

They'd only gone a few miles when she saw a car on the other side of the road in the gulley that separated the highway from the field next to the road. The car was definitely Hope's. She had her flashers going, and to Angie's horror, a black SUV was pulling in behind it.

"There. She's right there." She pointed toward the car and Estebe crossed the four-lane highway in a diagonal. Luckily there were no other cars on the road. As he pulled up, Angie could see Hope's face light up as she saw them.

Relief filled Angie but as she moved to unlock her seat belt, Estebe stilled her hand. "Wait a minute."

She turned her gaze toward the black sedan and there, sitting in the driver's seat, was a man in a black ski mask. Or at least she thought it was a man. Before she could study the figure, the car pulled out onto the roadway, did a one-eighty turn, and headed back toward Boise.

"I take it that wasn't roadway assistance." She looked at Estebe. "Why would someone be after Hope?"

Chapter 19

Angie called Ian as they bundled a frustrated Hope into Estebe's car. When he answered, she tried to sound cool even though every nerve in her body was screaming about what might have happened if they hadn't come on the girl and her stranded car just in time.

"Hey, can you have Hope's car picked up? It's on River Vista Highway about halfway to Meridian. I'll pay for the costs." She waved Hope's protests from the back seat away. "And have them look at why it broke down."

"From the tone in your voice, you're thinking it's been tampered with?" Ian had picked up on her concern easily.

"Maybe. And we weren't the only ones who arrived to help." She glanced at Estebe, who was watching her closely. "There was a black SUV there, but the guy must have realized that we had the problem in hand, as he just took off."

Ian understood her unsaid message. "You're thinking it was Evan and he's going after Hope?"

"Something like that." She didn't want to say more. Hope was already upset.

He didn't answer for a long couple of seconds. "I think I'll have Allen come out with me to pick up the car. He knows a thing or two about mechanics."

Relief filled her as she realized he believed her. Or at least believed her enough to get his uncle involved. "We'll make sure Hope gets safely home tonight, but call me with the name of the repair shop you take the car to. She'll need transportation to school next week."

As she hung up the phone, she glanced at Estebe. He'd read between the lines of her conversation. He nodded, then looked up into the rearview

mirror to catch Hope's gaze. "If your car takes too long, I can loan you
my backup car. It's not much, but it will get you back and forth to school."

"You don't need to do that. I can walk. The apartment isn't that far off
campus." Hope curled up on the back seat. She had her phone out. "That's
weird. My phone is dead. I was sure I charged it last night. But maybe not."

"We were trying to get a hold of you; that must have been why we
couldn't reach you." Angie turned back around to watch her. "How'd the
meeting with your professor go?"

Hope tucked her phone away. "It didn't. I sat there for over an hour, and
finally, one of students who has weekend class said he wasn't in. I guess I
must have gotten my days mixed up when his secretary called me."

"Oh?" Angie tried to sound casual, but her heart was beating too quickly.
"When did she call you?"

"He. His secretary is a guy. He called right as I was going into class on
Friday. I thought it was weird to be set up on a Saturday, but with all the
changes happening with them trying to replace Professor Monet, I didn't
question it. Maybe I should have." Hope twirled her hair and watched out
the window. "By that time, I was super late, and then the car just up and
died. I just had it in the shop for a checkup. Thanks for coming to find
me. That walk would have been a doozy."

"You should just find a phone and call one of us. We will come and get
you." Estebe turned onto the side street, then parked in the lot behind the
County Seat. He shut off the engine, then turned around in his seat. "Go
inside. Nancy's worried about you. I need to talk to Angie for a minute
about my schedule."

"Okay."

Estebe waited until Hope was inside before saying anything. "You do
not believe this was random either."

"No. Ian's going to go over to the car with Sheriff Brown and have it
checked out. I think the Good Samaritan with the ski mask had something
to do with her car breaking down. Although why he waited so long to
approach, I'm not sure."

"Maybe he didn't know her phone was dead. Maybe he waited to see
if she'd have help coming." He glanced at the kitchen door where Hope
had disappeared. "What I do know is we need to keep her safe. And I'm
not sure how we can do that without scaring her."

"Let's see what Sheriff Brown says about the car, then we can decide
what she needs to know. She can't protect herself if she doesn't know all
the facts." Angie got out of the car and stood, watching the building. "It

just makes me so mad that this one guy did this to her. All she did was offer him a ride home."

Estebe's chuckle surprised her. And when he saw that, he put his hand on her arm. "You are like the mama bear who's been watching out for the baby too long. Hope is an adult. She'll get through this. And she'll be fine. We will make sure of that. You are not the only one who cares for her."

True to his word, when the sheriff came to the restaurant that evening, Estebe stood by Hope and filled in the blanks when the girl didn't know the answer. As Sheriff Brown was leaving, Angie pulled him aside. "Do you think she's in danger?"

"Honestly, I don't know. That car of hers was just waiting to break down, so maybe it was just bad timing. But I don't like the idea of this guy wearing a ski mask. And I'm going to reach out to that professor and see if the appointment was really just a misunderstanding or if this was a setup. Any way you can keep her with one of you for a few days?" Sheriff Brown glanced over at Hope. "I asked if she'd go home to her family, but apparently her folks are in Tucson on holiday and she doesn't want to bother them."

"I'm sure we can work out a schedule." Angie glanced at the kitchen crew, who were right now gathered around Hope.

"I'm sure we're all just overreacting, but I'd feel better if she wasn't alone. I guess her roommate went home for a few weeks because her folks were concerned about her safety after this teacher's death." He set his hat on his head and nodded to Angie. "I'll let myself out. I've been here enough the last few months, I should know the way."

Angie wanted to be angry at the implication, but all she felt was weariness. She wanted this to be over. No more playing Nancy Drew, no Cops and Robbers. She just wanted to get back to the innocent life she'd lived before coming home to peaceful, scenic Idaho.

Felicia came to stand by her as servers busied themselves with getting the tables set up for the evening service. "What does Sheriff Brown say?"

"He's looking into it." She turned to her friend. "Hey, can Hope stay with you this evening? We'll have to figure out a schedule, but the sheriff doesn't want her alone."

Felicia nodded. "Let me get my calendar and I'll let you know what days she can stay here."

"Meet me in the kitchen. I think there are some others who will want to pitch in. Besides, the more places we stash her, the harder it will be for the guy to find her." Angie headed back into the kitchen to call an impromptu meeting. "Everyone gather around. We need to talk."

Hope came running to her side. "Angie, the sheriff thinks that someone might have done something to my car to make it break down. Tell me the truth, you don't think he's right, do you?"

"Honestly, Hope, I don't know what to believe. But the sheriff has asked for our help in keeping you safe. And mostly, that means not alone. Do you mind staying with Felicia tonight?"

Everyone was talking at once, but Angie held up a hand. "Let's let Hope talk first."

"I guess that would be all right. But really, I'm not in danger, am I?"

Angie sent Hope a supportive smile. "Let's go with the fact we all want to keep you safe. It will be like mini slumber parties."

They got out a calendar, and for the next two weeks, Hope had a place to stay and someone to get her to school and back.

Hope picked up the piece of paper that had dates and names and phone numbers, and a tear fell down her cheek.

"Don't cry. This won't last forever. Soon, the law enforcement types will find this guy and you'll be back being just another student on campus." Matt grinned at her. "Besides, you'll want to save your tears for the nights you stay with me. My place isn't as nice as everyone else's."

"I'm sure it will be adequate." Estebe glanced at the clock. "However, if we don't finish prep, we will not have a solid service. That is not acceptable."

As everyone made their way to their stations, Hope hung back with Angie. "I can't tell you all how much I appreciate this."

"You don't have to. Whether or not you like it, you're part of the team. How's the menu selection going for the recipe you're presenting at the next family meal?"

"There are just so many choices." Hope's eyes twinkled. "I'll have something amazing soon."

"I'm sure you will."

"Hope, please come over and help me with the potatoes," Estebe called out, looking over at the two women chatting.

"I better go. Thank you again."

Angie wanted to tell her that there was no need to thank her or any of the group. People came together for family. And that's what Hope was, like it or not. The group was all family.

Once service started, the unease that had hung around the kitchen lifted. The group worked like a well-oiled machine, and Angie marveled at the way they had come together, not only to feed the waiting diners but to support a coworker who had been a stranger to them less than a year ago.

Angie felt Felicia by her side before she spoke. "So this is weird, but someone wants to talk to you."

"Don't tell me they didn't like the entrée. I've been personally expediting all these plates and we haven't let one die waiting to be served." Angie wiped the edge of the plate she'd just taken from Estebe and then set it on a waiting tray. "Table six."

A waiting server picked up the tray and headed out of the kitchen.

Felicia waved Estebe over to the expediting station. "Can you cover for Angie for a minute? We've got a situation in the dining room."

Angie started to speak, but Felicia squeezed her arm, so she followed her out to the dining room. They paused at the edge, but Angie couldn't see anyone who even looked like they were looking toward them. She turned to Felicia. "Who wants to talk to me now?"

"Over here, by the door. Will you just tell him I'm done? He doesn't want to hear it from me." Felicia didn't let go of her hand and almost dragged Angie to the hostess station. There, sitting in the waiting area, was a clearly distraught Taylor.

He looked up from running his hands through his hair, and when he saw Felicia, he stood. "Look, I know I'm demanding, but you need to give me another chance. I can be more than just the head of the mission."

"I told you we are done. I'm sorry you felt the need to come out here and plead your case, but as Angie will tell you, once I make a decision, it's final." Felicia pushed Angie toward the guy.

Angie sent her friend a *what in the world are you getting me into* look, then turned toward Taylor. "I'm afraid Felicia's right. Once she's made up her mind, I've never seen her change it. Look, this isn't the best place for a scene. We've got a business to run here. Maybe you could call her tomorrow."

"No, no calling tomorrow." Felicia made swishing motions with her hands. "You need to leave now and go on with your life. I'm done playing whatever role you had in mind for me. For us."

"But I have tickets for the fund-raiser tomorrow. All the big hedge funds guys will be there, and they expect me to bring a date. You have to come with me. Otherwise, I'll look foolish. I'll lose millions in possible donations if they don't have faith in my ability to attend these social events." Taylor pressed his hands together. "Just go to this one party with me. You'll have fun. You can talk to these guys and maybe get some catering gigs for your restaurant."

"You want me to pretend we're still together so you can look good in front of your donor buddies?" Felicia's voice was cool, but Angie could hear the heat behind the words.

She watched Taylor's face go from devastated to hopeful as he considered the words. Then she hoped he wouldn't be as stupid as she thought he might just be. She closed her eyes when he opened his mouth.

"That would be perfect. I'll meet you at the Harrison House at seven. Since we're not really dating, there's no need for me to drive all the way out here to get you, right?" He glanced at his watch. "I'm so glad we got this cleared up. I need to get back to the mission and check on the evening shutdown process."

Felicia grabbed his jacket and he looked up at her in surprise. She waited until he was looking right at her. "Listen to me. There is no way I'm ever going to be your arm candy just because you've asked. I would rather spend my night fishing for crawdads out at the river than drive to Boise to this fancy shindig. Or maybe I'll just Daisy Duke it up in my fishing outfit and show up and embarrass you before I decide I'm done."

"You wouldn't do that." His voice trembled at the idea.

The horrified look on Taylor's face made Angie's lips twitch, but she didn't think laughing would be appropriate. "I think she would."

"You two are both crazy. I don't know what I ever saw in you." He stepped back away from Felicia's grip and moved toward the door. He paused before pushing it open. "I want you to know I did enjoy spending time with you, at least before you lost your freaking mind."

Angie stood by Felicia as they watched him get into his Mercedes and drive off. "I didn't realize you had decided you and Taylor were over."

"I gave him twenty-four hours. When he didn't even notice I didn't call, I called and left him a voice mail. I guess he got the message and came flying out here to save his fund-raiser." Felicia sighed. "It's hard being just another piece of arm candy."

"You were never just arm candy." Angie turned her friend away from the door. "You walked away from a ticking time bomb there. I think that guy is bat guano crazy."

"He had a great car, though." Felicia nodded to the dining room. "How many people do you think heard the final breakup?"

"Nobody. The wall here breaks up all that sound. Besides, we have that mood music going through the speakers." She put a gentle hand on Felicia's back. "Let's go back to work. I'll stay over tonight and we can have a slumber party with Hope and tell stories about the men who didn't deserve us."

As they walked into the dining room, a wave of applause started and then diners stood and clapped. One woman put a hand on Felicia's arm as she walked through. "That man didn't deserve you." Then she put a card in Felicia's hand. "But my nephew is single. Give him a call."

Angie pressed her lips together and tried not to laugh as they made their way through a room of diners and servers who were all telling Felicia the same thing. She'd stood up for herself and done good. As they entered the kitchen, Felicia leaned against the wall.

"You realize this is going to be all over town by morning? I don't think Taylor's going to be able to spin this to his favor anytime soon."

Angie handed her a bottle of water. "Especially not since a few of those hedge fund managers are here tonight for dinner and caught the entire show. You just sit down a minute and drink that water. You've had an exciting evening."

Estebe finished expediting a table, then stepped back around to the stove. He leaned over as Angie came back to her station. "The servers filled us in. I hear Felicia was very brave."

Angie looked over at her friend, who now looked more like she was in shock. "Brave and confident. I've never been so proud of her."

"Then I am proud as well." Estebe smiled over to Felicia, who had just looked up at them.

Then something passed between Estebe and Felicia that Angie couldn't quite believe. Was that a spark? As she looked back at Estebe, she thought she must have misinterpreted the look as he was back talking to Matt and finishing the last few entrees. *Curious*, Angie thought, but when she looked back at Felicia, she had already returned to the dining room.

Chapter 20

Angie left the apartment over the County Seat about midnight. Hope and Felicia were still talking and making a dent in the supply of beers they'd brought up from the restaurant after they'd closed the place down. But Angie had been drinking coffee, something she might regret when she finally climbed into bed, but she figured as tired as she felt, the caffeine wouldn't stop her from sleeping. She turned the music up and rolled her windows down as she drove home, thinking about her friend and her love life.

Felicia didn't fall easy, and Angie wondered if she'd really fallen in love with Taylor or if, more likely, she'd fallen for the ideal of Taylor. The mask the guy seemed to wear that changed depending on where he was and who he was with. Felicia had a soft heart, and meeting what she thought was a kind soul had probably blinded her to the fact that they were less dating than she was just another volunteer in the Taylor Mission show.

And maybe she'd imagined the spark that had flown between Felicia and Estebe. Because after that moment, the two hadn't been any different with each other than they'd ever been. Friendly, but not close. Even when they were closing up, Estebe was his normal self. He'd waited for Angie in the kitchen until she'd told him she was going upstairs with Felicia and Hope for a while.

Tomorrow, she'd have a talk with Felicia about Estebe and see if there was anything to this smoke she felt. Wait—tomorrow was Sunday, and she couldn't go into town and talk to Felicia. No, she was having dinner with Ian and his aunt and uncle. Her stomach clenched and she took a sip from the water bottle she'd tucked in the cup holder.

Now she really wouldn't get any sleep. What if Maggie didn't like her? She knew that Sheriff Brown was on the fence about her and Ian dating.

Would a bad showing from her make it hard for Ian to keep seeing her? No, that even sounded stupid. They were just people. And besides, she and Ian were just dating.

But the gnawing pit in her stomach didn't go away all the way home. After opening the door to let Dom out, she grabbed her flashlight so she could head out to the barn to check on Precious and Mabel. It was silly. She'd fed them well before she'd left, but you never knew. It was responsible pet ownership, although any farmer in the area would laugh if they heard her calling her hen and goat pets.

Mabel opened one eye, then closed it tight in the light. Precious was asleep on her straw, her back legs gently kicking like she was running in her dreams. Angie flipped the flashlight on her water dish and saw it was clean and filled. Then she turned off the light and used the moonlight to make her way back to the door, where Dom now sat waiting for her.

The barn was Precious's territory and the St. Bernard didn't take chances, even when the goat was fast asleep in dreamland. Angle closed the door and turned the latch. Weariness was starting to take hold now that she was home and knew her zoo was all right. Maybe she wouldn't have trouble falling asleep after all.

* * * *

The bright light bled through her eyelids the next morning. Angie rolled over and saw Dom sitting by the side of the bed, staring at her. She reached out and rubbed the top of his head. "You think I'm sleeping the day away, don't you, Dom?"

He licked her arm with his big sloppy tongue.

She peered at the alarm clock. It was after nine. Time to get up and get some breakfast. She'd never called Ian's aunt to see what she could bring, so she'd make her up a hostess gift instead. Angie had made several different types of jams that summer, and she would put a few into a basket with a fresh baked loaf of bread. That way, her hosts could have toast and jam for a few mornings next week.

After a quick shower and run to the barn, she got her prep done to make the quick bread. While she was in her fridge, she took out some bacon, eggs, and salsa. She'd make up two loafs of bread, and while she was baking, she'd make breakfast. Last night between service and the emotional roller coaster of Hope's safety and Felicia's love life, she'd burned away any food she'd eaten during the day, and now she was starving.

She sent a quick text to Felicia, asking how everything was going, but wasn't surprised when she didn't get a text back. The women had been still chatting and drinking when she'd left the apartment. Angie was glad that Hope and Felicia had bonded so quickly. She turned up the tunes and got busy doing the one thing that made her worries disappear: cooking.

By the time she was sitting at the table eating, her phone buzzed with an incoming text. She'd expected it to be Felicia, but instead it was Ian. He was done with his Sunday class and just checking in with her. She responded that she'd be ready at one, just like they'd planned. Then she set the phone down. The bread was in the oven. Breakfast was almost over. And she was meeting Ian's family that afternoon.

Pressing her fingers to her eyelids, she took a deep breath. She could do this. It wasn't a big thing. Except it was the first time she'd ever met someone's family. Todd's parents had been in New Jersey, and he'd gone home for the holidays without her, which should have told her something about where their relationship was heading. But instead, she'd made plans to come home to Nona's and that was that. Now, less than a year into dating, they were being put on parade. She decided she liked Todd's method of handling this part of the relationship better. It was less stress.

Because it wasn't real. She pushed the phone farther away and glanced at Dom, who'd lifted his head to watch her, hoping for some bacon leftovers. "You're lucky your life is easy."

He harrumphed at that and glanced toward the door. She suspected that meant *my life was easy before that goat came into it,* but she ignored the implication and went back to finish her meal.

Angie had finally settled on a pair of dress pants and a nice but comfortable blouse. She slipped on a pair of ballet slippers and added a silver chain with sparkles to the outfit. Then she grabbed a dark blue blazer that she hoped didn't make her look like a salesman and headed downstairs to wait for Ian.

The hostess basket sat nearer the edge of the table than she'd remembered, and as she walked into the kitchen, she saw the tablecloth slip closer to the edge. She ran and grabbed the basket before it toppled on top of Dom. He would have been surprised to get not only a fresh loaf of bread, but a few knots on his head where the jelly jars would have hit.

"You're becoming a little tricky with your thievery." She took the basket and set it on the cabinet, and then grabbed the tablecloth and folded it. "Am I going to have to lock you up in the mudroom while I'm gone?"

The look of horror on his face was priceless.

Angie laughed, which probably didn't help cement the threat in her voice. "No, I'm just going to have to keep things up where you can't get them. Of course, in a few months, that will have to be a special room on the roof. You're growing too fast."

He held out a paw and offered her a friendly shake to apologize for his dreadful manners and over-the-top need for her hostess gift. She shook, knowing this wasn't the last time she'd have to remember to keep things out of Dom's reach or keep Dom out of the room, which might be easier.

The sound of a car coming down the driveway caused Dom to run to the door and sit patiently, his tail wagging against the floorboards.

Angie glanced out the window and waved at Ian, who had parked and was heading toward the door. She slipped the jacket on and took a compact out of her purse to check her makeup for the tenth time since she'd put it on a few minutes ago.

After a slight knock, Ian came into the kitchen and gave Dom a quick hug around his neck. "Hey, big guy. Have you been a good boy?"

She laughed. "Hardly. We were just talking about proper punishment for eating the hostess gift I'd just recently put together."

"He ate it?"

Angie grabbed the basket and put it into Ian's hands. "If I'd changed one more time, this would have been just a good idea and my floor would have been covered in jam and broken glass. Things my Dom doesn't think about when he's figuring out a way to steal."

"Food. That's all he's thinking about. And as good as this bread smells, I don't blame him." He kissed her on the cheek. "You look lovely. There was no reason for you to get dressed up, but I have to say, I like it."

"You rarely see me in anything but jeans and T-shirts. I thought I'd like to play girl at least once." She glanced around the kitchen one more time. "Let me make sure everything's closed up. After seeing his new parlor trick, I'm a little hesitant to leave anything even close to his level."

She walked around the house, making sure the doors were locked, then met Ian out on the porch. She nodded toward the barn. "I should be back in time for evening feeding, right?"

"Unless you are one of the slowest eaters in the world, yes, you'll be back in time to feed Precious and Mabel." He took her arm and led her to the passenger side door. "Don't fret so much. This isn't a big deal."

Oh, but there he was wrong. She climbed into the truck and clicked on her seat belt. This was a huge deal. And worse, she wanted to get his uncle aside and talk to him about this Evan Morris character one more time. Especially now that she thought he was after Hope.

Thinking about that, she realized she hadn't heard back from Felicia. She grabbed her phone and there it was. One missed text. *We're making breakfast. Need something to soak up the alcohol. Have fun with Ian.*

"You have to deal with that?" Ian nodded toward the phone as he started the truck.

She keyed a quick *Thanks* and slipped the phone back into her tote. "Nope. I was just checking in with Felicia. She broke up with Taylor last night."

"I know." He turned out of the driveway and onto the road leading toward River Vista.

She turned toward him in the seat. "How on earth did you hear?"

"Your friend's scene was the talk of the social hour after church. By the way, the poll's going in her favor. Most of the congregation doesn't seem to like Taylor. And after this, they'll like him even less."

"Someone who was at the County Seat went to church this morning and gossiped? That doesn't sound very Christian." She grinned at him.

"Actually, I believe she was just concerned about the mental health and welfare of a community member. I'd say that concern falls under the tenets of the doctrine." He sped around an old Cadillac whose driver looked a lot like Mrs. Potter's best friend, Delores. "The gossip part was just a side benefit."

"You do know how to spin a good tale." She settled in for the ride.

He took her hand. "You really should consider coming to church with me more. You'll find out all sorts of interesting things about your neighbors here in River Vista. We're a hotbed of gossip."

"I'm not sure I really want to know about the secret lives of townsfolk." She turned up the radio. "I really love this song."

"Good distraction technique." He smiled at her and squeezed her hand. "This dinner will be fine. No worries at all."

Except when they got to the house, things weren't fine. A frazzled Maggie opened the door, took one look at the two of them, then let out a screech. "Allen, come take care of Ian and his guest."

Ian held on to the screen door and peeked in through the hallway. "There's no smoke coming out of the kitchen, so that's a good sign."

"Maybe I should go help?" She started to step inside when Sheriff Brown arrived at the door.

"There you two are. Maggie's just got a few more things to prepare, so why don't we go into the living room and have some iced tea." He held the door open and motioned them inside. "Come on now, you don't want all the flies to follow you inside, do you?"

Ian put a hand on her back and followed her inside. The sheriff motioned toward a room to the left, on the opposite side of the house from where Maggie had disappeared. Ian held up the basket.

"Angie brought this little gift along for you and Aunt Mags. I'm sure you'll love the jam." He looked around for a place to set it down. "Should I take it into the kitchen?"

Sheriff Brown grabbed the basket and set it on a desk near the doorway. "No, let's just give Maggie some space. She's a little nervous to have a real chef in her house for dinner."

"That's funny. I'm nervous to be here." Angie smiled, trying to ease the tension. She glanced toward the doorway. "Since we have a few minutes, I wanted to ask you what you'd found out about Evan Morris and why he's stalking Hope."

"You think he's stalking Hope? Why?" Now the eyes that had been friendly turned into cold blue steel, cop's eyes.

"I think he's the one who messed with her car. We saw a black SUV pulling up behind her, and it took off just as we arrived. Like he didn't want to be seen. I thought I told you all this when you interviewed us at the restaurant afterward. Maybe I'm getting things messed up." She nodded to a couch. "Can I sit?"

"Of course. Sorry, my manners seem to get lost when I'm in investigation mode." He sank down into a large recliner. "Look, I'm going to tell you something that might make you feel a little better about this Evan fella."

"Like he's in jail?" Angie felt Ian's foot kick hers, and she took a breath. "Sorry, go on."

"Anyway, I was told this under strict confidence, but since the guy has been such a problem, I think you need to know." Sheriff Brown leaned forward. "Evan Morris is with the US Marshals office. He's law enforcement. So you don't have to worry about him being the one going after Hope."

Angie didn't know how to respond. She'd been right, the guy wasn't a professor. But why the pretense? "So why was he following her? And who messed with her car? I don't think it just broke down."

"We're looking at that. The car's old. It could have just died." Sheriff Brown leaned back into his chair.

"Wait. You're telling me that Daniel Monet was in witness protection?" The implication of who Evan was had just hit her. "What did he do? Is that why we couldn't find him on the internet?"

"I didn't say that." A twinkle sparkled in Sheriff Brown's eye. "I don't think I even mentioned Daniel Monet. But if he had been in protection, it wasn't from the deeds he did back in England when he was friends with

Ian. At least, that's my impression of what's going on. They're keeping me pretty out of the loop on the investigation. All I know is Hope isn't considered a suspect anymore."

Angie thought about what she'd just learned. Daniel could have been part of some witness protection thing. It made sense why his history looked good on the surface but, when you went down a few layers, didn't hold up. "Sounds like he was killed because of whatever got him into this protection gig, and if that's true, you may never find the real killer."

"True. But as long as there's not some crazy running around here, I can't say I'm sorry about it." He must have seen Angie's reaction in her face. "Truly, I'm saddened by the death of our culinary professor, but honestly, it's not in my jurisdiction or my responsibility. If Ian hadn't been in contact with Daniel the night he was killed, I might never have known at all."

"Daniel called his handler," Ian mused. "That would be smart. He knew I recognized him. And if I'd been the nosy type, I might just have proven his new life was a lie."

"As it was, you took off to do just that before I could talk to you." Sheriff Brown refilled his iced tea glass. "That was probably why this Evan character arrived. He wanted to make sure his charge was safe."

"But he came after Daniel was dead." Angie still didn't understand Evan's role in this.

"He came as soon as Daniel called him." Sheriff Brown took a sip from his tea. Finally, he set the glass down on a coaster. "Look, I trust your instincts on this. I'm not saying there's any fire to this smoke, but I'll see what I can find out about our friend Evan. I may run into a few walls, but I'm going to try."

"One more thing before your wife comes back into the room." Angie leaned forward. "We have Hope staying with people for the next couple of weeks. Do you really think she's safe?"

"Probably. The only reason the police were looking at her in the first place is the fact she drove Daniel home that night and had the bad sense to stay for a drink." He turned his glass around on the coaster. "She didn't kill the guy. And if some hired killer did, he's long gone by now. I think she's as safe as anyone else walking the streets of Boise."

Chapter 21

"You don't buy Allen's theory about Hope." Ian waited until they'd finished dinner and were on their way back to her place to state the thought that had been running through her head for the last couple of hours. "I could tell at dinner. You were distracted and barely ate. Of course, Maggie talked enough for all of us, so I don't think she noticed."

"I'm so sorry. I didn't mean to be distracted." She slipped her sunglasses on. "I'm just worried. I know your uncle feels like this is all over, but it doesn't feel that way to me. And I still don't trust Evan. Federal marshal or not, the guy gives me the creeps."

"Well, if he was Daniel's handler, there's no reason for him to be hanging around here anymore. I think that's the missing piece that Allen found in your argument. He was so busy being bombarded with guys from Boise and then the marshal, he hadn't thought about why Evan was still here." He glanced over at her as they made their way out of the small subdivision where the Browns lived. "You should never have met him for coffee. I worry about you."

"I had enough people watching me." She smiled and squeezed his hand. "I'm sure the rumor mill hit your answering machine about who I was meeting before you even talked to me."

"Watching you is a lot different than keeping you protected." He focused on the road. "Sometimes you put yourself in dangerous situations and I don't think you even realize it."

"Well, now we know the guy who I met with was a federal law enforcement officer. I might have my reservations about the guy, but your uncle seems to think he's okay. I went to a memorial, but I took Felicia." She decided not to tell him about going to the college alone or searching

Daniel's house with Reana. She wouldn't win points in the argument with either of those. "Anyway, let's talk about something else. Dinner was nice."

"You're just saying that because you don't want to talk about this." He gripped the steering wheel and headed out of town. "The pork was burnt and the mashed potatoes were so overworked, they tasted like glue."

"She tried." Angie felt bad for Maggie. The woman had been a wreck from the moment they got there. "I thought I was nervous. Maggie was literally shaking when we sat down."

"She really isn't a bad cook. I mean, we do roasts for Sunday dinner all the time and she's never burned them. I think she just took on too much."

Angie knew the feeling. She was a little overloaded this week as well. "We'll take them out to eat next time. Maybe then we can actually talk and I can learn all your childhood secrets."

He laughed. "Maggie's not going to know any of those. My mum kept me off the family radar for a long time. Anything she's learned about my formative years, I've told her. So ask me if you have questions. I'm an open book."

"Hardly. We never talk about the past."

He pulled the car into her driveway. "You're right. We should spend more time just chatting. What's your plan for the rest of the night?"

"I'm thinking a long hot bath and a glass of wine." She sighed as she watched Mabel pecking around the barn. "After I feed and water my zoo."

"Go inside. I'll handle them. I owe you one for being such a good sport today. I promise, Maggie and Allen are good people and easy to get along with. You'll see."

Angie walked over to the door and let Dom out. "You don't have to do the feeding. I can."

"I know you can. I like to spend time with Precious, and Mabel tells me all sorts of things." He tapped his leg. "Come on, Dom, you're with me for a bit."

"I'm going to put the water on for tea, so come in when you're done."

He flashed a wicked grin. "I suppose that means you're postponing the bath part of the evening?"

"Stop it." She giggled. "Just come in and I'll see what I can round up for some type of dessert for the evening."

"Okay, but I really can't stay long. I've got a meeting with Mildred about Moss Farms tomorrow. Seriously, that woman needs to learn to make some decisions on her own." He waved her inside. "We'll talk later. Let me get the horde fed."

She put the water on for tea and found some cookies she'd brought home from the restaurant a few days ago. Then she pulled out her planner and looked at her schedule. She was supposed to have Hope on Wednesday, which would give them some time to cook together in her kitchen that night. She might as well enjoy the time and see how Hope was doing in her coursework. She made some notes about next month's menu and thought that maybe they would work out some recipes together.

Ian came in and washed his hands. He took the steaming pot off the stove and filled their teacups. "You have any time next week for me?"

"Did you bring your calendar?" She chose a tea bag and put it into her cup. "I'm booked Wednesday."

"I think we could do dinner Tuesday." He put his choice of tea into his water, then took out his phone. "Yes. Look, there's three entire hours not filled by something else on my schedule."

"And if you're not tired of me by then, I could come have lunch with you on Wednesday. I'm on Hope patrol that night, so I'll have to go into town and pick her up from school that afternoon."

"Do you really think this is necessary?" He keyed in their dinner date and then set the phone aside.

"Better safe than sorry." She shrugged off his look. "I know what your uncle said, but he's still having her car looked at. If he tells me it's just old, then we'll back off." *Maybe.*

"I'm heading back to town. I've got a hot date with a washing machine at the laundromat then I'm going over to do some grocery shopping. I know, you're dying to come along, but honestly, dear, I just don't think you can stand the excitement." He kissed her and paused, studying her eyes. "I do appreciate what you did today. I know Maggie feels better having spent some time with you. I'll set up something else soon."

"Not too soon." She grabbed another cookie. "I know they're nice people, but I stress out too much thinking about these encounters."

After Ian had left, she keyed in Felicia's number. When her friend answered on the first ring, Angie knew she'd been waiting for the report. "How's Hope?"

"Don't think you can get away with just asking questions. I've been dying here." Felicia laughed. "Hope's fine. She's watching cooking shows in the living room. It's like having you stay over. Anyway, she's here until tomorrow morning when Nancy comes and gets her for class. Nancy's mostly doing the pickup and drop-off thing since she's working that other job."

"Tell her I appreciate all she's doing." Angie decided to hold back for a while on what Sheriff Brown had said. Hope could stay with them for a few weeks. It wasn't going to hurt anything.

"I will. But spill. How did Sunday dinner go?"

Angie sighed. "It was a total disaster. And not because I was the uncomfortable one. The food, well, let's just say it was overdone and be nice about it."

"She burned dinner? Wow, she must have been more nervous than you were." Felicia called out to Hope in the next room. "Give me a second, will you?"

Angie sat listening to dead air when Felicia finally came back on. "I've got to go. Hope needs a few things at the store and I don't want her going alone."

"I'll stop by tomorrow. That way I can vent about the entire day." Angie said goodbye and looked around the small kitchen. Her chores were done. Ian had left. She'd talked to Felicia. She stood and went over to lock the outside door. Time for that bath she'd promised herself. She grabbed a bottle of wine from the fridge along with a wineglass from the cabinet and started to make her way upstairs.

Instead, she went to check the other doors on the main floor. They were still locked from when she'd left earlier. Maybe she was just being overly cautious, but she did live alone in the middle of farmland. She tucked a novel under her arm and put her phone in her jeans pocket. Now she could relax.

But after less than ten minutes in the tub, she was antsy. She knew someone had been watching Hope. Someone who had to be connected to Daniel and his whole secret identity thing. But every time she tried to think about who it was, all the roads dead-ended. There was no way that Tanya had killed the guy. And she didn't think Steve had it in him either. She'd never found the other student who had been obsessed with the professor, according to Barb.

And maybe she was just too tired to think straight after all of this craziness that had been her life lately. She climbed out of the tub, wrapped herself in her robe, and took the wine and glass back downstairs. Angie was too tired to even think about drinking. She'd fall asleep in the chair if she did.

She exchanged the wine for a bottle of water and started turning off the lights to head to bed. Tomorrow would come whether or not she was waiting for it, so she might as well be well rested.

* * * *

On Monday mornings Angie let the sun awaken her. She used the alarm clock on her phone for workdays, but when she didn't have to get up early, she liked to let the day start a little slower. She checked her messages and saw Ian had sent one around ten to say good night. She'd been asleep for a few hours by then. No text from Felicia, but since Hope had to be at school around nine, she figured her friend was up and about. She'd grab some breakfast fixings and head into town. She could cook while she talked, which always made her mind more focused anyway.

After finishing her chores, she packed the items she'd need to make breakfast into her basket and grabbed Dom's leash. "You want to go see Felicia?"

The quick bark surprised her, as he didn't usually respond verbally to her questions. But he liked Felicia, and Angie figured Dom knew what she was saying. Besides, he knew when she picked up the leash that they were going off on some adventure. She glanced at the sky as she loaded everything up into her car and smiled. She ran back inside for the backpack she took with them when they went walking and made sure she had some doggy treats inside. When she tossed it on the floor of the back seat, Dom sniffed the bag. He knew what was up. "We'll stop at the park for a hike on the way home. You've been home alone a lot lately, and I don't even have Erica around to come entertain you."

She'd gotten an email from Erica, who had told her she'd be back in a week but that her grandmother, Mrs. Potter, was staying with her parents for a few months. Angie thought that it might turn into a winter/summer type of arrangement with Mrs. Potter coming back to Idaho to spend the summers and staying with her son the other times. Even though she was happy the family was bonding, she'd miss talking to her. She made a mental note to give Mrs. Potter a call tonight and put it on her weekly list of to-dos for the next couple of months. What had that time management article said? What gets scheduled gets done. She didn't want to regret not staying in touch.

By the time she was in River Vista she'd thought through the recipe she wanted to make for Felicia, but she realized she hadn't let her friend know she was coming. She used her car's Bluetooth to make the call. When the call was picked up, she said, "Hey, I'm in town and thought I'd make breakfast."

"Come in through the front door of the County Seat. Don't go to the back parking lot."

Angie started to ask why but realized Felicia had hung up on her. She glanced at Dom, who watched her from his back seat perch. "Maybe you should stay in the car?"

The shake of his head made her laugh as she parked in front of the restaurant. The signage looked good and the outside made her smile. Of course, it needed to be swept clear of leaves again. Felicia had told her she was sweeping off leaves at least a couple of times a week. Maybe they needed to expand the cleaning crew to take care of the outside of the building as well. Or was that a separate landscaping company? She'd have to talk to Felicia.

After grabbing the basket and putting Dom on his leash, she locked the car. Big-city habit, but she didn't want to regret not taking the extra second to secure the vehicle. She unlocked and relocked the front door behind her once they were inside. There was enough light from the windows that she didn't have to flip on the overheads, and they made their way through the too-quiet dining room and into the back, where the stairway would take her to Felicia's apartment.

She found her friend at the top of the stairs, looking out the window toward the back parking lot. "What's going on?"

"I'm glad you brought Dom. I might just have to use him." Felicia pointed to the parking lot, where a dark Mercedes sat alone.

Angie angled to the corner of the window and saw Taylor sitting on the steps, his phone in his hands. "What the heck is he doing there?"

"Waiting for me to change my mind." Felicia rolled her eyes. "Apparently the boy has come to an epiphany and he's decided he loves me and can't live without me."

"You think it's a show?" Angie juggled the basket into her other hand so she could keep a hold of Dom, who'd already gotten bored with the greeting and was pulling to go into the apartment, where Felicia kept a bed on the living room floor for him. "Do you mind if Dom goes in? He's being a pill."

"No problem. I'm done watching him anyway. I turned off my phone after the first ten calls. Now he's just sitting there until I come out and let him explain. I've had enough of his explanations." She took the basket from Angie. "Ooh, what are we having for breakfast?"

"I thought I'd try out a casserole or two and see if we could upgrade them. The recipes might just go into the cookbook, but I thought we might do a brunch class at the first of the year. Maybe before Easter?"

Felicia shut the door and locked it. "I know he can't get upstairs, but just in case." She moved toward the kitchen. "Actually, I've been thinking about our hours issues. You want to increase staff hours? Why don't we open early on Sundays? We could nab the church crowd, maybe just have buffet and a few à la carte items, and that way, the staff would get more hours without us opening up another night."

"That's a really good idea." Angie took the basket from Felicia and started to unpack the contents. Her phone rang. "I wonder who that is?"

When she answered, Taylor started talking fast. "Don't hang up. I need to talk to Felicia and she won't answer. Tell her she needs to talk to me."

"Why would I do that, Taylor?" Angie shook her head, holding the phone out so Felicia could hear his ranting as well.

"Because I was stupid. I can't believe I just let her walk away."

She looked at Felicia, who made a slashing motion with her finger across her neck. "Look, I've got to go."

"Wait, just do me one favor. Could you ask her who she talked to at the last fund-raiser? I know there were some contacts she made that could be useful."

Felicia didn't wait for Angie to hang up. She pushed the little red button on Angie's phone and disconnected the call.

"I swear, if I ever go over the edge again for a guy, you have my permission to lock me in the walk-in until I come to my senses." She glanced at the supplies. "So, shall we get started?"

They spent the next two hours playing with a few different recipes, then Felicia got out the planner and they set a date to start offering brunch. "I'll talk to my servers on Thursday and see who's interested in additional hours."

"I'll do the same with the kitchen staff. I think this will be a great place to try out new recipes too. Remember, I'm doing a staff challenge for the next few family meals. Did you get into the lineup? Hope's up first." Angie held out a plate to Felicia.

"I know. She told me about what she plans to make. She's such a sweet kid. It's a shame she has to feel unsafe with all of this." Felicia took a heaping spoonful of the three finished dishes, then opened the fridge. "Orange juice?"

"Sure." Angie filled her own plate, then sat at the oversized breakfast bar. "According to Sheriff Brown, this might be over sooner rather than later."

"Did he find who killed Daniel?" Felica set the filled glasses in front of their plates and sat herself.

"Not really, but he's saying that Hope is off the suspect list." Angie took a bite out of the dish featuring scrambled eggs with locally cured ham and a cream sauce drizzled over the top. "We might just be able to get back to the business of cooking."

"With dishes like this, we're going to rock the Sunday brunch slots." Felicia dug into her breakfast.

Angie watched her eat and hoped that her problems with her former boyfriend would disappear as fast as the food.

Chapter 22

Angie checked out her schedule first thing Wednesday morning. She had one more day before her workweek started. Dinner last night with Ian had been just what she needed. Calm, easy, and enjoyable. She was in charge of Hope today, but she didn't have to pick her up in Boise until three. She'd made reservations at Canyon Creek for lunch with Ian at one. By the time they were done eating, it would be almost time to pick up Hope, and if it wasn't, she could use the time to do a quick stroll around the park on the greenbelt. The weather announcer had talked about snow coming into the valley by the weekend, so this might be her last chance for a quick fall walk.

Early-season snow never stayed long, but the chill that came with the white stuff would stay until spring decided to arrive. She and Dom would have to trade the hilly hiking trails for the more leisurely ones on the valley floor at the park. She should be working on a marketing plan for the restaurant's brunch expansion, but she just felt like playing hooky today.

Dom watched her from his bed. Sometimes she thought he could feel the energy come off her as she contemplated taking a hike. She checked her email—nothing urgent—then shut down the laptop. She'd work on the marketing plan on Sunday morning. Which would give her another excuse why she couldn't attend services with Ian. It wasn't exactly lying, more like creative planning.

She grabbed the hiking backpack and filled it with two bottles of water from the fridge. She had started using refillable bottles since her well water had tested clean and pure. Besides, she like the taste of the well water better than the bottled water she bought in bulk. She threw in a bottle of room temperature water for Dom and grabbed his leash. She didn't even have to ask, he was sitting at the door when she turned around.

As they were nearing the top, her phone rang. She glanced at the caller ID. "Felicia, what's going on?"

"I called to see if you'd done the marketing plan."

Of course she had. Angie couldn't get away with anything under her partner's watchful eye. "No, and you caught me skipping out on the chore. I thought Dom and I might get just a few more hikes, so we're out at Celebration Park. And when I get back, I'm having lunch in Boise with Ian."

"No rush, I was just going to see if you needed some brainstorming. But since you're off playing, I might just put in my yoga CD. I've been having problems concentrating. Especially since Taylor is calling every hour."

"He'll get the hint. Just don't pick up the phone." Angie sat on a bench the park had installed near the top of the hill. Dom sat on her foot, watching for stray rabbits. "I'll stop by after I pick up Hope. We can go grab some dinner together."

"Sounds like a plan." Felicia said her goodbyes and Angie rubbed the top of Dom's head. "See, we needed this hike because I'm going out to eat for lunch and dinner. And you know I can't just order a salad."

He woofed once, then stood and went to mark his territory on the side of the path. Angie took a sip of water, then returned to her hike.

She cut her timing close but she'd be able to grab a quick shower as soon as she got home. She changed into clean jeans and a cute sweater, and then gave Dom a quick hug. "I'll see you later. Maybe I'll bring over both Felicia and Hope tonight so we'll have a lot of company."

Dom went over and made three circles, then plopped into his bed. Angie thought the message was clear. All he wanted right now was a nap. And Angie's talking was disturbing his sleep time.

She checked her tote and made sure she had her phone, then started to head to the car. The phone rang and Angie was surprised to see Hope's name on the caller ID. "Hey, don't tell me you're already done with classes."

"Actually yeah. Nancy's here and she says she'll take me into River Vista. I'd like to go work on my recipe in the kitchen, if you don't mind."

"Sure. Felicia will be there, but if you can't get her to come down, Nancy has a key. Just make sure you lock up once you're inside the back door."

"Thanks. If this goes well, we'll have dinner ready by the time you come to get me." Hope sounded better than she had in days. More confident.

"Anyway, I'm meeting Ian for lunch. I'll probably be at the County Seat around three, three thirty?" She grabbed her keys out of her tote and went to the door. Locking it behind her, she left the house and headed to the car. "I'll call you if I'm going to be later than that."

Angie made another call, and when she got voice mail, she left Felicia a message about Hope being in the kitchen. She was starting to feel like maybe they were overreacting about Hope's safety. "One more week." She made a pledge as she drove into Boise. She'd keep up the precautions for one more week. Feeling comfortable with the decision, she turned up the tunes and sang along the rest of the way into town.

When she arrived, Ian was leaning against his truck, waiting. She kissed him on the cheek. "You could have met me inside. It's kind of chilly today."

"No worries. I wanted to soak in the sun as much as possible. I'm usually stuck in some office or meeting room during the day. And there's not a lot of sun once I call it in for the day."

"Just wait until February. We barely get any sun all month." She nodded to the restaurant. "Ready?"

"Which is another reason I'm standing out here. I almost forgot, I'm supposed to tell you to call Allen. I guess he has an update on what we discussed on Sunday? I told him just to tell me and I'd tell you, but he wants to talk to you directly." He held out his phone. "Here, you can use my cell and I'll go in and get us a table."

They walked into the lobby, and as soon as Sheriff Brown answered, Angie sat on one of the benches in the waiting area. "Hi, it's Angie. Ian said you have something to tell me?"

"I'm glad you called. I'm in Boise, talking to the primary investigators, but I wanted you to know that Evan Morris isn't on the job right now. He took an extended vacation a few weeks ago and hasn't returned to work."

"That doesn't make sense. Why would he come here to check on one of his witnesses if he's supposed to be on vacation?" The answer hit Angie fast. "He's not working as a marshal here, is he?"

"Appears not. And worse, no one has talked to him for a few days." Sheriff Brown paused, and even over the line, Angie could hear his thoughts grinding through his head. "It might not mean anything, but maybe you all still keeping Hope under wraps wouldn't be the worst plan in the world. At least until we can find out why Morris is really here. And please, no more coffee dates with the guy."

Without anything else to say, Angie cut the call short and made her way to the dining room. She filled Ian in on what his uncle had told her.

"So this guy takes personal time to come check out Daniel's death?" Ian sipped his tea. "That sounds suspicious right there."

"I know. But until they find him, it's going to be hard to know why exactly he's here. Unless he knows more about why Daniel was killed than he shared with the investigative team." She glanced through the menu. "I guess we'll find out more soon. Anyway, I'm starving. I took Dom on one last hike this morning, and I think I burned off all my breakfast before I got here."

They were sitting drinking coffee and sharing a couple of desserts when Felicia called.

"Hey, how are things going?"

"How did you know I was at the mission?" Felicia's question made her set her fork down.

"What do you mean you're at the mission? I thought you were at the restaurant with Hope." Angie was getting a bad feeling about this.

"I got a call from someone saying that Taylor had been hurt and needed me to come, but when I got here, he was fine." Angie could hear the car start up on the other side of the line. "I swear the guy probably had one of his lackeys call me, but he swears he didn't know anything about it. He called it a sign that I was supposed to come back to him."

"So you're not at the County Seat?" Angie saw Ian waving down the waitress for their check. He must have heard the panic in her voice.

"No. Why do you keep asking me that?"

Angie took a breath. Hope might be there alone, but it didn't mean there was a problem. "Because Hope's there alone. Let me give her a ring. Are you on your way back?"

"I'm downtown. I can be there in thirty minutes if traffic isn't bad."

"We're closer. I'll call you as soon as I talk to Hope." She stood as Ian signed off on his credit card charge. "I'm probably overreacting."

"Probably. But I need to go anyway." He walked her out to her car as she dialed Hope's number. The call went straight to voice mail.

She left a short message, hoping she didn't sound as freaked as she felt. She unlocked her car and climbed inside the driver's seat. "Sorry to cut this short, but I really don't want to leave Hope alone for long. Even if this thing with Morris is totally explainable, I'd just feel better if someone was there with her."

"I get it. Call me when you get there. I've got a meeting but I'll have my phone on me, so don't forget." He leaned in and kissed her. "I'm going to be worried about you if you don't call."

Angie held up three fingers in an imitation of what she hoped was the Scout salute. It had been a while since she'd been in the club. "I promise."

He shut the door and watched as she took off out of the parking lot. Angie waved as she turned onto the road and gunned the engine toward River Vista.

Over and over she told herself she was overreacting. She'd get there, Hope would be in the kitchen working on her recipe, and they'd laugh about her being so worried. That was the best scenario. Angie didn't want to think of the worst-case scenario. Or any of the ones in between. She made it to River Vista in twenty minutes, and she'd tried to call Hope six times during the drive.

She rushed up to the kitchen door and checked the doorknob. It was locked. She took a deep breath and unlocked the door. Then she stepped into the kitchen and her heart sank.

"Come on in. I can't believe how you're always in the wrong place at the wrong time." Evan Morris waved her into the kitchen with the handgun he held. "I was just telling Hope that she tends to take after you in that regard."

"Where is she?" Angie stepped inside and tried to not shut the door all the way. It might signal to someone that there was a problem. One of Sheriff Brown's guys did a walk through the business district at least once a day. Angie thought it was so he could get out of the station. Maybe he hadn't been by yet. She glanced around the kitchen and found Hope tied to a chair by the table. "Are you all right?"

Hope nodded and burst into tears. "I'm so sorry to get you involved in this. I was working on the vegetables, then a knock came at the door and I figured it was Felicia, but then he pushed his way in. I don't know what he wants, he won't tell me."

Angie took a step toward her, but Evan stopped her. "Now, let's not get so hasty. You forgot to close the door."

She shut the door and cursed herself for not asking Ian to come with her. Or calling Sheriff Brown with her bad feeling. Of course, had she been wrong, but she wasn't wrong and now there was trouble. "Tell us what you want and then leave. I don't want you upsetting Hope."

"What I want is to clear up a few loose ends. This one," Evan waved his gun toward Hope, "can put me at Daniel's the night of his murder. And now you're a problem too, since you walked into the middle of all this."

"You weren't at Daniel's." Hope shook her head. "When I left, there wasn't anyone around the house or parked nearby." Angie saw the blush on the girl's cheeks. "I didn't want anyone to see me leaving, especially since I went in for a drink. I didn't want the rumors."

"Not when you left the first time, when you left the second time." He pointed toward the table. "Go over and sit by her. That way I can keep an eye on you."

"How did you know I…" Hope shook her head. "I didn't even stop the second time. I saw the car in the driveway and just turned around and went back to the game. The man was disgusting. He told me he wanted to be with me, and then an hour later, he's with someone else? I dodged a bullet there."

Angie flinched at Hope's choice of words, but Evan either hadn't noticed or was focused on the story. "You drive a red Honda."

"I drive an old red Honda. It's a piece of crap compared to the one that was sitting in Daniel's driveway that night. I told the police this, or maybe I told my lawyer. I told someone." Hope struggled against the ropes. "Look, you take off, we'll stay here and give you time to make it over the border. All I want is to see tomorrow."

"Sorry, even if you aren't the one, I guess I've shown my cards too early. You two are going to have to—"

Before he could finish his statement, a hard-rapping noise came from the door. He looked at Angie. "This is a popular place today. Who else are you expecting?"

Don't let it be Felicia. She chanted the mantra in her head three times before looking at Evan. "I'm not expecting anyone. They'll go away if we ignore them." Felicia would have used her key—it couldn't be her.

As if to prove her wrong, the banging continued. "Open up, Angie, I know you're in there. I'm looking at your car. I want to get ready for the staff meeting before everyone else shows up in a few minutes. And besides, I have a pot full of chili to warm up."

"You're having a meeting here?" Evan slapped himself on the forehead. "This day just keeps getting better and better."

She watched as he considered his next steps. She could see on his face when he'd made up his mind.

"Okay, you're going to open the door, let this guy in, and then I'm heading out. I guess killing you two just got moved down my priority list. I'm more interested in doing whatever it takes for me to keep this lovely money I made in my bank account rather than the government's."

"You want me to open the door?" Angie stood and walked to the door.

"Slow down just a bit." Evan stepped next to her. "This is how it's going to go. You open the door, motion whoever's outside to go set the chili on the stove, and while you keep him busy, I'll sneak out. I'm going to keep an eye out on the place for a while. If you follow me outside or the police show up, I'll shoot whoever walks through that door in the next ten minutes. And once I start shooting, well, let's just say my trigger finger can get a little itchy."

"I'll do exactly what you say. I want you gone and out of here more than you know." Angie reached for the doorknob, keeping her face stone and her eyes on Evan's gun. "Okay, ready?"

When Evan nodded and set up to run outside as soon as the door cleared, Angie closed her eyes and took three deep breaths. She opened the door and threw it open. When Ian walked in with a Crock-Pot filled with what did smell like chili, her heart stopped. What was Ian doing here? Then, because Evan gave her a long stare with a wave of his gun, she took Ian's arm and led him toward the stove.

"Bring it over here." She let Ian put the chili down and watched out of the corner of her eye, as Evan ran through the doorway, pulling it shut behind him.

When Ian heard the door shut, he took a breath. "Are you okay? Is the door locked?"

Angie ran back to the door and threw the dead bolts. "It is now."

"Why on earth did you put yourself in danger?" She sank into Ian's arms, but then motioned toward Hope. "You untie Hope and I'll call the station."

"No need, they're out there now, picking up that piece of garbage." He held on to her as they walked over to the table.

"How did you know we needed help?" Angie liked the way his arm felt around her. She'd been scared out of her mind from the time she'd walked into the kitchen. Now she could actually let the feeling show. "And why in the world would he just take off like that?"

"Probably because of my clever announcement that all the staff was showing up in a few minutes. I was afraid that he was going to try to take one of you with him. But my plan worked." He untied Hope's arms, then rubbed where the ropes had been. "Are you all right? He didn't hurt you, did he?"

"I'm fine. I felt stupid. I can't believe I just let him inside. Teach me to start using the peephole. This means it's all over, right? I told him I didn't see him at Professor Monet's house, but he kept saying he saw my car."

"Yeah, that was weird. You saw the car there when you came back?" Angie sank into a chair next to Hope.

"The car he was talking about wasn't even my car. I saw it too when I went back to his place. I was stupid. I *was* going to sleep with him. But when I saw the car there, I figured he'd called someone else to meet him. He had said how lonely he was since he'd moved away from all his friends.

And how he didn't even have a car. He said he loved to drive. That he used to drive for a living. Which isn't so weird—chefs do a lot of side jobs just to keep the money coming in." Hope put her hand on her neck. "I'm done with men. From now on, it's school and work. If Prince Charming wants to find me, he better come with a job and a list of references before I'll even talk to him."

"Sounds like a solid plan." Angie looked up as Felicia came in through the dining room door. "Hey, there you are."

"Are you okay? You wouldn't believe it but there are police cars all around the building. I had to park at the Red Eye." She looked at the three of them sitting at the table. "I missed something. What did I miss?"

Felicia's questions were answered when Sheriff Brown came into the restaurant. Hope stood and quickly got him a cup of coffee. He sank into one of the chairs at the table where they'd all been huddled and took the cup she offered. "Thanks, Hope."

Angie waited until he had a couple of sips in before she couldn't help herself. "Do you need to interview us? He told us he killed Daniel. But why?"

"It's a long story. Daniel was in witness protection. He'd been a driver for a Canadian mob, and one day when he was sitting outside a mansion in upstate New York, the house was raided by federal officials. Daniel was offered a deal. Testify, move to the States, and he'd be protected." He drank more of his coffee. "Evan was Danny's handler. But he'd gotten in too deep on some gambling debts, and all he had to do to wipe them clean was get rid of one person."

"He said they paid him." Angie pushed a plate of cookies toward the sheriff. He looked like he hadn't eaten in days.

"I'm sure we'll find a substantial deposit into Evan's account. He's trying to play it off as an inheritance from a rich uncle, but my guess is he got a bonus if he killed Daniel before he could testify." Sheriff Brown picked up a cookie and took a bite. He pointed the cookie at Ian. "These are so good. Just don't tell your aunt you saw me eating sugar. I'm supposed to be avoiding it."

"Daniel wasn't a chef?" Hope seemed more shocked at this revelation than any of the other things that had happened that day. "He was just pretending?"

"According to his peers, Daniel wasn't a very convincing actor." Sheriff Brown finished his coffee and stood, taking another cookie. "I'll get your statements tomorrow. Right now I'm heading home to see my wife."

Hope sat staring into her cup of hot chocolate.

"Are you okay? It's over. You should be happy." Angie reached over and squeezed her shoulder. "Smile."

"I am happy. I'm just so upset over Daniel. Did you know he gave me a C on my last assignment? He said I wasn't portraying the image of a professional chef well enough. And he wasn't even a chef." Hope's eyes burned bright.

Angie picked up her cup and hid her smile behind the sip. Their Hope was back. Worried about grades and fairness in the world. She would be okay.

Chapter 23

"You're not going to believe this, but someone's here to talk to you." Felicia came into the kitchen as the crew was getting ready for Thursday's dinner service.

Angie set down the knife she'd been using to prep potatoes. "You sound like I'm not going to like this visit."

"I don't know. I mean, I'm not really sure why she's here." Felicia fell in step with her. "I'm kind of feeling like we should keep the doors locked on the County Seat until serving time. We're getting way too many drop-ins."

Angie hugged her friend. "The killer is in jail and Taylor has moved on. I don't think we have to worry about random visits anymore."

"You might change your mind." Felicia nodded to the hostess station where Tanya Livingston stood.

Angie hadn't known she could stop dead in her tracks until that very moment. In fact, Felicia turned back and waved her forward. It was too late anyway, Tanya had seen her.

She made her way to the hostess station. "How can I help you today?"

Tanya looked pointedly at Felicia, who shrugged.

"I've got napkins to fold." She left the two women alone.

"So anyway, I wanted to thank you for finding out who killed Daniel." She took a tissue from her purse. "I know you think I'm horrible, grieving over a man who's not my husband, but I loved Daniel."

"It's your life." Angie had a hard time understanding how Tanya could have fallen in love in the less than two months Daniel had lived here. "It's not my place to judge."

"Well, you're the only person who believes in that motto." Tanya sighed and put her tissues back away. "Anyway, when Sheriff Brown told me that man had seen me leave Daniel's and had thought it was that girl, well, it made me realize how close I came to being dead alongside him. I wanted to tell you that I'm going to fix my life. My marriage."

"Again, not my business." Angie wasn't sure why Tanya was confessing and listing off her turning over a new leaf goals, but she really needed to stop talking. "I've got to get back to work. Thanks for coming by."

Before she could turn, Tanya grabbed her wrist. "You don't understand. If that guy had realized I was the one who left Daniel's that night, I would have been dead. Over a little sex. It's really not fair."

Angie shook her wrist loose. "It sounds like you're having trouble dealing with the whole incident. Maybe you should find a counselor to talk to. I find that helps me when I'm feeling overwhelmed."

"Yes, I knew you would understand. Overwhelmed, that's exactly how I feel." She peered at Angie. "Do you really think counseling could help?"

It will get you out of my restaurant. Angie pushed away her first response because it was mean. The woman was having problems, and even though she was always a pain in the butt, this was a hard time for her. "Definitely. Now, I really have to get back to work. Lots of people to feed this evening."

"Oh, yes, I should let you go. Besides, Steve will be home soon. I like to be there when he comes home so we can talk about our days." Tanya smiled. "Thank you again for all you did."

"I really didn't do anything." She watched as Tanya winked at her.

"You keep telling people that."

Tanya strolled out the front door. Angie almost ran after her and threw the dead bolts, but she thought she might be overreacting. Just a bit. Felicia met her in the middle of the dining room.

"So what did the queen want to tell you?"

Angie explained how she wanted to thank her for saving her life. "And then I told her to go to counseling."

"And she didn't hit you with that purse?"

Angie shrugged. "Surprisingly not."

Angie went back into the kitchen and stood in the middle of the room for a minute, watching her team work. Hope was helping Nancy with the night's desserts. Matt and Estebe were talking about the football season and why the Broncos would be underestimated yet another year. She and Felicia had built this life, brought these people together and made a work family.

And even though bad things happened in the world, they didn't happen in this kitchen. Even having a killer hold her and Hope hostage hadn't changed the power of the County Seat.

She heard the door open behind her, and strong arms encircled her. She took in the smell that meant Ian and leaned back into his arms. "Did you come to have dinner with me before we open?"

"I decided I need to make sure I find time to be with you. You tend to get yourself in dangerous situations. If I'm around, maybe danger will pass you by." He kissed her neck, then stepped around her. "Estebe, I hear you might have access to some football tickets for next weekend?"

Angie smiled as the men started bantering back and forth. Prep was almost done and it was time to gather around the table and eat. Like a family.

Felicia came into the kitchen. "Do you mind if I eat with you guys tonight? I don't want to go upstairs alone."

"Of course. In fact, you should always eat with us. Your servers start showing up as soon as we finish, so this way, you're ready for them." Angie went over and grabbed the platters that Matt had started to set on the warming shelf. "Set the table for seven."

They worked together for a few minutes, then Angie called the others to the table. "Let's eat."

Ian sat next to her. Felicia started to pull out the chair on the other side of her and Estebe took it from her.

"Let me."

She slipped into the chair and smiled up at Estebe, who then sat next to her. "Thank you."

His face turned a darker shade, and Angie wondered if he was blushing. "You are most welcome. I would like to ask a personal question if I may? I was wondering if you were still dating Taylor."

"Actually, Taylor and I are done." Felicia took the platter that Angie handed her and filled half of her plate with a blue cheese, pear, and walnut salad with leafy greens. "I know, you wanted to tell me what a jerk he was. And yeah, you were right."

He took the salad and passed it on to Matt, who was listening to the conversation.

"That wasn't why I asked." He took a deep breath and then glanced at Matt, who nodded his encouragement. "I was wondering if I could take you to dinner on Tuesday."

Angie dropped the serving spoon she'd been using to get some scalloped potatoes. The clatter made Felicia jump. "Sorry."

Felicia looked at Estebe for a long time. Then she took the platter from Angie. "Dinner would be nice. Pick me up at six."

And then the rest of the table started talking about anything and everything except for the fact that Felicia and Estebe were going out on a date. Angie picked up her fork and started eating.

Ian leaned close and whispered in her ear. "Did you know about this?"

"Not at all." She watched the group as they ate. The world had just changed again. And for some reason, Angie thought it might not be a bad idea at all. And since she didn't want to make a big deal about it, she addressed the entire table. "I've been meaning to talk to you all about an idea Felicia and I have been bouncing around."

From the author:

One of my favorite recipes is Idaho Potato Pie. It's quick and easy to make but feels like a real meal rather than just sandwiches or a bagel. I grew up in Idaho, so I'm a potato girl and proud of it. I have an old picture of me at about two years old sitting with the bag of chips out on the front step. I look happy. My favorite school field trip was to the potato chip processing plant.

One day as I was thinking up a new recipe to make, I thought about how much I loved quiche. But I didn't want a salad with it, I wanted hash browns. The shredded kind that get so crisp and tasty? I came up with the following recipe. I hope you love it as much as I do.

Enjoy,
Lynn

Idaho Potato Pie

Preheat your oven to 350 degrees.

Line a pie plate with a premade pie crust. (You can make your own here but on most Sunday mornings, I'm looking for ease and speed.)
Inside the pie crust, layer the following:

> 2 cups of frozen shredded hash browns
> 1 cup of shredded cheddar cheese
> 1/2 cup of one of the following precooked meats
> Ham
> Bacon
> Sausage

In a bowl mix the following:

> 6 eggs
> ¼ cup of whole milk
> Salt
> Pepper

I like to add parsley or another herb here to brighten the flavors.
Pour over the mixture in the pie crust.
Bake for 30 minutes until the middle of the pie is set. Let cool 5-10 minutes and serve with a garden salad or put on the brunch table.

ABOUT THE AUTHOR

New York Times and *USA Today* best-selling author **Lynn Cahoon** is an Idaho expat. She grew up living the small town life she now loves to write about. Currently, she's living with her husband and two fur babies in a small historic town on the banks of the Mississippi river where her imagination tends to wander. *Guidebook to Murder*, Book 1 of the Tourist Trap series, won the 2015 Reader's Crown award for Mystery Fiction.

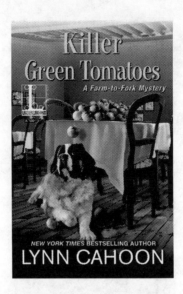

The time seems ripe for success as Angie Turner opens her farm-to-table restaurant in her Idaho hometown—until her new tomato supplier is accused of murder and Angie has to pick the real killer...

To Angie, nothing tastes more like summer than her Nona's fried green tomatoes. Eager to add the recipe to the menu at the County Seat, she's found the perfect produce supplier—her sous chef Estebe's cousin, Javier. Just one problem: ladies' man Javier's current hot tomato, Heather, has turned up dead, and he's the prime suspect. Somehow, between managing her restaurant and navigating a romantic triangle between Estebe and Ian, the owner/manager of the farmer's market, Angie needs to produce evidence to clear Javier—before this green tomato farmer gets fried...

Who Moved My Goat Cheese?

A Farm-to-Fork Mystery

FIRST IN A NEW SERIES!

NEW YORK TIMES BESTSELLING AUTHOR

LYNN CAHOON

Angie Turner hopes her new farm-to-table restaurant can be a fresh start in her old hometown in rural Idaho. But when a goat dairy farmer is murdered, Angie must turn the tables on a bleating black sheep . . .

With three weeks until opening night for their restaurant, the County Seat, Angie and her best friend and business partner Felicia are scrambling to line up local vendors—from the farmer's market to the goat dairy farm of Old Man Moss. Fortunately, the cantankerous Moss takes a shine to Angie, as does his kid goat Precious. So when Angie hears the bloodcurdling news of foul play at the dairy farm, she jumps in to mind the man's livestock and help solve the murder. One thing's for sure, there's no whey Angie's going to let some killer get *her* goat . . .

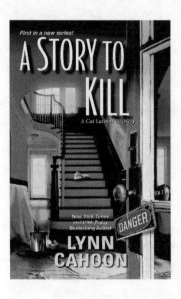

Former English professor Cat Latimer is back in Colorado, hosting writers' retreats in the big blue Victorian she's inherited, much to her surprise, from none other than her carousing ex-husband! Now it's an authors' getaway—but Cat won't let anyone get away with murder...

The bed-and-breakfast is open for business, and bestselling author Tom Cook is among its first guests. Cat doesn't know why he came all the way from New York, but she's glad to have him among the quirkier—and far less famous—attendees.

Cat's high school sweetheart Seth, who's fixing up the weathered home, brings on mixed emotions for Cat...some of them a little overpowering. But it's her uncle, the local police chief, whom she'll call for help when there's a surprise ending for Tom Cook in his cozy guest room. Will a killer have the last word on the new life Cat has barely begun?

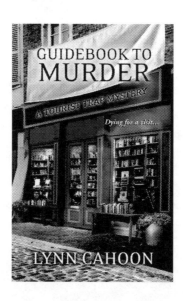

In the gentle coastal town of South Cove, California, all Jill Gardner wants is to keep her store—Coffee, Books, and More—open and running. So why is she caught up in the business of murder?

When Jill's elderly friend, Miss Emily, calls in a fit of pique, she already knows the city council is trying to force Emily to sell her dilapidated old house. But Emily's gumption goes for naught when she dies unexpectedly and leaves the house to Jill—along with all of her problems...*and* her enemies. Convinced her friend was murdered, Jill is finding the list of suspects longer than the list of repairs needed on the house. But Jill is determined to uncover the culprit—especially if it gets her closer to South Cove's finest, Detective Greg King. Problem is, the killer knows she's on the case—and is determined to close the book on Jill *permanently*...

Printed in the United States
by Baker & Taylor Publisher Services